SHANA YOUNGDAHL

A CATALOG OF BURNT OBJECTS

Dial Books

Content Note: This novel touches on topics such as alcohol addiction/AUD, domestic violence, anxiety, PTSD, wildfires, and death.

DIAL BOOKS
An imprint of Penguin Random House LLC
1745 Broadway, New York, New York 10019

First published in the United States of America by Dial Books,
an imprint of Penguin Random House LLC, 2025
Copyright © 2025 by Shana Youngdahl

Visit us online at PenguinRandomHouse.com.

Library of Congress Cataloging-in-Publication Data

Names: Youngdahl, Shana, author. • Title: A catalog of burnt objects / Shana Youngdahl. Description: New York, New York : Dial Books, 2025. | Audience term: Teenagers | Audience: Ages 12 years and up. | Summary: "A girl struggles to figure out her estranged brother, a new love, and her own future just as wildfires beset her small California town"— Provided by publisher. • Identifiers: LCCN 2024055022 (print) | LCCN 2024055023 (ebook) | ISBN 9780593405512 (hardcover) | ISBN 9780593405536 (ebook) • Subjects: CYAC: Family life—Fiction | Siblings—Fiction | First loves—Fiction | Wildfires—Fiction | California— Fiction | LCGFT: Novels. • Classification: LCC PZ7.1.Y8124 Cat 2025 (print) | LCC PZ7.1.Y8124 (ebook) | DDC [Fic]—dc23
LC record available at https://lccn.loc.gov/2024055022
LC ebook record available at https://lccn.loc.gov/2024055023

Printed in the United States of America • BVG

ISBN 9780593405512
10 9 8 7 6 5 4 3 2 1

This book was edited by Jessica Dandino Garrison, copyedited by Regina Castillo, proofread by Kenny Young, and designed by Maya Tatsakawa. The production was supervised by Jayne Ziemba, Nicole Kiser, and Vanessa Robles. Text set in Calisto.

The authorized representative in the EU for product safety and compliance is Penguin Random House Ireland, Morrison Chambers, 32 Nassau Street, Dublin D02 YH68, Ireland, https://eu-contact.penguin.ie.

For Paradise,
the town that built me

If you look at Sierra on a map, you'll see it's shaped like an obtuse scalene triangle. You won't see all the backyard beekeepers, grow operations, and do-it-yourself houses. Flatten our town out like that and it'll look ordered. Contained. But Sierra is part of a wild that rolls down off the mountains and reaches between the suburban-style houses, trailers, and cabins. A wild that creeps out from behind the oak and pine, in the shape of foxes, deer, and mountain lions. A wild that comes up on a sudden rush of wind. We put down our roads, build our houses, but the wild is still there. Prowling.

Anytime I talked about how small Sierra was, my gramps would say, "Sierra's on the Road to Nowhere, Cappi." Then he'd sing a few lines of that Talking Heads song. I'd tell him the song was a metaphor, not a literal road to nowhere. He'd shake his gray ponytail and say, "It's good to be from nowhere. A guy like me can have a view like this." He'd point to the canyon, where the afternoon light glowed an orange no photograph could capture, and the mottled greens of pine, oak, and red-barked manzanita above the river made you feel like you'd walked into a landscape painting.

Gramps wasn't wrong. You really can't get anywhere from

Sierra, at least not quickly. Sierra's shaped by canyons on the east and west, mountains to the north. The lower town limit's a crenellation of hills that folds into California's great valley, growing its rice, almonds, and smog. The three main roads out trace the canyons' edge in winding lines. No highways. No fast escape.

Living in Sierra was like being a fish trapped in a pond where the feeder creek dries up most of the year. If you wanted out in any permanent way, you had to plan, and hope the waters ran high so you could swim for your life if the chance came. At least that's what I thought. I never imagined we'd be—well, you know. No one imagines it. You just—can't.

Gramps teased me for wanting to leave. He really thought there was no better place on earth. He always wanted to grow the town, welcome newcomers. He knew all about Sierra. He'd built it. Not the roads, but the houses. Hundreds of them. He tried to preserve the trees when he could. He said they make the town. Roots, you know.

Once, Cecil Ito took Gramps and me over Sierra in his little three-seater plane. From up there it looked like there was no town at all, just three roads twisting through trees. After we came down, Gramps brought me his Talking Heads LP and said I should keep it. We listened to it on Dad's record player in the living room as we looked at a map of what we'd flown over. I said the map made Sierra look tame, but the view from the airplane made it seem all wild.

Sierra wasn't either. Not really. It was both. A wild filled with people, living in houses my gramps built, nestled between the trees. Under the greens. Perched on the edges of canyons or tucked back from the twisting pavement. People lived. Thousands and thousands hidden on roads that led nowhere.

EIGHT WEEKS BEFORE

"Honey, ask your brother if you can grab something," Dad said as he stepped into the driveway.

"Don't," Beckett called. "Only a laundry basket's left."

"Really?" I said, looking at the two boxes in Beck's hands. His cuticles were frayed, and his arms, strained by weight, shook. A heavy feeling expanded in my center. I tried to ignore it. My brother was alive. Home. Sober. That was good.

"I'll get the laundry," Dad said.

"Hungry, Beck?" Mom eyed how his shorts hung too low on his hips.

"Starving," he said. His voice was a fake cheery that made me wonder when he'd last eaten. Heat blew in the open door with the scent of dried grass and pitch. A guy jogged down the middle of the road, his footfalls slapping the concrete, dark hair peeking out from under an orange bandana. I'd been seeing him running all summer and wondered where he came from. He was cute, but didn't he know about heat exhaustion? It was ninety degrees and climbing.

Dad returned with the laundry basket in one arm, head turned away. When he got close, I could smell why. He shut the door and stumbled. Cursed. Clothes spilled across the floor as Cheerio, our cat, darted under him. She looked up, her gray face indignant. A pair of boxers hung over one ear and down her body. Dad scratched her head with his free hand, called her a "stupid cat" in a baby voice, and picked up the underwear with two fingers. Cheerio lifted one white paw to swipe at the fabric, and then stretched out across the entry floor.

"Don't worry about that, Dad. I got it," Beckett said, appearing empty-handed. He hummed as he scooped up the musty clothes.

Dad handed the basket over, saying, "I'm going to tell your gramps you made it—he was hoping you'd be here for lunch." Beck nodded as Dad slipped out the front door.

"Did you give up bathing and laundry?" I asked, lifting my foot to stand in tree pose.

"Yeah. It's a standard part of rehab." Beck arched one eyebrow.

I took a deep breath, swaying on my standing leg as I pressed my palms together because I was not, absolutely not, going to let my brother unbalance me in all the ways he used to. I was not going to hide in the closet if he yelled. I was not going to ask Mom to stock the kitchen with unbreakable plastic cups. I was going to trust him. Even if three years ago he shattered a dozen glasses while I hid in the closet. He was on the mend now. I could stand to be in the same room as him. On one leg even.

"Come on, Caps. Gotta get used to my rehab jokes."

I teetered but didn't fall. I'd recently mastered keeping my foot way up on my thigh above the knee. I felt powerful.

"So is bathing against the rules? Do you have to get dirty to get clean?" The corner of my mouth ticked up as Mom shouted from the other room:

"Caprice! You know cleanliness is an inappropriate metaphor for sobriety!"

"Sorry," I mouthed. Beckett grinned.

"Easy joke," he said. "Try harder." I inhaled slowly, wondering if maybe Beckett and I would be siblings who laughed together again. His expression shifted. "Didn't Mom tell you? I went to Davis—to see Mason. I—stayed awhile."

"Oh," I said. She hadn't. Mason was Beckett's best friend from forever who now "lived" at UC Davis Medical Center. Beckett had walked away from a totaled truck with a few bruises and Mason, six months after the accident, had air mechanically pushed in and out of his lungs. Mason couldn't talk, or even blink in reply, and I wanted to know what Beckett had done there, and if it was even safe for him to visit right after being discharged. But the best support for people coming out of rehab, according to the internet, was to focus on the present and not ask too many questions. So I didn't.

"The Vanagon doesn't have a shower, but I'm thinking of trying to install one." He smiled, same as when we'd sneak down to The Last Dam Stop: Gas and Grub and buy candy we weren't allowed at home. I chewed the inside of my cheek. Was he joking? It wasn't funny.

"Laundry is downstairs. That way, remember?" I said, pointing. Once he would have tried to knock me out of my pose. Now he shuffled past me politely, but the basket bumped my hip anyway and I dropped my foot to the floor. He stopped, reaching out his free hand to me. I brushed it away and focused hard to keep my yoga face relaxed.

"If you fall, I will catch you, I will be waiting," he sang, words from an old song. Beck was lead tenor in the Sierra High Singers. More than once, deals were made that kept him performing despite his rule-annihilation and spotty grades.

Once he was out of high school, there was no more chorus to keep him in check. There were years we barely saw him. Then, after the crash with Mason, he got worse and worse for two months until finally he'd begged for Mom and Dad to help. They found a rehab facility on the coast with an opening. He'd been there the last four months.

Now my brother was back. My sort of sad, broken, too-skinny brother with a laundry basket and two boxes to his name. He didn't look menacing. But he was an unknown variable. The peace and calm we'd found without him was probably about to evaporate like water off the cracking clay of Sierra soil.

All I really wanted was to get through the coming year without any big surprises, finish the app I was developing, and get into college. That was my program. My plan.

Beckett looked at me from behind a strip of greasy hair, and he must have seen how hard I was working to keep my yoga-relaxed face on, because he said, "I'm not a meth lab, you know. I won't explode."

I smiled at that. A little.

"You sure?"

"I smell bad, but not that bad." His voice was smoke-worn and tired.

I swallowed. Technically, Beckett suffered from substance use disorder from alcohol, but I knew it led him to some pretty dark stuff, though no one had ever bothered to tell me the details and I didn't ask. My brother joking about how a meth lab smelled made me feel off, and a little scared. Was he serious? Did he really know? Or was he teasing me? I didn't know how to ask, and I felt like I did when Cheerio disappeared at night, and I was stuck alone imagining the worst: foxes and bobcats out for her soft belly.

In the year after Beckett dropped out of college, we did a few family therapy sessions that he didn't bother showing up for, and Mom started taking me to yoga and stressing the importance of "routines to promote calm and order." I suspect she also put a reminder on her phone to tell me "Don't drink!" and "Make good choices!" at regular intervals, because I heard those phrases so often, they must have run on some kind of programmed loop. For three years before the accident, Beckett had worked various jobs in Willow Springs and had shown up at our house irregularly, usually drunk, often in need of money, never without a fight. The night of his crash with Mason, my parents woke me in the middle of the night to go to the hospital, where we found my brother cussing out an orderly.

Our family had been through enough. Now I just wanted to hang out with Alicia and plan our futures, hers in music, mine in computers, drawing creative energy from each other like the Merry Pranksters, only without all the acid.

Beckett turned toward the stairs. His best friend was never going to be the same. There was no way around that. I felt a tremor in my chest. Like a bird was trapped there, beating its little wings against my ribs. My brother fought battles I'd never understand. And the knowledge tightened around me, crushing my words. I slipped my phone out of my pocket and texted Alicia.

Not in a coma wasn't the right answer, though I thought about it.

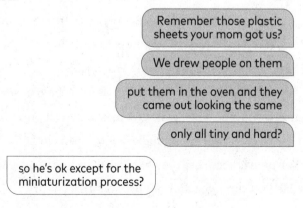

> can we carry him in our pockets??

> is he shatterproof????

> 1. Yes 2. No 3. I hope?

> IF Beckett returns from
> rehab THEN shatterproof

I laughed. In third grade, Girls Who Code taught us to make jokes like they were computer commands. Back then they were more: *IF eat beans THEN fart*. But over time, things got abstract.

> IF Beckett THEN prepare for chaos.

I'd typed that one to Alicia a thousand times. It meant I was locating breakable objects, developing an escape plan, and trying to keep everyone calm and happy. In the past it was impossible. But I'd tried. I'd been trying since I was ten. Now it felt a little less impossible to try to be hopeful.

I pocketed my phone. Alicia and her little sister, Jenny, got along fantastically despite the eight years between them. They had some kind of natural sibling code. Beckett and I never did.

I grabbed the almost-full bucket of water from my shower and lugged it downstairs.

"Here," I said, handing it to my brother.

"Thanks." He dumped the gray water in the old top-load washing machine. This was a long-standing conservation effort—collect shower water and use it to clean clothes.

"Welcome home," I said as he turned around. I opened my arms. He half shrugged and stepped into them.

He smelled like sweat and dirt and tobacco. He was home. Alive. Trying.

"I'm glad you're back," I said. I meant it. Even as that little bird in my chest struggled to flutter.

"Me too. But if you didn't leave me any hot water, I'm going to kill you." He tugged my wet hair.

"I didn't know when you were coming! There's this cool technology called texting. You should try it."

"I need a new phone."

Right. Mom said he wanted a new number too because there were lots of people he was trying to leave behind. People who wouldn't understand he wanted to be sober. But not being found in Sierra was going to be like speaking binary code. Just impossible.

"Get on that, after you shower. You smell like one of Gram's compost piles. And please *please* forget to collect the water. I don't want to wash my clothes in your funk."

He almost smiled, palmed his whiskers, and left the bucket on the floor next to the washer as he stepped away. "Can I borrow a razor?"

"Ugh. Gross. Why don't you have— Never mind—" I swallowed. "There are disposable ones in the drawer. Right-hand side. Don't use mine."

"Aw, Cautious Cappi," Beckett said, and for a second, his old grin appeared. The one that showed how his right front tooth had shifted slightly sideways because he never wore his retainer. Then he shook his head. "You're lucky."

"Understanding basic hygiene isn't luck," I said.

"I never paid attention to that stuff," he said.

"My program is simple—wash hands, don't touch things other people's fluids have, and avoid everything you've ever done," I said, chipper, stepping between him and the sink. "You've made high school easy."

"Was that a thank-you?" he said, arms loose at his sides. His PANIC! AT THE DISCO shirt was coming unstitched at the hem.

"Yeah," I said. Maybe it was. "Thanks for keeping the druggies away."

"Protection's like the first job of a big brother."

I tried to smile but my mouth didn't cooperate. I was thinking of five years before, when I was twelve, and I'd tried to keep him from driving when he was so drunk, he could barely walk. I'd hidden his keys, but he got the spare Dad kept in the downstairs cabinet. When I realized he was leaving, I ran out front and tried to pry them from his fingers. He elbowed me and I fell on the pebbled paving stones and cut my knee. Angry, I screamed, "Do whatever you want!" and went in to stanch the bleeding. He didn't come home the next morning, or the next. My terror was matched only by the silence of the house. Nobody played music. Nobody talked. I told my parents what happened, sitting at the table tracing my scab. Owning up. That still made me angry. The guilt. As if a middle-schooler with gumby arms could stop a drunk sixteen-year-old from doing what he wanted.

Beckett dropped his arm across my shoulder. "Be warned, you're on your own navigating the nerds. I only weed out the losers like me."

"You're not a loser," I said, but it didn't come out convincingly. We both knew I'd called him that countless times.

"Thanks for the faith—" He paused. "So, any *special* nerds?"

I shook my head.

"But you're building that app the parents can't stop bragging about—isn't that bound to impress some—"

"Admissions teams and scholarship committees? Hopefully."

Beckett blinked and then stuck his chin out. "I was going to say *hot nerds*."

"Uh, do you remember high school?"

"Not really, no." His smile dampened.

"The only people who are impressed by me building an app are our parents, Cecil Ito, and the computer club. That's Alicia and Mo."

"Mo's not make-you-sweat material, I take it?"

"Ew." I swatted his shoulder. Mo, a sophomore who Alicia and I called our little brother, was so far from hotness, he was practically Antarctica. "The Sierra High dating pool is incestuous and small. It's not worth it."

Beckett looked at me sideways.

"It's true! I've already dated Grayson, the one person I haven't known since kindergarten, and he turned out to be a jerk."

Beckett chuckled. "Maybe that was the problem. There's nothing wrong with dating someone you've known forever."

"Uh, yeah there is. I mean, Micah Feldstone might be cute if I could forget how he sat next to me in second grade munching his scabs."

Beckett made a face but then said, "How hot is he? Maybe you could—"

"Even if I *could*—and I can't—Micah and Alicia dated all through eighth grade and he seriously broke her heart. For months she only listened to music in minor keys."

"She did?"

"She wanted to feel her feelings."

"Huh."

I shrugged. "Honestly, what's the point of dating? High school relationships don't last. There's like a two percent chance."

"Ice cream doesn't last either, but it's still worth it," Beckett said, poking me in the stomach.

I poked back.

"I think your app thing's awesome," he said, turning to go back upstairs.

Really? He looked back. Did he see something on my face? Some secret joy, some relief? "Dad said it was, anyway," he added.

Oh.

"So . . ." he said. "What's it about?"

"It's so tourists—" I began, and a look flashed across Beckett's face that said Sierra doesn't have tourists. No beach. No General Sherman Tree. No Winchester Mystery House. Certainly no Disneyland. "It's a prototype. Something that could grow beyond Sierra. But Gramps was going on about it to Cecil, and he wants to invest."

"Real money?"

"Not Monopoly money." In the world of app development,

the twenty thousand Cecil was giving me wasn't a lot. But in Sierra, it was huge. I didn't know people had money like that just sitting around to invest in anything, but a high-schooler's project? It was wild.

Beckett ran his hands through his hair. "You're earning back the college savings our parents blew on me, then?"

I looked up expecting to see his grin, that crooked tooth, but his gaze was on his Vans, tracing the edge of the tile. "Beck—you know—I—everyone wanted to help." He shook his head and then stepped toward me, swinging his arm up and dropping a hand on my shoulder. A heaviness bubbled in my stomach and I blurted, "Twenty thousand won't even cover my first year unless I get serious scholarships, and I'm supposed to pay some of that to my team, so—"

"Hey, I'm a dropout who defaulted on my loans. I get it." *Oof.* He squeezed my shoulder, then fell back so I could go up the stairs first.

We found Mom in the kitchen, straight-backed at the marble-topped island, her lips tight, next to our slump-shouldered dad. I could almost hear them silently shouting, *You're not worried enough!* and *You need to relax!* Mom sliced a cucumber and Dad folded meat onto the bread.

"Look—it's the two people responsible for creating you and keeping you alive," I said.

"Despite your best efforts," Mom added, cutting a sandwich in half and smiling.

Dad raised one eyebrow and popped a piece of turkey in his

mouth. My parents rarely agreed on anything Beckett-related.

Gramps's head was in the refrigerator. "Well, here he is! My Beckett Bear," he said, turning with the tea pitcher in his hand. Beckett made a sound between a laugh and a sigh as he stepped toward Gramps.

"Gramps refuses to believe you're no longer ten," I said.

Gramps winked at me. "He can't be! 'Cause then I'd be . . ." He set down the pitcher and held up his fingers like he was counting. Beck's eyes stuck on Gramps's thinning ponytail. "Well, come on, then!" Gramps opened up his arms for a long hug.

"Be careful, he hasn't showered yet!" I said.

"Caps said I'm worse than Gram's compost."

"Good compost doesn't smell"—Gramps paused and smiled at me—"that bad. We'll put up with you," he said to Beckett. "We're eating outside anyway."

I pointed to the sliding door. "Right this way, Beckett Bear."

Beckett stepped past me onto the deck, where Gram was parked in the shade. Dad and Gramps had picked her up from the care facility earlier.

"Gram!" Beckett leaned down to kiss her head. Wow. I couldn't remember the last time I'd seen that.

"What trouble could a handsome man like you have been in to say hello like that?" Gram asked.

"You don't want to know," Beckett said, sitting down.

When I was maybe eight and Beckett twelve, we were in the garden with Gram. She said, "Some seeds take to the wind. Others grow right in the soil where they're dropped. Some get carried off in the belly of an animal to be shat out somewhere new." Then she looked between us. "What kind of seed are you?"

"Wind!" I'd cried, opening my arms and imagining I was floating on the canyon breeze.

"Naw, you're shit seeds," Beckett said, eyes gleaming.

"*You* are," I'd said, shoving him with my shoulder.

"*Smells* like you are," he said.

Gram smacked him hard then with her garden gloves. "Go turn the compost if you've got shit on your brain."

Beckett's face went blank. My throat tightened. My eyes stung, but I didn't let tears fall.

"Go on now, it's not like I hit you," Gram said, her voice all honey and flowers. It was *exactly* like she'd hit him. Sometimes she called those whaps "love smacks." They weren't usually hard, but they were hits. I never got one.

"*Wind* seeds land in shit anyway," Beckett grumbled to me, as if I'd been the one to slap him. Maybe because I kept sitting next to Gram, pressing my fingers into the dirt, maybe I kind of had.

"Boys," Gram had said then as Beck slunk away. "At least they grow into men, right?" I'd thought she meant strong builder-types like my gramps. But now I realize Gram was all innuendo no matter who she was talking to. I stayed next to her in the garden, tucking seeds into the ground. I felt bad for Beck, even if he'd been a jerk. But not enough to join him turning compost.

We didn't know then that the disease was already taking root in Gram's brain, and it made her act more unpredictably than ever.

"She doesn't remember us anymore," I said, looking at Gram now, her silver braids coming undone. I wanted to love her in an uncomplicated way. But it was hard to tell where she ended and her illness began.

"I don't remember the name of the restaurant I worked at last year, so—" Beckett half smiled like it was somehow the same. I wondered if it bothered him at all.

Mom and Dad came out, passing us plates, sandwiches, cucumber slices, salt and vinegar chips. They settled on opposite sides of the porch. Gramps followed with cups of tea sweating in the heat. He pulled a chair up next to Gram, settling his hand on her leg.

"It's good to be home," he said. I wanted so badly to welcome him back, to forgive or forget or whatever I needed to do.

"It's hard to stay away from Sierra, isn't it, boys!" Gramps said.

"Oh Glenn, don't start," Mom said.

"What?" Gramps put his hands in the air. "Growth! That's the future."

"Town's bigger than it needs to be already, Dad."

"You're saying that 'cause you're no longer building up here," Gramps said, leaning forward as my dad rocked back.

"Gentlemen," Mom said, "we're here to welcome Beckett home. Not to argue."

"Well, thanks for raising the population back up," Gramps said, his blue eyes sparkling.

"Where are we?" Gram asked.

"At my place, Mom," Dad said.

"Don't you try to trick me, Dylan!" Gram raised her finger at my dad.

People think computers are smart. But they aren't. They're just fast at doing what they're told. But once they learn something, they don't forget. Sure, a virus could wipe them clean, but even then, memory can be restored. Backed up. No one had figured out how to do that for people. I wondered if it would ever be possible—to download your memories—and then restore them. Could that kind of thing work for Gram, or Mason? Who would invent something like that? A doctor? A computer scientist? Both?

An acorn woodpecker tap-tap-tapped. The Hernándezes' rooster crowed. Our backyard looked across the canyon—trees and red dirt, our ridge and the next. Below us, the snake of the river. I could feel Beck's eyes on me, but neither of us spoke. What was he thinking? Was he worried about being back? Was he really happy to be here? I didn't know, and I didn't ask.

I wasn't sure how much time we should spend together now that we were all acting out the one big happy family. Still, I sipped my tea, and flashed Beckett one of my practiced yoga smiles. It was the best I could do. I hoped it told him I was trying. If he could, I could.

Program for Trying to Be a Good Sister While Avoiding Beckett-Induced Chaos

IF Beckett is working with Gramps, make coffee and send him off with two cups.

THEN:

1. *Work on app 45 minutes*
2. *Yoga 20-35 minutes*
3. *Work on app 60 minutes*
4. *Snack*
5. *Repeat until 3 p.m.*

THEN run the following:

IF Beckett is smoking on the deck THEN take a shower.

IF Beckett is reading on the couch THEN work in the garden.

IF Beckett is in the shower OR going for a drive THEN stay in the house.

IF Beckett is with Gramps, Mom or Dad THEN join in family conversation.

A basic rule: IF only Beckett is HERE then Caprice is NOT HERE.

FIVE WEEKS BEFORE

Alicia:

you might be a stalker

Caprice:

Maybe *he's* the stalker.

This guy jogs by *my* house. Every day.

Even when it's 102, and there's air quality alerts.

you got to get a pic

Um, who's the stalker?

he must be hot if you wait at the window!!!

Computer work is hard on the body.

I can't help it if he always runs by when

I'm taking a yoga break

Yoga: n. 1. ancient practice that melds breath and body,

2. looking for smokin' hot athletes from your front window

ALICIA!

I can't help it

Where'd he come from?

Why don't I recognize him?

he's probably that kid from preschool that moved away

you know the one who ate paste???

now he's back, fit, hot and waiting for you.

Axel was a ginger.

oh, that's right, Axel, cool name.

Yeah, too bad he turned out to be a weapons enthusiast.

1. you've got something against stockpiling now???

2. how do you know that?

3. you going to tell me how things are going with Beckett?

1. Ha.

2. He's one of Kim's cousins.

3. So far Beckett chaos-meters are very low

and it's been weeks!!!!

maybe it's the new normal?

Like year-round fire season &

epic floods after years of drought?

capybara!

I know, I know. I'm trying.

so. is running-hottie there yet????

"What's up?" Beckett said, a glass of iced tea in his hand.

No. Beckett is.

I palmed my phone and held it behind my back.

"Yoga break," I said, and then, "There he is!" realizing too late I'd spoken, not texted.

Beckett, a cat waiting to pounce, said, "Who?"

I turned. Beckett was right there. "I don't know. He runs by a lot—"

"So you're worried he'll collapse from heat exhaustion."

"Kinda." Did my brother know me so well? "But also, where'd he come from?"

"Let's find out," Beckett said, that exhilarated note in his voice like when he'd say "Let's run down to the river!"

Before I could even turn, he was out the front door calling, "Hey! Hey! Excuse me!"

Oh no. I almost dropped to the floor under the windows. Then messaged Alicia instead and drifted after my brother out the door.

Remember when I said Beckett-caused chaos was low?

Looks like that's over.

In the road, the runner slowed and put his hands to his chest like *Me?*

"Yeah, you," Beckett said, striding toward him, tea glass in hand. The paving stones burned my feet, so I hopped to the tiny patch of yellowing grass under the pine. Cheerio appeared and rubbed against my bare ankles as the guy jogged in place, pulling off his chunky headphones.

is he juggling your
Gram's teacups again?

Ha. No.

He's introducing himself
to running guy

OMGOMGOMGOMGOMG!!!!!!!

I held my phone behind my back. Beckett asked, "Are you unaware of heat stroke, or training for a desert marathon?"

The runner shook his head, confused, and Beck took a step back, pointing at me. "My sister says you sprint by all the time. She's worried she'll have to resuscitate you."

The guy, who looked about to dash off, froze when he saw me. He smiled and I realized he was beyond cute. Not sports model—too lanky—but something better. More peculiar. Brown eyes. A smile to make any orthodontist proud. His nose was crooked, like maybe it had been broken and never healed right. And there was something in the flush of his freckled cheeks that made the crooked nose feel like it was probably from an excited puppy, not a fistfight. His eyes locked on mine, and I was aware of my yoga-wild hair, sweat, and the fact that I was staring.

"You're worried about me?" he said, and I could hear something in his voice. Delight? I met his eyes, and his smile widened.

"Exercising when it could risk breaking your body's ability to regulate temperature is not super smart," I said.

He cocked his head, but the smile didn't leave. "I just moved from Willow Springs. Midday here is like dusk there."

"Not exactly," I said.

He was almost laughing now. Was I running the flirt program well? "Okay, yeah," he said. "Technically it's more like five degrees cooler up here."

I crossed my arms. *Technically* correct.

"If you're new, Caprice here is the person to show you around town," Beckett said with a Vanna White gesture. "She's working on this app to try and get tourists to Sierra. She has investors. Not bad for a high school kid."

Was my brother bragging about me? To a boy who was pruning access to my dorsolateral prefrontal cortex simply by standing there?

"An app builder, huh? Did you know Googleplex is going to be underwater by 2050?" the guy asked.

Oh no. Was this perfect out-of-town boy a mansplaining technophobe? Was he going to lecture me on the amount of energy it takes to make a microchip? Or the negative planetary impact of server farms? Or go off about the impending financial collapse because AI is going to take everyone's jobs?

"I guess billionaires can afford to not care about sea-level rise," I said, and then added, after a noticeably awkward pause, "Jerks."

"Jerks?" Beckett laughed. "They offer you enough pay and give you a motorized scooter to zoom around their fancy flood zone, and you'll be one of them too."

I was tempted to say *What do you know?* He hadn't been around. He didn't know that what I wanted had far less to do with how much money I could make than how much I could do. Sure, I was starting with a tourist app, but I might end up building hard drives for human memories.

Running guy, for his part, started to jog in place again, like he wanted to get out of our sibling moment but wasn't sure if he should. I counted his feet hitting the gravel five times before Beckett said, "Iced tea?" and pointed at his glass and then to our house. It took me a half second to realize he was inviting the guy in.

The runner looked thirstily at the glass and shook his head. "Thanks, but I've gotta run."

"Literally," I said.

Running guy's smile did not falter. "I'll see you around if you go to Sierra High. I'll be a senior."

I hopped from one foot to the other because even the grass was scorching. "Go Beavers!" I said. The Golden Beaver was our much adored and much mocked Sierra High mascot.

"Fastest Dam Builders in Town," the runner said, still smiling. My insides turned larval.

"Dam Spirit already," Beckett said. "Guess you're fitting in."

The guy flushed. "Tea another time, then?" he said to Beckett, but with his eyes very much on me.

Beckett said, "Let me get your number. I just moved back after three years in Willow Springs. It'd be nice to know someone new. I'm not, but also, I am." It hit me then that my brother really had lived in Willow Springs. And I knew almost nothing about it.

"I'm River," the kid said, his eyes on me. Was *I* supposed to be taking his number too?

"Beckett. And this, again, is Caprice."

River's brow creased and he looked at our house like he was trying to figure out what kind of people name their kids after an avant-garde playwright and, literally, a whim. Or maybe he was appreciating the garden.

He wore one of those survival cord bracelets, and the sweat pools on his shirt were somehow the opposite of disgusting.

> His name is River.

I typed to Alicia like a clod instead of inputting his number. But he was giving it to Beckett, right? Not to me.

> He's going to Sierra High.

> A new senior

My phone almost slipped out of my slick hands as it vibrated.

> WHAT?!?!?

I wished Alicia was home every day.

River tugged his earlobe and resumed his run-in-place jog. "See ya," he said to the space between Beckett and me, "probably tomorrow," before launching into a sprint so fast, I swear the colors of his shirt blurred.

"Bye," I said. It came out small and I wasn't sure he heard it with the thirty-five mph winds he was creating. My face burned. Had he noticed me noticing him all summer? Other than the Grayson disaster, I hadn't dated anyone. And this guy, who I did not know, looked at me like he was coded to look at nothing else. Me! I wanted to kill Beck and hug him. Instead I said, "What was that about?"

"Just trying to help you navigate beyond the nerds," he said, taking a swallow of his tea.

"By embarrassing me?"

Beckett squinched up his nose. "I embarrassed you?" He looked surprised. "I wouldn't worry about it, Cap. I'm pretty sure if you just breathe near him, you'll clinch the deal."

I decided to ignore this. "You know half the cross-country team are serious stoners," I said.

"Caps, *Gramps* is a serious stoner. I fail to see the problem."

"Gramps quit," I said. My phone vibrated.

Alicia:

She sent the same message—six times with an increasing number of exclamations points. The last took up three rows.

"He didn't have to do that," Beck said. "I never liked weed."

I crossed my arms, tucking my phone in the crook of my elbow. How did I respond to that? Had he not read the family guide we pored over getting ready for him to come home? "For all we know, this River kid could be a serial killer," I finally said.

"Oh right. A guy shows up who didn't eat his scabs, and looks at you like that, but you don't know him—so he's definitely Jeffrey Dahmer. That tracks."

"Yeah, okay. But he *may* have eaten his scabs. We weren't there. Now he probably thinks I'm some stalker who wants to resuscitate him," I said.

"That is a problem. Resuscitation is not sexy. The mouth-to-mouth part can induce vomiting."

"Gross," I said.

Beckett swirled his tea. The ice rattled. He leaned toward me and the cold glass grazed my arm. "Gramps really ripped up his plants?"

"If by 'rip up,' you mean, did he repot them and drive to the Homesteaders' house? Then yeah," I said, and punched him in the arm, a little harder than I should have.

Beckett held the tea glass to his bicep. "He didn't have to."

"He didn't mind. We're all glad you're—"

That's when a car pulled up, and a blond girl with blue tips got out, squealing, and running toward my brother. Beckett handed me his iced tea with a grin and said, "Looks like my lucky day. Now Cappi, what are you going to do for River's number? My room could use a vacuum."

"I don't want River's number," I said.

"Sure you don't," he said, turning to face the girl who launched herself at him, threading her legs around his middle and giggling. That's when I recognized her. Kylie LaGrasse, Beckett's prom date.

"Since when do you notice when a room needs to be vacuumed?" I asked, but Beckett didn't answer. His face had disappeared behind a tangle of blond and blue hair.

I guess my brother had been found by someone he was happy to see. She didn't even need his new number.

OBJECT: Dried Prom Corsage

LOCATION: 15 Sierra Way, Sierra, California

RESIDENT: Kylie LaGrasse

....

I want to be clear: I was never in love with Beckett Alexander. Okay, maybe I was sort of in love with Beckett Alexander. But only in the way everyone was. I wasn't ever his girlfriend. Not really. We did go to prom, and kiss, and—we had an understanding that went on for five years or so. It's good to have a nice guy to call when you want to make a mistake, you know? I mean, not that Beckett was a nice guy, nice guy. He drank a lot. And he was unreliable as all hell. But he was sweet. Safe. He didn't push things.

I knew I wasn't the only girl. I was okay with that. It didn't start on prom night—must have been six months before that—fall—when the nights were still warm, and we'd party in the woods north of the dam. Beckett tasted like rum and said I was more beautiful than the stars. I told him he was full of it, but I really wanted to make out with someone. He was game. I don't even remember how we ended up going to prom together. There was no promposal, that's for sure.

I didn't keep the corsage because of Beckett. Honestly, I was surprised he thought to bring me one, but his aunt ran the flower shop, so I guess that's why he remembered. It was gorgeous—five tiny blue lilies surrounding two white orchids. Beckett had an orchid on his lapel to match, their petals velvet-soft. They were probably the nicest flowers anyone had at prom. It's silly, I know, but I loved prom. All the different groups together for a final dance. One last chance to dress the part of adults before we really were living it.

The flowers matched my beaded flapper dress and Beckett's blue tux. I still have those, thanks to digital picture packages and cloud storage. You can't see the flowers in detail. But we look happy. Laughing, open-mouthed, my bobbed hair curled along my chin. We looked like a couple. Like we didn't have a care in the world. Beckett was drunk, but only a little bit. We stayed at prom until the last song. We sang along and cheered at the end. Later I found him passed out on the bathroom floor, the lilies of his boutonniere crushed, a glass of what I thought was orange juice next to him. I made sure he was lying on his side and unclipped the ruined flowers. Then took a long swallow of that juice and immediately spat it out. It was mostly vodka.

Beckett. I knew I couldn't get too close. I knew he had these big cracks in him and if I wasn't careful, I could fall through. Sometimes, it made me sad, but mostly, we had fun.

The next day, I had a headache and some of the beads had fallen off my dress, but my corsage was still in good shape. I coated it in hairspray and hung it on a hanger in a dark corner of my closet, checking on it every few days, spraying it as needed. When it was *dry, I set it on my bookshelf. I had lots of things, so sometimes I won-der why I think about that corsage so much. I guess because prom was this important night from high school, and because Beckett, maybe like Sierra, was a habit hard to shake. Despite all logic and good reason, I returned. I still see all the good. Even now.*

I never thought of myself as someone who loved high school, or who was popular or who cared about those things. But the truth is, I was kinda popular. In my own way. And I did care. It was fun—to be there, to cheer. That's the real reason I went with Beckett. He took the spotlight, you know? Good and bad. If you were with Beckett, you would be seen. On prom night, I wanted to be seen. And I was. I guess now that so much is gone, it's those memories that matter, you know? The times we were together, the times we danced.

FIVE WEEKS BEFORE

The next morning when I got up, Kylie was pouring herself a cup of coffee in my kitchen. I guess I shouldn't have been surprised, given her greeting the day before. I tried not to stare at the mascara under her eyes. She offered me a weak smile. I did one of those finger waves and tried to lift the corners of my mouth. When she gestured with the carafe, I set my left-handed mug on the counter and nodded my thanks. I'd barely woken up—it was too soon to talk.

"Ah, I did smell coffee! You make enough for me?" Mom strode into the kitchen wearing black yoga pants and a green PrAna top that matched her eyes.

"Someone made a whole pot," I said, setting out Mom's mug. Kylie filled it.

"Beckett," she said, pointing to the deck. "He's smoking. I hope you don't mind, but I can't be near it."

"Me neither. There's enough smoke in the air these days," Mom said like it was normal to be talking to Kylie at eight a.m. "I'm Irene. Nice to meet you."

"We actually met like three years ago, but you might not remember—I'm Kylie."

Mom snapped her fingers. "Of course, prom! I didn't—sorry—"

"It happens. It's the hair." Kylie pointed to her platinum and blue.

I opened my mouth to say something nice, like *It suits you*, or to tell her the biology teacher still raved about her detailed animal drawings even though she graduated years ago, but Beckett slid open the door and boomed, "Mom, you remember my friend Kylie?"

"Friend?" I mouthed. Mom managed a warning headshake before plastering on her helpful Elementary Staff Face and said, "I do now! Did you get something to eat?"

"Beck made me a bagel." She pointed to an empty plate.

"I'm thoughtful like that," he said, dropping a hand to Kylie's shoulder before turning to me. "Caps, why are you up? Did you bypass the programming that makes teenagers sleep late?"

"I've got stuff to do," I said.

"App-y Cappi, always on track," Beckett said, and I didn't know if he was taunting me. Yesterday he'd seemed proud, but with Beckett, I never knew.

"Not too much work today," Mom said. She knew Alicia was coming home.

"We're going swimming," I told her, and wondered if I should ask Beckett to come. But I didn't want Kylie to join. What would I say to a girl who'd just slept with my brother—on the other side of the wall from me? Alicia would want me to ask. But it was her first day back. I thought of all the times I'd tried to follow Beckett and Mason on their bike rides, all the times they wouldn't let me. I'd end up sulking with Gram, digging in her garden to bury the sting.

Beckett took three bagels from the bag and started juggling them. Kylie smiled. "I remember you doing that with—ugh—something else at Mason's birthday party senior year."

At Mason's name, Beckett dropped one of the bagels.

Kylie reddened.

Mom, who hadn't heard, said, "Beck—people are going to eat those."

"Sorry," Beckett said, and scooped it up. "Don't worry, I'll eat that one."

"No, I'm sorry." Kylie's voice was soft. "I mean—" She looked between us. Lost. Beck set the bagel on the counter and bagged the other two.

"It's okay," Beckett said. From the way he crinkled the plastic and tensed his jaw, it didn't seem okay. I thought of this red fox I'd seen years ago. I'd been helping Gramps on a worksite, and there it was, white-tipped tail twitching. I'd stared at it for a minute, two minutes, three. Our eyes locked, like we understood each other. Like we had some connection that was deep and unspoken. But when I told Gramps, he chuckled and said, "Wild animals only look you in the eye if they're going to attack. You're lucky it didn't come running at you, Capybara." And then he chased after me shouting, "I'm going to get you!"

And even though I laughed and knew a fox wasn't a real threat to an eleven-year-old, something in me felt drowned. I thought I'd had a moment with that fox, but Gramps said it wanted to hurt me. How had I gotten the message so wrong?

It's how I felt with my brother most of the time. Like, maybe it was better to run than stay and risk more misunderstanding. That was why I'd been avoiding him.

"Look," Beckett said—he was talking to Kylie, but his eyes were on me. "I think about what happened to Mason all the time. You bringing him up doesn't remind me. I'm going to see his mom today—if you want to come?"

Kylie chewed her lip. I wasn't sure if Beck was talking to her, or Mom, or me.

"Oh—I—work—pretty soon actually." She didn't know where to look.

"I've been meaning to visit Candace," Mom said. "I'll go with you."

Beckett nodded, arms across his chest.

"Take her flowers," I said. "I'll cut something." I liked Candace, but seeing her now made my skin cold. For a while after the accident, I was delivering flowers to her house all the time. I don't know who was sending them, it might have been Adrienne. But it was silly. She wasn't there. She'd practically moved to Davis. But now she was back home. She needed to work.

Kylie's watch beeped. "Yikes. Gotta get moving. Nice seeing you."

I mustered a "Have a good day."

"Come back anytime," Mom said. I had to focus on the fern in the window so I didn't repeat *Come anytime*, like Beckett might have if *I'd* been the one to host a sexy slumber party.

I did not even raise my eyebrows as Beckett followed Kylie to the door. He was out of view when I said, "Nice to see Beckett has friends."

"Don't be like that," Mom said.

"Like what?"

"You know," she said, lifting her coffee mug in the air. "It *is* nice—Beckett's young and—"

"Don't say anything about men and urges."

Mom made a face like she'd bitten a pickle. "Caprice Alexander, who do you think raised you?"

"Apparently someone not bothered by a strange girl in the kitchen at dawn?"

"Not when my adult son, who's been locked away from the world for months, brings her home, no. I'm not."

"But what if she—"

Mom's hand went up. Her nail polish was chipped. She picked at it when she was stressed. "Your brother needs friends," she said, "and you need to trust him."

My skin prickled, and I felt hollowed out. How exactly was I supposed to do that?

"Five bucks says she's a Scorpio."

"Mom!"

"You're right, she could be an Aries, Scorpio moon—and I don't know, Pisces rising?"

I gave my mom a look.

"You're a Taurus—of course you're dismissive." She put her arm around me as I continued the side-eye. "At least Alicia's finally back, so you'll have something to do," she said, changing the subject. "I was about to send you to Mariana and Jake's, so they'd know how awful it is when she's gone all summer."

"Hey! I kept busy!"

"Exactly. You need fun. You should take your brother with you—Alicia won't mind."

"Alicia just got back," I said. "Beckett had plenty of fun with his own friend."

Mom gave me that long stare. Her eyes seemed greener as they widened slightly with disappointment.

"I'll go cut some flowers for Candace," I said, because okay. She was right. I was awful. But I figured I should get to have Alicia to myself at least for a day. I slipped out the back door, grabbed the cutting shears from the potting bench, and clipped a nice summer bouquet for Mason's mom—echinacea, Blue Boa, and Shasta daisies from the garden I took over when we had to move Gram. She taught me everything I know about flowers. Now sometimes it stung that she could still name them and not me. I was arranging the stems when Beckett returned from his extended goodbye. He chuckled at his phone.

"What?" I said.

"Oh, I'm letting River know you won't be here to watch him run by later."

"You are not!" I lunged for his phone. He held it out of my

reach. I jumped, trying to knock it out of his hand. My shoulder hit him hard, and the phone fell into one of Dad's potted succulents. We hadn't squabbled like this since I was probably ten. I was half laughing, half-mortified, fully desperate.

"Careful with the plants—you know how Dad—" But Beckett was fast. He picked up the phone without pulling up any of the trailing stems of the burro's tail and held it tight to his body.

"Hmm, I wonder if he's curious what *you're* doing. Maybe I'll take an action shot to send." He clicked the camera.

"No!"

He held up the picture of me—braless in my tank top and kitten PJ shorts. I jumped to pull his arms down. He pushed me into the wall near that ugly vase Mom's famous artist friend made. I squeezed his neck and hissed, "If we break Mom's vase, she will murder us."

"But Dad'll thank us." He stepped away from the wall, putting a few feet between us and the vase, then he pried my arms off his neck and twisted so he was facing me. He grinned. I grabbed his fingers, squeezing until the phone fell out of his hand.

I pressed the home button. Locked. Beckett slapped his knee and laughed. "Of course it's locked, tech genius!"

"You suck," I said.

"Only with consent."

"Ugh, gross. Go away."

"Whatever."

His phone vibrated. I stared at it.

"You want to know what River said?"

"Why are you such an—agent of *chaos*?"

"Cute," Beckett said, holding my gaze for a beat as if daring me to tell him off. "I'm glad you recognize my superpower." He picked up the flowers. "Thanks for these. Tell Alicia I said hi."

I *did* want to run from him now—seething and screaming at myself for not putting River's number in my phone the day before. He didn't seem to be on social. I'd checked. Multiple times.

I heard Beckett call to Mom and then sing *I was following the, I was following the pack,* and with a click of our red front door, they were gone.

"Slow down." Alicia was way ahead of me on the trail that wound into the canyon. "Did music camp have an athletic program this year?" Sweat trickled under my CAL T-shirt as I hustled to keep up.

"Moonlight hikes had multiple perks," Alicia called back. "And then the grandparents kept me marching through museums."

"Jealous. Tell me more."

I meant it, but Alicia waved me off. "You really should have been down here all summer, Cap."

"Alone? Who would keep the creeps away?"

"Your long-lost brother?"

"He hasn't been here *all* summer. And you know how it is with Beckett. I—I can't say anything right around him. Plus, why swim with someone who won't appreciate my hot new bikini?"

Alicia tossed her box braids. "I appreciate your new swimwear, Caps, but I'm not the target audience. Why didn't you invite Running Boy?"

"I don't have his number."

"Bad reason." She held up a finger. "Beck has it."

"I wasn't about to vacuum Beckett's room for it."

"Beck knows when a room needs vacuuming?" She stopped in the middle of the trail.

"Surprising, right?"

She didn't answer. "You brought water?"

I nodded and handed her a bottle. She never remembered water or maybe she knew I'd always pack two. We'd stopped in a shady spot before a little bridge over a flume—these manmade streams that ran along the canyon's side. Originally, they'd had something to do with mining and now were part of the dam's hydroelectric waterway.

Alicia passed the bottle back. "Thanks." Then she grinned. "I had a lot of what you've been missing this summer, and you've been missing a *lot*."

"Yes! Spill it!"

She twitched her nose and started walking again. I ran my hand along a manzanita as we passed and curves of its red bark shed into my palm.

"Really?" I said. "You're not going to say more about French Cello Man?"

"First, the Beckett update."

"Kylie LaGrasse was breakfasting with us, so—"

"Well—that's good, right? I mean, he was probably hurting for it after—"

"You sound like my mom," I said.

"Did she offer to do Kylie's chart?"

"Didn't even ask her sign. Wild, right? She speculated after, Scorpio-Pisces-something rising."

"You paid a lot of attention to that—for a Taurus."

"Ha, ha." We'd reached the spot where the canyon edge was so narrow, the trail went onto a bridge a foot above the flume. Our steps rattled the metal grate, and the water below us gushed. The air tasted of dust and pine. I always felt dizzy as we reached the midpoint of the suspended pathway. Walking against the flow of the water did that. I took a deep breath to rebalance before putting one foot in front of the other like a gymnast. Following Alicia, I stepped off the walkway and onto the crossbeam to inch my way to the flume's edge and balance on the lip of the half-pipe.

Alicia crouched for the drop, and I said, "Dad's angling for family therapy. All of us this time. It's because I didn't go to the exit conference or whatever."

She looked up, top lip curled. I knew she thought I was wrong not to go to that counseling session the week before Beckett left rehab. My parents said it would be supportive to go, but I didn't see the point. I wasn't the one making the rules, I wasn't going to enforce them. I was just the sister. Plus, it was a four-hour drive, and I had an app to build.

Alicia jumped to the soft earth below. "You out of my way?"

I called. Then saw her shuffle out from under the elevated canal and hold on to a baby pine tree. She gave me a thumbs-up.

I dropped, landing in a squat and tipping back onto my butt.

"French Canadian Cellist details PLEASE," I said as we slid together between the manzanita and pine, the dirt staining the pockets of our cut-offs auburn.

She smiled. "A moonlight cello solo is probably as good as you'd imagine."

I laughed. "Not something I have ever imagined. Did it result in a lot of, shall we say, *physical* education?"

"Oh, it did!" Alicia grinned. "So therapy—Will you go to that same person in Willow Springs?

"Um, you did not change the subject again."

Alicia chucked me on the shoulder. "Some details stay in the make-out cabin."

"Really? Wait—there was a *cabin*?"

She gave me a moony grin. "I told you we played 'Kaze No Torimichi' from *My Neighbor Totoro* for the final concert, right? Piano and cello are natural companions."

"Like bees and flowers," I said.

"And that performance won us a donation to charity."

"And you picked the vaquita, right?"

"Yes! Thankfully he was on board. The poor panda of the sea! Only ten left! Ten—"

"And all because of people fishing with illegal nets," I said, finishing her rant.

"Yeah." Alicia shook her head. "I guess if I win classical fest this year, that could be my charity."

"Good idea. Now, please! Tell me how you harmonized!"

Alicia raised an eyebrow. "You are thirsty. Anyway, Mom can get you names of other therapists."

"You think I need to deal with my anger?" I was joking. Trying to.

"Yep, Capybara. I do."

Ouch. Not even a sarcastic response. I swerved to avoid a patch of poison oak. The air cooled and the ground flattened out. "You forget what he was like, Alicia," I said.

"Um, like the time he was throwing dishes at your mom? No, I remember." We'd reached the banks of the Plumule River.

"The water's low," I said, but I was thinking how selfish I was, not inviting my brother. Selfish and unsupportive. "Have you ever seen it this low?"

Alicia looked up and down the waterline. "When did it last rain? February?" She stretched her arms to the sky and exhaled. Maybe we were done talking about Beckett. She said, "It's so good to be home."

"Is it?" Alicia and I had been plotting our escape from Sierra for as long as I could remember. But as one of the few Black people in town, she had to deal with shit I didn't. The racism, microaggressions, and even a general thoughtlessness that seemed to type people who looked like me as "Sierra," even though this place was inhabited long before white people claimed it. "Last year you were in a funk for weeks after coming back," I said.

"Well, this is our senior year, so it'll be different. And this is the best place in town," she said, slipping off her purple Birks.

We'd come out on a little beach. Across from us, a sheer wall of serpentine glowed greenish yellow in the midday sun. The water was low, but it still rushed over the rocks upstream and pooled in front of us, dark blue, and deep enough to jump. We dropped our things, stripped down to our bikinis, and splashed in. I floated on my back; Alicia swam a kind of breaststroke with her head above the water.

"Yeah," I agreed. "It is."

We sat on the boulder in the sun, our swimsuits dry again. My thoughts had turned to the app—how to capture this place for it—get good pictures—when we heard footsteps thudding down the canyon side.

"Great. My first day back and we have to share?" Alicia shaded her eyes with her hand. There were so many amazing spots you could reach without having to fling yourself off a flume and butt-slide down a canyon wall, so this one was usually vacant.

The skittering and crunching continued. Then, across the sunlit water, a familiar hunch topped by a head of light-brown curls emerged from the trees.

"Beckett?" I burst out. He wasn't alone. Behind him, stepping onto the beach, blinking into the light, was Running Boy. River. River! I held tight to the rock.

"Beckett!" Alicia called, all smiles and waves. "Who's your friend?"

River held up a hand. Beckett flashed that lopsided grin and sang, *"Moon river wider than a mile."* His velvet tenor reverberated through the canyon.

"Cute," I called, before Beckett could get to the lines about heartbreakers—the ones that made all the middle school girls swoon when the Sierra High Singers used to perform for us.

My brother wasn't fazed by my tone or death glare. He said, "At least I didn't find you two skinny-dipping, then you'd be mooning River."

Alicia ignored this and said, "Ah, the famous Running River." She lowered her voice and said to me, "That's why you almost fell off the rock!"

"River," Beckett said, "Alicia Johnson, expert pianist, programmer, and the sole reason my sister ever leaves the house." I opened my mouth to protest, but he met my eyes and said, "Mom wasn't sure where you went, but I figured you knew the best spot."

We did. Because he'd shown us when he was fifteen. Mason was out of town, and probably because Alicia was over, Beckett asked if we wanted to see the best swimming hole in Sierra.

I fixed my gaze on the serpentine rock. If I'd asked him to come, then he couldn't have ambushed us. Ugh. And now River was here, and I was in my hot new bikini—in my peripheral vision, River peeled off his shirt. Um . . .

"Welcome back!" Alicia called across the water.

"Thanks—you too."

"Come on out!" she said, gesturing to the rock. "Plenty of room."

Alicia pressed me with her eyes. I could almost hear her saying, *Relax, your brother is fine, and you can totally talk to a half-naked boy while wearing the equivalent of a bra and underwear.*

Beckett and River jumped in. I tried to watch the water, the light on the canyon walls, but my eyes tracked River as he swam. Like it was automatic. *Damn.*

Beckett climbed up, holding on to his shorts so they wouldn't slide off.

"You don't have trunks?" I asked.

He shook his head and sat down, darkening the rock with water as he squeezed his shorts out like a sponge.

"Careful, Beck! My phone!" I said.

"You swam out here with your phone?"

"Girl's talented. Once she brought a whole picnic, and nothing got wet," Alicia said. "Today, though, she's taking pictures and making notes for the app. Sometimes she even talks to me"—Alicia paused and gave me her little devilish eyebrow dance—"about the parts of the app I'm helping with."

I half snarled and half smiled. I'd only taken three pictures while she was texting with Cello Man. I was relieved she was up for it—for being on my "team," as Cecil called it—on top of all the other senior stuff we had: college and scholarship applications, AP exams. She was also prepping for North State Classical Fest. And since she couldn't decide between college or conservatory, she was applying to both. That we had time to sit in the sun on a rock at all was kind of amazing.

"Appy-Cappi and Alicia-Apps!" Beckett said with a clap. "Practically Steve and Steve."

And when he looked between us, I saw for a sec how lonely he must be. Twenty-one, sober, his own best friend unable to even blink a hello.

And then River was there, wet head popping up over granite, glistening like a slow-motion shot in the *Baywatch* episodes Gram loved. Only this boy was better—less muscle-popping, more long and lean.

"Uh, hellooo," I said.

"Beckett told me if I wanted to see you today, I better come with." He smiled, pushing his hair off his forehead. My lungs constricted. *Air.* Then River shook off like a puppy—it was such a strange move, head to tail, complete with a smack to his ear to dislodge water. I was cured. I could breathe again.

"In the flesh," I said, which was maybe not the best thing when so much of my own was showing. But I couldn't really tell if he was checking me out.

"So Beckett," Alicia said, "what do you think the three best places in Sierra are?"

"Oh"—Beckett wrung his hands—"here, Impregnate Point, and—"

"Impregnate Point?" I asked.

"Some name," River said, squinting against the sun.

"He means Wayson Heights," Alicia said.

"Oh, right." How had I not heard that one before? "People say the view rivals the Grand Canyon." River nodded.

"What's the third?" Alicia asked, poking Beckett's leg.

"My house, specifically, my bedroom."

"Ew, Beck, don't be gross," I said.

"I wasn't," Beckett said. "It's great in there—the shadows of the trees in the afternoon, the blue walls—that bed Gramps made for me, the stars Dad and I painted on the ceiling— they're real constellations."

"Maybe we should put your room on the app," I said. "It appears to be a popular destination."

Beckett tossed a pebble at me. "You can't put this spot on the app, or Impregnate Point."

"Yes we can," I said.

"Do you want them flooded with people?"

"I hate to break it to you, Beckett Alexander," Alicia said, "but the internet exists, and this spot is on it." She waved a finger around the canyon.

"An app's different. It won't be some obscure website built by a techno hippie in 1998. People will use it and see pictures and come. They'll ruin it."

I leaned back and felt the rock warm under my palms. "You sound like Dad. And who knows if anyone will even use the app. Most of them just hum away in obscurity."

Beckett met my eyes. What did he see? A bunny maybe, about to dart away. Why'd he come down here? Was bringing

River a gift? A joke? Did he really want to hang out with us? Finally he said, "Dad's right about lots of things."

Huh. I didn't expect that. "Well," I said, "nice you think people will download it. And if they do, it's crowdsourced, so if I don't add this spot, someone else will."

"And, *bam*!" He clapped. "Erosion."

"Seriously? Since when has trail quality been your cause?" I said.

"Um—he does have a point about erosion," River said, looking down.

"You're a soil expert?" Alicia asked. "I thought you were here to check out Caprice's hot new bikini."

I don't know who went redder, River or me. After a second he met my eyes. "It is a very nice swimsuit."

"Thanks," I said, and tried to swallow my smile while turning to my brother. "Beck—if the app takes off—and it's a big if—it'll help pay for college."

Beckett narrowed his eyes. "See, I told you. Enough money and a scooter, and you'll do anything they ask."

"Oh, you're one to give life advice?" I said, and Alicia audibly gasped. Birds suffocated inside my lungs.

Beckett twisted a curl around his finger. "Nope. Definitely not."

Alicia jostled Beckett's shoulder. "Caprice didn't sell her soul to Elon Musk. She's just trying to get out of Sierra."

"I get it," River said. "I signed with Oregon to run

cross-country for the environmental engineering degree. I like to run, sure, but mostly it's the other thing."

"Environmental engineering's cool," I said.

River smiled, looked like he was about to say more, but before he could, "The app is going to be good," Beckett said. "Because everything Caprice does is good." What was that note in his voice? Anger? Envy? "She should be careful what she puts on it."

"If you feel so strongly about it, maybe you should help," Alicia said.

"Great idea," Beckett said. "I like this girl. Is she in charge?"

"Ali," I said cutting my eyes to her and ignoring my brother.

"What?" She opened her palms to the air. "He likes me." She grinned. "And we could use more help." My skin felt tight. Did my brother like *me?* I honestly didn't know. Still, Alicia had a point. It seemed like Beckett believed in my app. Maybe even more that I did, if he thought it'd be so popular, it would cause environmental impact. Sure, I'd been avoiding him, but if he helped, it could be fun—like we were working on those Rube Goldberg machines we'd made as kids. Plus, we'd be a team. It wouldn't be just us.

"Okay," I said, chewing on the side of my lip. I could probably get him on my side about most things. Or Alicia could. I swallowed, forcing the lump out of my throat. "But you can't code—"

Alicia said, "Beck can be an ideas guy."

"Alicia likes my ideas," Beckett said. He stretched his arms to the sky. "I'm in. River should help too. He's practically a tourist—"

Alicia clapped. "Yes! New-kid perspective!" I shook my fist at Alicia. She blew me a kiss.

"Sure," River said. Our eyes met. His were dark and hazel. For a second I forgot how to breathe.

"Okay," I said after a beat too long. "The goal is to finish the app and launch it at Dam Days."

"You ever been here for Dam Days?" Alicia asked River. "The town, like, dresses up as construction workers or dam engineers, and the rest like hippies."

"Our family has a long-standing parade rivalry," Beckett said.

River widened his eyes.

"Gramps's business," I explained, "Alexander Construction. It represents the dam workers. Even Frank Wants Flowers, the flower shop our gram started that our aunt runs—"

"That's the hippies," Beckett finished.

"Their grandparents' marriage is like the union of the two," Alicia added. "It's some serious small-town white people stuff."

"Damn," River said with a little smirk.

"Exactly," I said. "The town tries to point out how people lived here way before the dam—this is Maidu land—but my Gramps says Dam Days really is about trying to connect the anti-growth residents and the pro-growth residents through a celebratory flashback to 1968 when the town incorporated, and it mostly leaves out the people who were here first."

"Sounds . . ." River rubbed his jaw.

"Tiny-towncore?" Alicia offered.

"Yeah," River said, laughing.

"It's not without its problems. But Gramps says it's good for growth," I said.

"And Dad says it's a way to remind people that we'll always be a small town," Beckett said.

"And," Alicia added, brushing pebbles from her palms, "the hospital's extra busy with accidents. It's like our own special New Year's or Fourth of July."

"Caps here," Beckett said, nodding to me, "was seriously competitive about the float as a kid. Total flower-child demon." I tried to remember how I acted getting ready for the parade, but it was all a blur of flower crowns, float decoration, and Gram getting me to spy on Gramps, so we could be sure to one-up them in the parade. I couldn't remember anything about Beckett except how he always rode with Alexander Construction—well, until he got so drunk, he fell off the float. After that he didn't come. I felt Beckett's eyes on me. "But for all your Dam Pride, you still knock the Beavers—"

"Beckett, enough with knocking beavers," Alicia said.

"There's never enough knocking beavers," Beckett said.

I felt my ears redden. River had turned pink too. I wanted to push Beckett into the water.

River said, "Yeah man, that's a little—"

"Sexist? Homophobic? Childish?" I offered.

"Caps, *why* are you so damn serious!" Beckett tossed a rock into the water. "Get it? Dam serious? I was joking." Beckett grinned. River gave Beckett the side-eye. "Yeah, I can be a lot sometimes." Beckett lay back on the boulder. "Fun fact—I can't remember the last time I was sober here."

We went quiet. I thought about that first time he brought Alicia and me. Was he drunk and we didn't even know?

"Anyone else hot?" I stood, ending the very long silence.

"Well, *you're* boiling," Alicia said, eyebrow arched.

"Stop!" I flailed my hands in her direction, feeling the stupid grin on my face.

"Swim time," I said.

Beckett stood and glanced at Alicia. I saw a hint of his *I'm plotting something* smile as I launched myself into the cold water.

My foot grazed the mud at the bottom. I came up, swam a few strokes, closed my eyes. Opened them, and then River was there, beside me. How is it fair that boys swim shirtless? And how was this boy rewiring my brain simply by floating next to me? His eyes flecked like mica. Our hands brushed, the contact electric. "Wow," I said.

"What?" His hand bumped mine again. I thought, *IF contact with River THEN electric-eel-level shocks.* Somehow I turned on my belly and swam to the rockslides. I could feel his eyes on me.

"River, watch Cappi!" Beckett yelled.

"As if he's looking anywhere else," Alicia called.

I sat, and was washed down the stone slide, surfacing again in front of River. My leg grazed his and I had to fight to regain control of my prefrontal cortex. He swam to the rock himself, slid down with a whoop and a splash. When he resurfaced, we bobbed silently, eyes on each other. I was aware of every inch of my skin, of the musk scent of the mud from the shore, how the ripples River made brushed against me, his eyes glinting brown and gold in the afternoon light.

He looked up the canyon where the shadows were growing long. "Oh! I gotta get going. Preseason practice starts at five."

"Oh, *Should I stay or should I go?*" Beckett sang.

Alicia laughed.

River looked at me. I could tell he wanted me to follow. Cute as he was, I wasn't going to make it that easy.

"I'll go with you," Beckett said.

"Hey Beckett," Alicia called when the boys were standing on the shore. "Funny that Caps didn't come down here all summer because she was worried about creeps, and then you showed up." She cackled.

Beckett ran splashing back at her.

I had no idea how to talk to my brother about anything that mattered. But if we worked together on this app, maybe we could figure it out. Maybe he would know I was trying.

Alicia and Beckett were laughing as I turned and watched River pull on his shirt. He met my eyes. Oh. I'd been caught. And it didn't feel bad. He smiled. I could float on that feeling forever. I don't know how much time passed, but then Beckett called to River, "Wanna race?"

I turned around, slid under the cool water, and when I surfaced again, the boys were gone, and our clothes were missing from the shore.

OBJECT: Clay Angel with a Chipped Wing
LOCATION: 32 Pine Crest Avenue, Sierra, California
RESIDENT: Illana Moon

A group of graduating Sierra High Singers gave the angel to me at their graduation. They'd nominated me staff speaker that year, and I'm pretty sure they also put me up for Teacher of the Year. I won for the county, but choir teachers can have a disadvantage at state. At some level, the judges don't take you as seriously if you're teaching singing and not math, even though I can promise you I kept more kids at Sierra High than any one of my math colleagues—no shade to my math peeps! I love you, nerdy number Beavers! But let's be real—my singers graduate. I've kept some well-known troublemakers not only on campus but gotten them to show up sober and in suits on Saturday mornings to sing at the old folks' home. And that's the thing, I guess—that angel—it reminded me that I don't just love my job because I get to sing every day. I love my job because of how much these kids need to sing. You can listen to music others make nonstop in your earbuds, but that doesn't give you the same good feeling as joining your voice with others. Of practicing together so long and so hard that eventually you sound like heaven. You see, that angel was each one of my students. No matter what they did outside my class, no matter what mistakes they made, or what *they were dealing with, they could show up and sound like heaven. They could bring their gift to the world. So no, it's not just that I get worked up about my clay angel, it's that this happened to my kids. This town's kids. You know when that angel fell and chipped, I cried. Well, that sure seems silly now that it and so much is gone, doesn't it? No time to cry. I got to help us remember how to sing.*

THREE WEEKS BEFORE

"Oh!" Alicia tapped the long window of the choir classroom, where, on the inside, River rocked back and forth on his toes like he might want to sprint out of there. She turned to me. "Caps! He's a choir boy! If you're lucky, he can teach you the magic of the serenade."

It was the first day of school and hot as Hades in the outdoor hallways of Sierra High. Alicia waved wildly, but River didn't see us. The scent of smoke from a wildfire somewhere layered in with the sweat, fruity lotions, and body sprays of the crowded sidewalks. Alicia stopped at the choir room door. "You're coming, right?"

"*He's* in there. I'll get more work done in the library." It was my free period, when I was supposed to work on the AP Computer Science class I took online. Sierra High didn't offer it. Alicia swung her I'M HERE FOR THE FUN bag into my hip.

"Depends, Capybara, on how you define *work*."

"Ali! I don't even know if he likes me. He hasn't run by again."

"Oh come on. He hasn't run by because preseason is no joke. Did you see Mitchell's post about his feet?"

"Ugh, yes and gross. I didn't know toenails could do that."

"Oh, I did." She made a face. "I'm sure River'll keep his socks on in class. You saw what a gentleman he was, even faced with you in that spicy swimsuit. None of that *I'm talking to the boobs* stuff. I mean, he was glancing, so clearly the guy was working hard to keep his id from taking over, but—"

"I'll see you at lunch," I said, trying to pull away before he spotted me.

"Come in! Adrienne's stupid insistence that we take time off to *readjust to the school year* means I am not going to be seeing you enough. My Cappi-meter is low, look—" She went slack-mouthed and moved her arms like she was running out of batteries, an act she'd been doing since third grade.

"We just sat together for two classes, Alicia."

"Thank God! I almost got hives from that calculus syllabus. If you weren't there—I would've—"

"Been just fine."

"Without my breathing instructor? No way. Weekly tests, Caps! Not quizzes. Tests!"

I put my hands on her shoulders, guiding them down from her ears.

"Thank you," Alicia said. "Now, Cappi, time for chorus—a little River will do you good. Look at him in that button-down and his running shorts for the first day of school. If he scrambles your language function, it's okay. He might not even notice."

I turned back to the windows where River had spotted us and now stood on the other side of the glass, looking kinda like a puppy in one of those adoption cubes. "Come on," Alicia said, tugging my arm. I let her drag me into the classroom as she whispered, "You see how he's gazing right at your"—she bumped my hip with hers—"face?"

Heat surged up the back of my neck as we practically slammed into River inside the door. I squeaked out a "Hey," and added a finger wave. Then immediately wanted to hide my hands but—damn—pocketless skirt. *IF dressing up for the first day AND bound to encounter cute new guy THEN prepare with pockets.*

Alicia said, "Were you in on the great clothing steal?"

"Huh?" River looked confused. His button-down was blue and undone and, under it, his T-shirt read MIDDLE-EARTH'S ANNUAL MORDOR FUN RUN.

"Innocent as a baby," Alicia said. "As I suspected."

"What's she talking about?" River asked.

I stared at the gold flecks in his eyes until Alicia jostled me. "Oh—my brother," I said.

When I didn't say more, River sort of shrugged, his arms loose. "I didn't know you were in choir."

"She's my moral support," Alicia said, dropping her bag on the piano bench and sitting down. She pushed open the key cover and played an arpeggio.

River's brow furrowed.

"Alicia's the accompanist. And I—"

"Accompany *me*—" Alicia said, with a few dramatic Fifth Symphony chords.

"Emotional support," I said. "Not musical."

Alicia lowered her voice. "It's true—Caps here can't tell her bass from treble."

"Music's my super dysfunction," I said.

"You can't be that bad," River offered.

"IF you wait around long enough THEN she'll sing AND—" Alicia cringed.

"IF you start THEN I'll leave."

River looked—what? Embarrassed? Perplexed? About my singing? Our goofy code-talk?

But he said, "Don't." And he put out his hand but stopped just short of touching my arm. Then, after a pause where his ears turned red, he added, "I've been in ten different chorus programs, and I've never had a student accompanist."

"Well," Alicia said, "I'm frankly fantastic." She started playing the Moonlight Sonata, then switched to the "Maple Leaf Rag" for a few measures, before rolling into a Taylor Swift song that got half the classroom belting it out. River met my eye. There are no lightning bugs in California—well, I've never seen one. Dad claims there are. Alicia told me how at music camp out in Illinois they'd appear out of the darkness, making a sudden sparkle of light. That was what I felt then. All flicker. All over. Alicia stopped playing, but the room went on singing. She looked up at River. "I wouldn't have pegged you for a singer."

"If you move a lot, it's a good elective. Most schools have it."

"Do you like it?" I asked.

"Don't hate it. Might rather build hydroponic gardens or something. Or maybe my own heat pump."

"Huh," I said, and Alicia played some chords that meant *Damn.* Or possibly *HEAT PUMP!!*

The bell rang, and Ms. Moon scuttled in, loaded down with three tote bags she dropped next to Alicia; then she clapped her hands together. "Okay, okay, places everybody!"

"I'll disappear to that corner," I said, waving to Violet Homesteader, Kim Chase, and Mitchell Wheeler, who, as if already adapted to our new status as seniors, scurried in the door seconds after the bell. Mitchell smiled and settled on the bleachers next to River, probably bonding over mutilated runner toes.

"Caprice, won't you sing with us this year? It's your last chance," Ms. Moon said, but before I could say *I still don't have my brother's voice,* she turned back to the room, introduced herself to the new students, and ordered Alicia to play a warm-up.

I settled under the window and pulled out my laptop. I glanced up, and saw River, shining like a god with the sun slanting through the window, mouth wide as he sang *"Ah, Eh, Ee, Oh, Ooh."* My god. My brain. My heart. My hormones. I was not going to be able to work. I logged into my online classroom but could barely read. I clicked through the module, pretending I was absorbing it, but my eyes kept pulling back to River, who was now smiling at me around his vowels. *Ah, Eh, Ee, Oh, Oooooooh.* I closed my laptop. Might as well surrender.

My phone vibrated. I turned it over to flip on DO NOT DIS-
TURB but saw:

Cecil:

> Can you meet Friday afternoon
> with your team?

I stared at it. Why did Cecil want to meet? We didn't meet.
After our initial talk, we typically texted or talked quickly by
phone. I swallowed.

> Probably—I'll need to ask.

I hovered my hand over my phone unsure of what else to
say. I settled on:

> Why?

> I want to meet them

> And make sure we're on the same page.

Huh. What did that mean? I tried to make eye contact with
Alicia, but she was too focused. Usually, that was what I liked
about accompanying the accompanist—she focused, and I
focused. We worked like gears clicking together. But now I
needed her.

Ms. Moon stopped the singing and ordered the class to read
through the syllabus. I slipped up to the piano to show Alicia
my phone.

"Friday works for me."

"Right, but—"

"Caprice, you may join us in song, or you may sit and be

silent. Alicia—can you give us a D?" Alicia struck the key. I mouthed "Sorry" to Ms. Moon while slipping Alicia's phone onto the piano next to her sheet music.

Then I texted:

> What if he has a problem with the team?

> you're worried what he'll think of beckett

> Kinda. Okay, yeah.

Ms. Moon crossed the room and stood behind Alicia. "You need both hands for class, Ms. Johnson."

Alicia dropped her phone into her bag. Her eyes were wide and a little sad as she mouthed "Everyone loves Beckett." I shrugged. Because yeah. I was pretty sure asking Beckett and River to work with us on the app was the right thing to do, but most people thought of Beckett as a loveable screw-up who was not to be trusted. Cecil was an old family friend, though, so maybe—

Alicia mouthed *"Stop freaking out,"* and nodded toward River. I focused to pick out his voice, deep and full. A voice that could cross canyons. It sent me midair, and I replaced my app worries with this program: *IF boy sings Ah, Eh, Ee, Oh, Ooh THEN lightning bugs will spontaneously hatch west of the Mississippi.* River's eyes locked on mine, and it looked like he forgot what came next—*Oh, Ohh,* or *Eh.* He stopped singing. The room flickered bright. Alicia was right. Everything was going to be okay.

My dad was really obsessed with making sure I knew role-playing games. I got into it because what seven-year-old isn't excited to play a game that takes hours with their dad? He even decided we should make custom figures. He went all out, bought a 3-D printer and set up a workshop in the garage and everything. The modeling software was tricky, but he worked with me to translate my little-kid scribbles into actual things that we printed and painted. We finished the set and played two or three games before Mom threw him out saying he had expensive obsessions and needed a job. He moved to Yuba City after that, and I only saw him once a month—usually I'd pack up those figures and we'd play a game. We rarely had time to finish. I taught my cousin Kim to play, and Mo too. I could make them again, I guess, but it wouldn't be the same. The files—everything—all of it's gone. Even if I had the designs—which I don't—and could print them, they wouldn't have the same little-kid paint job. Some things you can't replace.

TWO AND A HALF WEEKS BEFORE

Friday. I climbed out of Gramps's truck, pulling my shoulder bag over my head and straightening my dress. Light blue. Slim stripe. Alicia was waiting for me in the parking lot of Hole in the Dam Donuts, leaning against her silver Saab in a black skirt and a short-sleeved coat. Summer concert gear. Totally together. If only I could hand off the meeting to her—she looked like a boss even in her trademark purple Birkenstocks. I looked like I was going to a wedding and my strappy sandals were held together with superglue.

"Don't stand around here sweating," Gramps said. "Get some treats for your meeting. Layla's always got that A/C blasting." He pulled out a twenty and stuffed it into my hand. "And you know it's your job to eat them. I always say, never—"

"Take money for a job you can't finish," I said. "Thanks. But you don't have to pay—"

He stuffed his hands in his pockets so I couldn't return the cash right as the boys pulled up in River's truck. In the last week, I'd only seen River at school—firefly glimpses across the

choir room. Practice ate up all his time. This app and everything else ate up mine.

"Um, wow," I said, trying to moderate my voice as I took
in River's Sierra High T-shirt and track shorts topped off by a
gray linen sport coat, then Beckett's ripped jeans and Dad's old
Red Hot Chili Peppers T-shirt. "This is your business casual?"
I could just imagine Cecil's face.

"It's what we got," Beckett said, like he knew it wasn't right
but accepted it. I started to sweat.

"Well," Gramps said, looking between my brother and me
like he had thoughts. But all he said was, "I'm off." And with a
salute and a honk, he was.

"Did you know River's carbon neutral?" Beckett asked as we
tumbled into the arctic air-conditioning of Hole in the Dam. "His
truck runs on vegetable oil, and he never even buys new clothes."

"Sometimes I have to for cross-country."

"Hold up," I said. "Your truck runs on vegetable oil?"

River nodded, but before he could say anything else, Alicia
leaned across me. "Please tell me you buy new underwear."

"Uh, yeah," River said, pink spreading down his neck.
"Recycled cotton though."

Alicia mouthed "Recycled cotton," and my insides turned
to popcorn.

"Caprice Alexander!" Layla Montoya waved as I approached
the counter. "How's your gram?"

"Depends on the day," I said lightly. Gram loved Layla

and her dogs—when they ran by, Layla would stop and Gram always had treats in her pockets.

"Can we get a mixed half dozen?" I said.

"And five coffees," Beckett added. Right. Coffees. I held my breath. I could do this. I just needed to trust my brother and keep my eyes off River and his upcycled everything.

"Don't say anything stupid," Beckett said, grabbing a coffee and the donut box. Could he tell how nervous I was? My sweat had turned icy.

"Thanks." I picked up a cup, tipped toward him, and led the way to the big corner table.

"Big brother's looking out for you." He set the box on the table. "Are we allowed to eat these, or . . . ?" He sat down practically drooling.

"No. They're just decorations." I dropped into the chair next to him.

"They could be. I don't know how this kind of meeting works." His curls hid his eyes.

"You think I do?" I'd been raised around two family businesses, but Alexander Construction was all Gramps. And we didn't have real meetings at Frank's. Mostly we joked about getting gored by geraniums. I tried to focus on my feet under the table—all four corners like in yoga. But I was distracted by River plopping into his chair, a coffee in each hand.

Then Cecil strode in, salt-and-pepper hair shining. Beckett leaned over and whispered, "He already gave you a pile of money. You're golden as ever."

Golden as ever. Is that what Beckett thought? About me? I crossed my arms over my chest. River, who had stayed at the counter chatting with Layla, jogged to our table as Cecil sat next to Alicia, her hands in her lap like she was about to raise them to an invisible keyboard and perform.

"Caprice! Is this your team?"

"Uh, yes," I said.

Cecil looked right at Beckett and asked, "You're on it?" Beckett nodded. Cecil struggled to rearrange his face from disappointed to blank. I'd been worried what Cecil would think. Now my hands turned to fists under the table and a swell of fury rose in me. How dare he judge my brother. He had no idea. I took a subtle breath and tried to clear my throat.

"My brother," I said, smiling, going for confident, "is excited to help streamline the user experience." Beckett made a face that said *What are you even talking about?* My cheeks tightened. "And Alicia," I continued, "brings musical *and* common sense to code and design."

"I make things more elegant," she said as Cecil took her hand over the table, bypassing my brother. How was Beckett supposed to have a chance in Sierra when people snubbed him like this? I tried to let the thought go with a sharp, quiet exhale.

"And this is River," I said, not adding anything else; I mean, why was he here, really? Because he spontaneously generated bioluminescence in my brain? Because he was friends with my brother? River took Cecil's hand. Beckett picked up three donuts like he might want to juggle them. I widened my eyes.

"Riv's our tourist," Beckett said. Did he feel slighted? He didn't seem to. He was all curls and smiles.

"The new kid, actually," River said.

"Excellent!" Cecil said, clapping his hands. Beckett passed a donut to Alicia and the other to River.

"So, tell me how's it going," Cecil said.

I tried to make my shoulder blades slide down my back like in yoga. But nope. I felt them rise to my ears. "I'm working on a demo," I managed, but my voice sounded too high. I paused for a slow breath and continued. "The app launches to a map of town. A tutorial will show users how to add sites. Here's a list of the places we'll add as examples."

I passed him a paper.

Cecil glanced at it and said, "So your crowd-sourcing idea, how does it promote business?"

"By showing what we think is best about living here," I said, trying to sound sure.

"Like the best swimming spots," Alicia added.

Cecil waved his hand. "No one is buying anything at the river."

"Soil erosion," Beckett mouthed at me. Under the table, I ground my heel into his toes.

My brother flashed a pained smile and said, "Cecil has a point. But also, if you're going to put swimming spots, or, say, Impregnate Point on there, won't the anti-growth folks come after you?"

How'd my brother have a boardroom voice in a donut

shop? And how'd he manage to say "Impregnate Point" without Cecil raising his eyebrows? Beck continued, all casual confidence:

"If our swimming holes get too much foot traffic, or if there are suddenly fifteen or fifty more cars at every lookout, imagine it—trash, erosion, smokers forgetting this town is literally a tinderbox"—he mimed ashing a cigarette—"poof!" Beckett shook a curl out of his eye. He would know about the smokers. My surprise anger shifted targets now. I wanted to slug my brother.

Cecil made an excited clicking sound. "He's right!"

"Okay," I said slowly, trying to take back control, cursing myself for not having talked with Beck *before* the meeting. Why'd I think he'd change his mind from when we were swimming? Or just go along with what I said? I mean, this was Beckett. My mouth was dry now. Cecil leaned over the table and picked up a donut. Right. No one had even offered him one. Or a coffee. The extra one just sat in front of River, steaming.

"How about this," Cecil said. "You could limit the map to just downtown? Less environmental impact that way, more businesses. Or maybe you have other ideas, considering all this—" He moved the hand with the jelly-filled in a circle.

"Absolutely," I said, because there didn't seem to be another answer.

Cecil pointed to his watch. "We can check in again in a few weeks. I've got to run now—another meeting across town. Thanks for this." He held up the jelly-filled.

My jaw fused, but I managed a smile, though I probably looked like some terrifying doll from the window of Way Back Antiques. "Thanks," I managed, and it didn't totally sound like a growl.

"Great!" Cecil stood and in seconds was out the door.

"That went well." Beckett leaned back in his chair.

"Sure, if I'm building an ad for the Chamber of Commerce." I dropped my head to the Formica table. "Who wants to rethink with me?"

"Raincheck," Alicia said. "I've got to practice." Her fingers played an imaginary piano.

"I can," River said, "after I drop off your brother. Just a sec." He went back to the counter as Layla disappeared into the kitchen.

Oh. *Well.* I perked up. Maybe the day *could* get better.

I bit my lip to keep a smile from spreading. Maybe River and I could finally be alone.

"I need to help Gramps at the lumberyard," Beckett said, then added, "But it shouldn't take long. If you guys'll wait, I can come."

Ah. Never mind.

"Can someone get the door?" River called. Layla was handing him two big jugs. "I got some oil for the truck."

"And a job!" Layla added. Her smile lines deepened as she gave River's shoulder an affectionate shake. "Delivering for me Saturday and Sunday mornings."

"When I don't have a meet."

"Nice!" Beckett said. "I can cover when he's busy."

Layla narrowed her eyes. "Does your car run on cooking oil? 'Cause donut-smelling delivery's the sale's pitch."

Beckett's mouth twitched. "Maybe it could. River?"

"It's a Vanagon, right?"

Beckett nodded.

"Then, yeah. I think so."

Oof. Beckett was making friends. That was good. But I couldn't stop myself hoping the idea might gather dust, like that drum kit my parents bought Beckett in middle school.

In the parking lot, River finished loading the jugs into the back of the truck.

"See ya!" Alicia called as she slipped into the Saab.

"Bye! Tell the Frenchman I say bonjour."

"I'm really practicing piano, Cap. The vaquita need me to win this," she called over the *Spirited Away* soundtrack blasting from her speakers.

"Win it for the sea pandas!" When I turned back, River was already in the driver's seat. Beckett was nowhere to be seen. I took a breath and opened the truck door.

Inside, the vinyl bench seat stuck to my knees. "Um, River, I think it's so hot in here, your seats are melting."

River laughed, then reached across me and grabbed a crank on the passenger door. "This truck's pre-power windows," he said. Our heads were inches apart as he rolled the window down. His elbow bumped my thighs and I felt hotwired. *Why,*

why, was my brother not just leaving us alone? I flattened my spine against the seat and River smiled, his eyes half-closed, revealing two tiny freckles on his right eyelid.

Was it weird to want to kiss someone's eyelid? Or to even have this thought after my brother sabotaged my meeting and now I had to rethink the whole app? A hot donut-scented breeze rolled in and River, still leaning across me, tapped his fingers quickly on my now-open window frame, smiling shyly with those hazel eyes. I almost leaned in. I almost just went for it. But then he moved back behind the steering column. I swiveled toward him. Magnetized. Probably grinning like a fool.

And then before I could even get a word out, Beckett was back. Opening the passenger door and motioning for me to slide over. I gave him a look.

"What? You don't want to sit closer to his stick?"

"Where you been, Beck?" I said, trying to sound chipper as I slid over and realized the stick shift was going to be sitting pretty much right between my knees. I smoothed my skirt. River accidentally touching me while he drove wasn't the problem. My brother ready to comment? That was. I went yoga-posture perfect, and squeezed my legs together like Gram said she did when she was a girl, and her parents made her keep a penny between her knees all through church.

"So, uh—" River's teeth went into his lip. He tinkered with the plastic wrapped around his steering wheel, then knocked a set of glass straws around the cup holder, bumping my knee with the back of his hand and sending a ripple up my spine.

The imaginary penny between my knees flattened like in one of those souvenir machines. "So what's up with Cecil?" River said. "He listened to Beckett more than you." Surprised, I glanced from River to my brother, who was staring out the open window, then back to River, who was staring at me.

"Caps can't be blamed if she brought a brilliant team," Beck said, clicking his seat belt.

"True," I said, not wanting to get into it. Plus, I'd read on the Al-Anon website that sometimes choosing to do nothing was empowering. Maybe I could say nothing. Do nothing. Walking into a room with Beckett meant all eyes went to him, for better or worse. I should have been better prepared. It wasn't fair of me to be mad, really. It was partly my fault.

River tapped the plastic and said, "You should be able to make the app how you want, though. It's your design." He started the truck.

Huh. Nice he thought so. I forced a smile but shook my head. "Cecil's backing this. What he wants matters." I felt heavy. I wasn't going to give the money back, say, *Sorry, I can't do this.* But if my team wasn't even backing me, if my own brother wasn't, maybe my idea was bad.

"Are we waiting for someone to buckle their lap belt or what?" Beckett asked.

River's eyes were on me. Intent with what? Curiosity? Concern? He said, "I don't know where I'm going."

"Turn right," I said.

"Uh, no. Go left," Beckett said.

"In what universe is it faster to get to the lumberyard by going left?"

"Mine." Beckett grinned. "I like the long way around."

River turned right and when he did, his leg jostled against mine. Did he do it on purpose?

"Here are some places we can all agree should go on the app"—I pointed—"the Dam Museum"—its sign boasted HOME OF THE ORIGINAL DAM MODEL!—"and of course, Liquor of the Dam'd."

"Stay away from the Hell Boy," Beckett said. "And pretty much everything else in there."

Was he talking to me, or to River? Because didn't he know that repeatedly finding him in our bathroom covered in vomit, starting when I was ten, was enough to get me to steer clear of Hell Boy? As far as I was concerned I was never going to taste alcohol. River's leg against mine jostled me out of my head. "Turn right up here, before Sierra Market—best fries in town. Then Burrito Junction—on the right, endless chip baskets. And Sierra still has a butcher—parents dig that." The sign said WHAT'S YOUR BEEF? SIERRA'S SOURCE FOR DAM FINE MEAT.

"Lot of businesses for the app then," River said.

"*Money, money, money,*" Beckett sang.

I elbowed him.

"You're so jealous of my pipes," he said.

"Hardly."

"So why do you look like you did when we were picnicking at the lake and Gramps teased you for singing off-key and you got so mad, you ran away?"

I bit my lip. I knew what he was talking about. Gram's birthday. All the girls dressed like fairy queens: Mom, Gram, Adrienne, and me all in flower crowns and tutus, big butterfly wings. When I sang, I thought I'd sounded as magical as I felt. Then Gramps went and joked, so I ran off and hid in a hollow tree. Everyone was freaking out until Beckett found me.

"You were supposed to be watching me."

"I was a ten-year-old at a lake! I was not in charge."

"You don't even know when you *are* in charge."

"What's that supposed to mean?"

It meant he had no idea when he took over. And he took over. All the effing time. But I couldn't say that. I'd said enough. I needed to be supportive. Accepting. Let him know he was loved. I ground my molars.

"So—um—am I still going the right way?" River said.

"Yeah," Beckett and I said together.

"So, I think," River said, "if you can figure out the erosion thing, that swimming spot should go on the app."

"Hm," Beckett said. "I see you chose your side."

"There aren't sides!" I said. "I just need to make this thing. Cecil needs to like it. And *we* need to figure it out together because you are part of the *team* now."

"*The more we get together, together, together, the more we get together, the happier we'll be,*" Beckett sang.

"River, do you think there'd be legal ramifications if I removed his vocal cords?"

"*For my friends are your friends, and your friends are my friends,*" Beckett continued.

"Probably," River said. "But they might be worth it." River downshifted as he reached the stop sign. His knuckles neared my knees, sparking a firefly.

"You wouldn't dare!" Beckett shoved me and I crushed into River's side. When I pulled myself off him, dizzy from the charged contact and the scent of forest soap, Beckett mouthed "You're welcome," and flashed his turn-tooth smile.

I looked away. "Turn left," I said, trying to discreetly keep contact with River's arm. I didn't like my brother's methods, but I did like being this close to River. "It's right after the Feeney Brothers Law Offices."

As River parked at the lumberyard my phone vibrated.

Alicia:

DID YOU DITCH YOUR BROTHER YET??!!!

Alicia

Stop yelling

And. I wish.

We're waiting for him

to help Gramps

WHY? YOU COULD BE KISSING INSTEAD!!

You're the one that's always telling me

to hang out with Beckett!

YEAH BUT NOT WHEN
YOU COULD BE HEADING

TO IMPREGNATE POINT WITH RIVER

OMG WHY do you call it that?

WHY DON'T YOU?!

DROP HIM OFF WITH
WHAT'S HER NAME

ANIMAL DRAWING GIRL

Kylie?

YES!

IT'S TIME FOR YOU TO GET

WHAT YOU'VE BEEN MISSING!

She hasn't been around in weeks.

YOU THINK HE CARES?

How about you leave me alone
and call your French Cellist?

I'm practicing.

Uh, no. You're texting me.

this left-hand sequence is hard

And then Beckett was back, opening the door to the truck,
and I'd wasted my minutes alone with River texting.

"I found the specs for a typical Vanagon conversion," River
said, holding up his phone.

Oh. River had been focused on Beck's van. What about the
app? Wasn't *that* our plan?

"Beck, didn't you say seven corporations pollute more than all individuals combined? Kinda looking like you think your actions matter."

Beckett smiled. "Look, if I can deliver donuts in a car that *smells* like them and do some spare-change worth of good, I'll take it."

He had a point. If converting the car meant that Beckett could have a job, that was important, right? And if someone in town who wasn't family was willing to take a chance on him after everything, I couldn't resent it. Even our aunt Adrienne didn't want him to work for her. He was a little shit at the meeting today. And after. But maybe he was pissed at Cecil shunning him like that. Maybe that's why he'd sabotaged me.

River was still looking at his phone. His tongue went between his teeth. "Yeah, we can do this!" Then he looked up at me. "Caprice—crap—you wanted more help today, and I got so excited about—"

"It's fine," I said. Because it was. Or at least it should be. Beckett needed friends, a job. He'd been through enough. And I could work on the app alone. I was good at that, and maybe that was the better way to get it done after all.

On the drive home, River talked about relative carbon footprint of biodiesel versus gasoline, the expense of electric cars, and the waste generated by people getting new cars more often than they needed. We crested the hill near the Anglican Church and a deer jumped out of the trees. River shifted to avoid it. His leg fell against mine again. He gave me a little sideways smile. I spent the drive thinking—*IF you meet River's eyes THEN electrically charged space particles will shimmer blue and green through the air AND a billion fireflies will spontaneously appear outside their climate zone and fill your head.*

I wanted help on the app, but the truth was, by the time we got home, I wasn't thinking about anything but River. I focused on that feeling as I worked in the living room, while River and Beckett disassembled the Vanagon in the driveway. When River left for practice, the look he gave me was intense enough to fuse my vertebrae. Something was happening. I could wait.

OBJECT: Pinch Pots Made By My Niece and Nephew

LOCATION: Even Frank Wants Flowers, 300 Staff Road, Thousand Oaks Center, Sierra, California

RESIDENT: Adrienne Alexander

I never wanted kids. Never even really liked them. But when my brother and Irene moved back to town, I decided to take being an aunt seriously. I was not prepared for how desperately I would love my nephew. He was all chaos and curls. He could climb anything. You took your eyes off the kid for a second and he was scaling the bookshelves. It was marvelous. I had no idea the phrase "climbing the walls" was literal until I met that boy. When his sister was born, she was so soft and small, and that kid adored her. They couldn't let her cry herself to sleep because they'd find Beckett in there with his hand through the crib rails. Irene and Dylan were beside themselves. It was cute. I never babysat; my parents did. But I would show up and give them a trampoline or take them to the Sacramento Zoo. When I officially took over as owner of the store, they made me these pinch pots. Beckett's was green with a tree; Caprice's yellow with a square at the bottom she told me was a robot. I kept them on the counter by the register. Beckett's held my business cards. Caprice's was the take a penny, leave a penny bowl. People around here still use cash, so it was useful. Sometimes I wonder how much cash burned in the *fire, how many people kept envelopes of it in their nightstands. And how many of them were also the ones who didn't have insurance. Thankfully I did. For my place and the store. I had to list everything for them. Even those pinch pots. Insurance makes you list a value. It made my heart ache to write "handmade business card holder." And "handmade change bowl, thirty dollars each." When I knew they were priceless.*

ONE WEEK BEFORE

"I hear Beckett crashed your end-of-summer swim party with Alicia here, stole your clothes, and is now dismantling his car. So I guess he's doing all right, then?" These were Aunt Adrienne's words to me when I arrived at Even Frank Wants Flowers the next week. Alicia was already wiping down the front window, perched over the display of fairy yard ornaments, crystals, and house plants.

"Ali! You ratted him out before I could! No fair!"

"You were late. What was I supposed to do? Keep the gossip from her for"—she looked at her watch—"ten whole minutes? No way. Not after she made us take time off to settle back into school, and as soon as I walked in the door I had to wipe some kid's snot off the windows."

"Fair. I'll do the bathroom."

Alicia smiled. "I didn't tell her how we've been scheming to get you up to Impregnate Point with River, but we've failed because Beckett is attached to you both like some sucker fish—" She puckered her lips and blew me a kiss.

"What!" Adrienne dropped a stack of invoices and pointed at Alicia. "You were holding back the good stuff."

"Adrienne!" I dropped my head to the wall.

"If your dad hung out with some guy I was into when we were in high school—" Adrienne bugged her eyes at me.

"Please no stories about the dark days before social kept people from taking their clothes off everywhere," I said.

"Fine," she said, "tell me about this boy."

"Cappi's full-on love-zombied, and she just met him," Alicia said.

"I am not!" But the blood rushing to my face told all.

"Oh, come on Caps, we're not twelve! I get it. He's smart, cute, and carbon neutral."

"Is he a wind farm?" Adrienne asked.

"Seriously," Alicia, said gaining composure, "he wears only used clothes."

"And converted his truck to cooking oil," I said.

"Cute and carbon neutral, huh? Sounds like a guy you should be careful hanging out with at Impregnate Point."

"Don't call it that," I said.

"You want a list of people I know who were conceived up there?"

I said *no* at the same time Alicia said *yes*.

Adrienne laughed. "Fine, I'll tell Ali when you're doing deliveries. There's a Cappi Surprise Sunrise in there today," she said, and Alicia giggled.

"What?"

"Nothing," Alicia said. "I know you like those." When I was little I had "opinions" about floral design. At seven my favorite color was yellow, and all I would say when Gram and Adrienne asked me what I thought of an arrangement was "More sunflowers! Yellow roses!" That's how the Cappi Surprise Sunrise Bouquet was born. I still felt warm inside when they were ordered.

"Now get to that bathroom," Adrienne said, swatting me with a bit of raffia. "And so you know, there's a big box of condoms in the cabinet."

"We've been meaning to ask you about that, actually," Alicia said.

"None of your business." Adrienne pointed the raffia at Alicia. Adrienne was a committed single lady. We knew she dated, but no one stuck. "Seriously," Adrienne continued, "take some. Either of you. Both."

I must have been redder than a Valentine's bouquet. Adrienne, like my gram, was too much sometimes. "You're lucky I'm still working for you," I said, breezily. "I have investors now."

"*An* investor," she said. "Don't get a big head. You have deliveries to do."

"And a bathroom to clean," Alicia added.

"Right, right."

"Grab some condoms while you're in there!" Adrienne and Alicia called together and then they both dissolved into giggles as I disappeared into the back room. Adrienne whispered "Cappi Surprise!" I shook my head.

After the bathroom was clean and citrus scented, I slipped into the best place in the store—the cooler—to grab my deliveries. Full buckets by type and color filled the floor, and finished arrangements lined the shelves. When I was little, Gram would bring me in while she selected flowers or changed the water, and then we'd pretend I was Alice in Wonderland and the flowers could talk. I had great conversations with gerbera daisies. Roses were more standoffish. You know, thorns.

"Delivery duty," I said, exiting the cooler and squeezing past Adrienne with the Cappi Surprise in one arm and an arrangement of pink and yellow roses Adrienne had tagged for Gram in the other.

"The Cappi Surprise should be your last delivery." She smiled and tucked another arrangement of peonies in the crook of my elbow behind the Surprise. "Text me when you're done, and I'll clock you out. The longest route possible shouldn't take more than an hour," she said. Her hazel eyes lit up like Dad's. "No stopping to work on the app, okay?"

I nodded, hiding my nose in the roses.

"Not even a picture."

"Not today," I said.

Adrienne gave me a little salute that showed off the three tulips tattooed on her inner arm. I didn't salute back. My arms were full of flowers.

After dropping off the peonies, I pulled into Gram's complex, a white building surrounded by trees and wide meandering walkways. Dozens of brightly painted birdfeeders made by Sierra Ridge fourth graders dotted the grounds. I parked by an overgrown azalea bush and left the car running so my last delivery wouldn't wilt. I half ran through the glass doors, signed in at the desk, and charged down the antiseptic-smelling hallway to Gram's room. We'd done what we could to make it feel comfortable—papered half of one wall with flowered cards, brought a few things from their house: a vase, a couple teacups, her wedding photos, a sunflower quilt. Still, it never felt comfortable. There was a curtain to pull around her hospital bed, and the smell was always wrong, ammonia under floral potpourri.

"Adrienne!" Gram said as I plastered a smile on my face. It wasn't that I didn't want to see her, but sometimes delivering flowers to my own gram was the hardest part of my job. Everyone else was happy to see a flower delivery girl. Even the people who were mourning. Flower delivery means you are remembered. Except when I bring them to Gram. Then I'm faced with how much she's forgotten, including the existence of me.

I dropped a kiss on her silver head. Her braids had come unpinned. I had to deliver that Cappi Surprise, or I would've stayed to cross them over her head the way she liked. She didn't realize they were down, but that wasn't the point. "I brought you roses," I said.

"You've been up to no good, then?" she joked.

"Is being ravished with roses not good?"

"Oh, you girls. You think you invented sneaking around, but—"

"Uh—please. I don't want to know what you did when you were sneaking around."

Gram's eyes glinted. "Oh, I'm not going to give you any ideas."

"You have before," I said, shaking my head, wishing I could shed the memory of her telling me details of boat parties gone wild. It stung that she remembered those and not meeting me at the bus after school with flowers—how we walked home and made up songs so I would remember the names; *dahlias and delphiniums, de-de-de-de-dee.* How she never told me I couldn't sing.

She clicked her tongue. "I wouldn't let you steal my secrets."

"Gram, you don't remember." I fussed with the roses.

"I'm no gram, and I don't forget a thing," she said. She looked at me, her eyes clouded with cataracts. "I feel everything in my bones." My throat tightened. Gram used to say, "Bones don't lie, you listen to them bones of yours, Caps, and you'll be just fine." At night I'd put my ear up to my bones imagining they'd whisper to me. Eventually I realized she was talking about a feeling, and I couldn't help but hope that even if she'd forgotten me, she remembered, somewhere in her bones. But it didn't seem likely. She didn't even remember being a gram. That she remembered things like dancing topless on a houseboat might have been funny if it didn't hurt so bad.

Gram started humming, "Sugar Magnolia."

"Head's all empty and I don't care," I sang along, tuneless as

usual. Gram tapped her fingers on the edge of her wheelchair. She used to dance, arms in the air, and my gramps would sing the line, "She can make happy any man alive," and then whisper to me, "But she picked me, can you believe it? Pinch me!"

Her humming stopped. I refolded her blanket and by the time I'd finished, her eyes were closing. She'd sung herself to sleep. We'd been able to talk, joke, sing. It was as good a visit as we'd ever have now. I dropped a kiss on her forehead. "Love you," I whispered. She was softly snoring. It didn't matter. I said it to remind myself.

I pushed out the glass doors into the heat, and forced one of those long exhales like in Tuesday yoga class. The kind that has a little whistle to it.

Then I saw someone sitting in my car—Mom's car. No—two someones. Without thinking, I ran over, shouting "Get out!" as I pulled my phone from my pocket—to do what? I didn't know—call Mom? Then curls and the slumping shoulders came into focus. Beckett. I felt sweat slick across my forehead. A frustrated scream froze in my throat. I stopped. Because next to him was a taller boy with dark hair. River. I forced a breath, then tapped the window. Beckett's green eyes met mine, all sunlit water.

"Oh hey, Caps." He rolled down the window and smiled. "River and I thought maybe we should steal Mom's car before someone else does." River waved from the passenger seat, and I couldn't tell if the look on his face was embarrassed or excited.

River was here. I felt full of static. Standing with dripping knee pits in the parking lot of an elder care facility was hardly the way I wanted to greet this boy. "Who's going to steal a car from here?" I said, trying to open the driver's side door. Beckett held it closed.

"You know some old people are on seriously popular drugs, right? Mason used to have a guy who'd sell him whatever he managed not to take in a month. The stool softeners were a letdown. Unless of course you were already on something that plugged you up—and then it was sort of a bonus." Beckett rolled his head on the headrest. "Count that as another way you're lucky, Caps—you don't know the seedy underbelly of a place like this. You get to drop off your flowers and roll on. Whereas I"—he tapped his chest—"confront my past every time I visit our grandma."

"Are you—" I stopped because what was I going to say? When my brother said things like this, like he was joking but he wasn't, I felt like I'd done the Dam Dip—Sierra's January jump in the reservoir—all tingly and freaked out, unable to put a thought together.

Beckett tossed his curls, "I'm not seeking a geriatric dealer if that's what you're asking."

"I wasn't—I—" Why couldn't I talk? Why did I feel like someone tossed a bucket of ice water over me?

The car door swung open and Beckett slid out of the driver's side. In the passenger seat, River continued to weave his fingers together, pulling them apart. Making a steeple, tapping index finger to thumb. "Hasn't River told you that idling for more than ten seconds contributes more greenhouse gases to the environment than restarting your car?"

"Seems like he told *you,*" I said before I could control myself.

I stood in the open door but didn't climb in. River still sat, kneading his hands like dough.

"You wanna ditch my brother and hang out with me? I only have one more delivery." I nodded to the Cappi Surprise in the back. River's cheeks bloomed rosebuds.

"We, uh—"

"River's my personal low-carbon chauffeur until we can get the part for the Vanagon."

"It's only fair," River said as he got out of the car and came to stand on the driver's side. "The conversion's more complex than I thought."

"Huh." I turned back to my brother hoping that could help me avoid the messy feelings roiling in my belly. "You're really here to see Gram?"

"You really think I suck," Beckett said.

"Only with consent," I chimed.

My brother smiled like he approved. "Gram will like River—don't you think?"

Oh no. If Gram woke up, she would very much like River.

I turned to him. "Did Beck warn you about Gram?"

River's eyebrows came together.

"She will *love* you," Beckett said. "Hopefully I'll get to see a hot nurse too."

"You're gross," I said.

"Yeah, Beck, that's a little—ugh," River added.

Beckett held up his hand. "Says the guy working so hard to look my sister in the eye." He offered his turn-tooth smile, curls falling into his eyes, and he was that kid again who always got away with everything. "I'm glad you appreciate us saving Mom's car. She'll love to hear you left it running with the keys in it for twenty minutes."

"It was five."

He tapped his phone. His timer was running: "Nine minutes and fifty-two seconds. Plus, however long it was running before we got here."

"You are such a—"

"Wonderful brother?" Beckett stuck his hands in his pockets before walking toward the entrance.

"Enjoy your last delivery," River said. His eyes met mine, dropped down, then came back to mine. I nodded, wings aflutter behind my rib cage. River's smile flashed and he put his hand up to his mouth like he knew he'd disabled my language program. Did he wonder what could happen if we were ever alone? I watched as he followed my brother into the blinding white building.

It wasn't until the stop sign near Way Back Antiques that I remembered I hadn't checked my delivery sheet for the Cappi Surprise. I flipped the invoice over. Huh. My name and address were on it. Did Adrienne make me a back-to-school bouquet?

I was about to reach for the card, but the guy behind me

tapped his horn, so I drove. When I got home, I tugged the card loose from the arrangement. It read:

Maybe it's a basic rule, but IF you meet a girl that you can't stop thinking about THEN send her flowers —River

Caprice:

IF a boy you can't stop thinking about sends you flowers,

THEN invite him to hang out.

River:

I'll keep that it mind

Ha

You knew about the Cappi Surprise Sunrise?

It's not on the website—

I'm the webmaster so I know—

I'm a man of surprises—

u like it?

I love it

It's my bouquet!

Thanks

I worried it'd be like

if u got me Pokémon trading cards—

cute—but not what I'm into now.

I guess I better return those.

Ha ha

So now you're into?

1. Reversing the ecological disaster

2. Girls who code

3. Running

You're into Alicia?

Well, kinda.

But only as a friend.

I'll break it to her gently

Thanks.

I do have a thing for
your grandma though—

I think it's mutual

Oh no. She woke up?

Did she try to feel your muscles?

Twice!

And it's only been ten minutes!

I'm hoping she's going for a third.

Huh. She really puts the
power in power nap.

But you know she can't code right?

> Bummer.

> I'll have to introduce her to
> an AI who can help with that

> Ha-ha

> if you're done flirting
> with my grandma

> do you want to hang out?

> Always. All the time. Right now.

I didn't type this, but I thought it: *IF a boy you like responds to*
"do you want to hang out?" with "Always. All the time. Right now."
THEN reassemble your body from the vapor it became.

My phone lit up again.

> Except I'm hanging
> out with ur brother . . .

> Right.

And just like that I transformed from vapor to puddle. I
knew River and Beck had a Willow Springs connection, the car
project, and my brother was lonely and River wasn't a reminder
of his past. I got it. I did. But—I really, really wanted to be alone
with River. I stared at my phone and wrote:

> Let's all hang out then?

OBJECT: Abacus
LOCATION: Ridge Rock Apartments, Unit 4, Sierra, California
RESIDENT: Candace Hildebrandt

My son was smart. He was going to be the first of us to go to college. He loved math. I always thought maybe it was because of that abacus I gave him for his fourth birthday. He learned to add on that thing, and then multiply and divide. He'd click the colored beads into place and later I started using it to balance my own checkbook. It made me feel in control, to keep track of money that way, maybe because people pray on beads too, so clicking them was a prayer that helped me make ends meet.

I bought it from one of those catalogs that promise to make your kid into the next Einstein or something. I fell for that stuff too much, played classical music to my belly before the kid was even born. I wanted him to have everything I didn't. And he did. He was studying math at Willow Springs. I thought he might be a teacher one day, right here at Sierra High. He laughed at that because except for that choir teacher, he never much liked authority, but I said that kind of job had benefits and retirement. I never had that. Makes a big difference, that stuff.

He dropped out after his first year. "Taking a pause," he called it. Every time he visited, he promised he was planning to go back.

"You know, Mom, when I'm ready to focus." The funny thing is, I never worried about him when he was with his friend Beckett. They were charming, those two. Fun to be around. I knew they drank too much, sure. But boys do that, you know? I asked Mason about it. He said they were fine. They weren't. We still talk about it. He knows now. Beckett comes around still and that helps some. People think I should be mad at him, but I can't. When you don't have much left— well, you know.

I kept that abacus in the kitchen all those years. I was even using it that morning. But I didn't think to grab it. I got my wallet, go-bag, medicines. A photo album from when Mason was little. I was lucky to be home. To have been able to grab anything at all. I drove out of there and went straight to Mason at UC Davis Medical Center. I told him all about it. Even if he can't hear me, I think he knows. I'm living down here now, even found a job. It's good to be closer to Mason, but I don't much like the traffic and how much more I've got to pay in rent.

I was on the back deck, waiting for River and Beckett after Gram's. My belly felt full of feathered creatures, and my attempts at calming them with four-part breathing were worthless. Gramps must have seen me from his yard, because he came ambling over.

"Whatcha thinking about?" He settled beside me on the glider.

I couldn't hide the grin. The worry. Or the blush. I wondered if he could hear the wings in me.

"That boy's really got under your skin. Wooing you with flowers." He smiled.

My shoulders tensed. Welcome to Sierra, where your gramps gets a play-by-play of your love life.

We rocked back. Gramps rolled the seat forward. "I know what you're thinking, Cappi. You can't blame Beckett or Adrienne for their gossip."

"They *both* said something?"

"It's been all over your face for weeks. But with those two

hollering—well—figured I better say something too." He elbowed me gently.

I buried my face in my hands.

"Don't make this into another one of your reasons to leave town, Capybara. You know that boy would never have known what flowers to get you if it weren't for Frank."

"Good old Frank." The story went that Gram thought it'd be funny to name her shop for someone not her husband and send a message that men like flowers too. "Give the town something to talk about," she always said. That's why the store was called Even Frank Wants Flowers. Alliterative. Simple. And, knowing Gram, full of opportunities to joke about stamen, pollination, and birds and bees.

"See? Sierra's not so bad," Gramps said. "Your beau gets you flowers, and you get to look at a view like this! A man like me can have a view like this!"

"Gramps, I know you love the view."

"You'll see how good it is someday. More people will move in, make it better. Livelier."

"Dad doesn't agree."

Gramps chuckled. "Well, your dad figured out this was the place to be, and boy am I glad. If he hadn't come back, I wouldn't be sitting here, seeing my granddaughter almost all grown up. Not wanting to share Sierra with more folks—that's his problem."

"We would have visited you," I said, trying to divert him from thoughts of my dad.

He shook his head. "Not the same. After that heart attack scare when you were little, I figured I was lucky to see you learn to ride a two-wheeler. But this—old enough to be falling in love?" He whistled and looked out across the canyon. "Not everyone gets a life so lucky."

We rocked back. I remembered that heart attack. The ambulance in the driveway. Gram crying, her garden gloves still on. Dirt on her face. Dad and Mom rushing around. Beckett disappearing into the canyon with Mason and no one but me noticing they were gone. My eyes stung thinking about it. I put my hand on Gramps's elbow, wondering if I should say something about growing up next door, about how happy I was he still remembered me, knew me so well, and how thankful I was to still have him. Instead, I gave him the side-eye and said, "Who said anything about love?"

Gramps chuckled. "I suspect no one has." He stretched his arm around my shoulder. "Not yet. But I see the way he's scanning for you every time he's with your brother—hoping you might pop out from behind a tree or something."

I curled into Gramps's side, laughing.

"I know a thing or two about things," he said, and the wind came up, almost strong enough to rock us all by itself. "Red-flag warnings tonight. You might luck into no school if they cut power." The power company cut service when winds were too high. Dad said they did it instead of upgrading their old fire-causing equipment like they should. Gramps said they did it to protect us. I figured it was both. Power grids weren't built for a warming world, but I wouldn't say that to Gramps. I wasn't sure he believed in climate change.

Gramps hugged me to his side and said, "Imagine, you could spend the whole day tomorrow with that boy. In the dark!"

"Gramps!" He was as bad as Adrienne. Time in the dark with River was definitely not something I wanted to talk about with my grandpa.

He laughed. "Every now and again, I've got to say what your gram would."

I settled my cheek on his shoulder. "Maybe for my next app, I should build a power-outage predictor? The snow-day one is super popular."

"I figure you could build anything, Capybara, if you set your mind to it."

"The same's been said about you," I said, and Gramps smiled. We rocked long enough that I didn't even need to focus on my breath to feel calm.

Then: "Caprice!" Beckett shouted. "Hurry up!" As if he couldn't text? Where were we hurrying to?

"Sounds like the boys are here." Gramps squeezed my shoulder.

"Cappi!" Beckett shouted from inside the house now.

"We're out here," Gramps called.

Beckett stuck his head out the sliding door. "River's got to let his dog out—let's go."

"Now hang on a second," Gramps said. "I need to talk some business with you. How about you let the kids go, and we talk."

Beckett stepped onto the porch, pulling the door shut behind him. "Oh." He tucked a curl behind his ear. "Okay. I'll grab us some iced tea." He turned to go inside.

Gramps winked at me. "I suppose you'll be thanking me."

I dropped a kiss on his sandpapery face and gave his silver ponytail a gentle tug. "I love you, Gramps."

"Well, don't go thinking I did this all for you—I do need to talk to our boy."

"Sure," I said, flying off the porch and practically levitating through the side yard where River waited in his truck. I climbed in.

"Hey—um, thanks for the—" I swiveled to face him. His hand went to my elbow. He was smiling and I wondered if he felt full of feathers too.

His phone lit up and he grabbed it out of the cupholder. "Oh man. We've really got to get going. My moms are freaking out. Where's Beck?"

"He has to talk to Gramps—"

"Oh." River's hand went to his hair. And then he grinned. "Let's go!"

River drove south down the Ridge Road. The ponderosa pines thinned, and the sky opened over the golden hillsides. My ears popped with the change in elevation. River braked at a blind curve, and at first I thought he was being extra cautious, but then he turned onto a dirt road I hadn't noticed before.

That's the thing about Sierra. You can feel like you know the town so well—you can have a job where you drive all over—and still you can be surprised by roads suddenly appearing between the hillsides.

We bumped down a rutted, gravel drive until the house came into view. At first glance, it was towering, set into the hill, a few ponderosas around it, one yellowed by pine beetle. I counted three stories. But as we drew closer, I could tell it was ramshackle. The front was all windows set between wide logs—full trees stripped of their bark— and the back seemed to extend into the hillside. Room after room, each constructed of slightly different materials. There was an unfinished unattached garage of particle board, and on it someone had painted a gnome in a purple hat standing with a mushroom, and below it was an actual matching ceramic garden gnome. Between the house and the garage sat two new rain barrels and a pile of PVC pipe.

"My moms inherited the house from their adopted grandmas. I know it's—well, unique."

I chewed my lip, examining the hand-hewn logs. I guessed someone—or more likely a rotating cast of someones—had built onto it over and over.

"Looks like pretty standard Sierra," I said, and just as soon knew it was wrong. Because if this was "standard Sierra," then our house was something different. I don't know if River heard me. I hoped he didn't. He was out of the truck and jogging to the glass front door, where, on the other side, a black Lab stood wagging its tail.

I slid out of the truck.

"This is Spock," River said, opening the door so the dog could get out and patting its head. A giant cowbell dangled from a rope next to the door. A metal chair sat on the porch, slightly rusted. From the rafters hung a pottery bell with a painted-on goldfinch and a driftwood clacker that thumped in the breeze. I'd gotten Gram one like it when I was little. I bought it at the Dam Days craft fair with my own money. We'd hung it outside her kitchen window.

On the porch, Spock sniffed my hand, then nosed my crotch.

"Go on, Spock," River said, his voice slightly higher than normal. "Come on in."

River kicked off his sneakers and slipped on the oddest flip-flops I'd ever seen. I bugged my eyes. "What are those?" Two identical smaller pairs sat next to the door.

"Oh! I made these. From recycled tires and twine."

"You are committed."

"I just don't like waste. Or buying things. I'm thirsty," he said. Uh. Yeah. Me too. "Tea?" He ushered me into the kitchen, where one wall was lined with jars of oats and dried beans, and along another was a huge cook-top at the end of a wooden counter. He filled two glasses with ice, then poured from a ceramic pitcher.

"I want to show you something—" I followed him into a hallway lined with packed bookshelves, except for one filled with pictures—and in the center an 8x10 photo of two women in wedding dresses, swinging a tiny River between them.

"I swear, people who didn't go to their parents' weddings are missing out. That day was seriously fun. This way."

The wings in my chest expanded as River led me into the room walled with windows. He took my tea and set it on a tray—then pointed to a ladder. "You okay to climb?"

"A loft?"

"My room."

I wiped my hands on my skirt, my palms so sweaty, it might be dangerous to climb. Also my skirt was—well, a skirt. "Maybe you should go first?" I said, fidgeting with my hem.

The loft was spacious, half the size of the large room below, with one wall of windows, two of slant ceilings, the fourth not a wall at all, but a split-pine railing. A mattress on the floor with blue sheets, a fuzzy green blanket. I took a step toward it. River tugged a rope and the tray where he'd set our teas pulled up even with the railing.

"Oh hey! Beckett and I built something like this for our tree house."

River handed me my tea. "I know," he said. I took a sip. Beckett had told River about that. Huh. I was never sure what my brother remembered. Or cared about.

River's hand touched my elbow, and my posture went instantly yoga-teacher perfect as sparks seemed to fly up my arms and out my fingertips.

"That's not what I wanted to show you," River said. "Here." I'm pretty sure I lifted off the floor and floated with him as he guided me to a wall completely covered in diagrams. Pencil sketches labeled with careful print—all caps. SOLAR LAWN MOWER. TREADMILL WASHER DRYER. RAIN BARREL AND GRAY WATER PURIFICATION.

"You made these?" I asked.

"I designed them. I haven't made them all." He dropped his hand from my back and pointed to the rain barrels. "I'm working on this one now." He smoothed the corner of another. "And this one's my truck."

"Wait—you—you didn't use plans?"

A faint blush crept up River's neck. He looked down, shy to admit how supremely cool this was. "I made changes from other plans, so—"

"That's still amazing."

"Yeah, I want to start my own business someday, for afford-able green living."

I wanted to reach out and touch him, but my glass was still in my hand. *IF finally alone with the boy you've been wanting to kiss AND there is a bed THEN kiss and kiss and kiss and kiss.*

I turned to him. My fingers touched his survival cord brace-let, this boy who'd sent me flowers. This boy who designed things to make the world better. This boy leaned down. I felt myself lifting, practically floating toward him—

"Rivvvv-eeeeee?"

I jumped back, spilling tea over my hand and knocking my head into the slanted ceiling. "Ouch!" White pain crackled across the back of my head.

"You okay?" River asked.

"Yeah." Just slightly hurt and super disappointed.

He called, "Be right down!" He touched his thumb to my lips before turning to the ladder. It took all my focus to not fall as I went after him.

His moms were in the kitchen, unpacking cloth shopping bags.

"You must be Caprice," a woman with short hair and glasses said, extending a hand. There was dried clay on her arm and paint splatters on her T-shirt. "I'm Megan, and this is Kate." Kate wore a cream pantsuit, her sandy hair pulled half up. She nodded at me.

"Nice to meet you both," I said, taking Megan's hand. Her bracelet said *BREATHE*. I inhaled.

Then Kate said, "River, you know the rule about not being home alone with girls," in a voice that made me feel scolded by a librarian.

"I was showing her my designs," River said.

"Is that what the kids are calling it these days?" Megan whispered out of the side of her mouth. Her nose had the same sharp slant as River's, and with the green glasses, the snark, and the clay bits, it made her far less terrifying than her wife.

"My brother was going to come with us," I offered, "but my gramps needed to talk to him."

"We're going back there now—" River started. *We were?*

"You can't. Remember we have a dinner with that friend of Beebe's in town?" Megan said.

"Ugh—no."

"Well, you're coming. We'll drop you off, Caprice," Kate said. "You live on River's running route, right? So it's on the way."

"Oh, thanks," I said. A few minutes later, we climbed into the back of his parents' car. I texted River:

> if school's canceled tomorrow

I'll plan to be busy

with u

I didn't text back, just met his eyes. And *IF a boy looks at you like that, THEN pray for high winds and a dark day.*

OBJECT: DIY Designs for Improving
Carbon Footprint and Eco Living
LOCATION: 4 Arborage Road, Sierra, California
RESIDENT: River Parker-Holt

....

I don't even know how many there were. Fifty? Seventy-five? I started designing things before I could even write, and by age twelve I was working on a series of DIY hacks for the environment. Megan said that my mind for building things must come from my dad, but I never gave him much thought beyond the birthday cards he sent every year. I designed things because I knew that the people who drove Teslas never lived in my neighborhood. My moms did okay. I was never hungry. But until we moved to Sierra, we didn't own a house. It was so lucky, that house. They were tired of moving. Always moving. Sometimes for better jobs. Sometimes because landlords can tell you to. Twice because our neighbors threatened them. Once because the property owners came and ripped out the trees in the yard. I kept my designs through all the moves, carefully untaping them from my walls, then putting them back up. Some I made, but most I dreamed of making when I had the time and supplies. I'm trying to redraw them now, on a tablet this time so I can save them easier. But it's hard to remember them all. I might never. Maybe that's okay. The best ideas are always there, right? I believe that. I have to.

ONE DAY BEFORE

The winds died off the next day, which meant school followed by a busy week. It seemed impossible to hang out with River. He had cross-country practice, then an out-of-town meet that kept him busy all weekend, and when he was free it was always when Adrienne needed me at the shop. And I wasn't the only one annoyed. The Vanagon was still in pieces in our driveway. Beckett needed River's help to install the part they'd been missing. So when we finally found time, I wasn't sure we'd actually be alone.

I was trying to focus on the app. But all I could think about was the casual way River had touched my arm at choir Friday morning, and how he'd set his hand on my back for a moment in the hallway on Tuesday. He understood that school was not the right vibe for a first kiss, but I was starting to wonder if pulling him into the trees by the art room might be okay. I checked my phone for the three hundredth time to see if he was back from his race, and then hid it from myself under a pillow. I was about to make some actual app progress when Beckett banged in the front door, a gust of warm wind behind him, a flush in his cheeks. His words tumbled out, loud and fast. "Caps! Listen to this—I ran into Cecil at a meeting and—"

"Wait, Cecil goes to meetings?" I swiveled away from the computer.

"Yeah." Beckett combed his hands through his hair. "That's why he was so weird to me at Hole in the Dam, we'd just been at one, and so seeing me after threw him I guess—"

"You didn't tell me?"

"Uh, meetings are anonymous. Anyway, he told me I could tell you because today we went over to Hole in the Dam after, and we figured out some things about the app."

"You what?" I said, positive I didn't hear him right.

"You know how he wasn't sure about the—"

"Go back to the part where you figured things out without me."

Beckett put up his hands. "We just—"

If my eyes were lasers, they would have cut my brother in half. Seventeen thousand times.

He took a step toward me, "Caps—I'm trying to help."

"Well, you're not." I stood up, crossing from the desk to perch on the edge of the couch, keeping the front door in sight.

His look was pointed. "I know you care about this. But you've got to work with Cecil. He has a vision. We've—"

"You really don't get it."

His expression flattened. His chest expanded with a deep breath. He met my eyes. "I don't think—"

"What? You don't want to talk about how you always take everything over? The treehouse? Our parents? Even River. Everything is *always* about you, and I can't complain about it. Because then I'm the asshole. And that's fine—but my app, Beck? You don't even understand how it works."

"Like the code? That doesn't matter. You said so yourself."

My head flashed with heat. Was I talking in 1's and 0's? How did he not get it? "You—you don't understand anything."

Beckett pressed his palms into his eyes, then dropped them. Glanced up. He didn't look angry, exactly. He looked exhausted. His voice wavered when he said, "You really want to go there? Because I promise, you have no idea the extent of what you don't understand."

If my breastbone were a plate, he'd shattered it. Or maybe we'd both done it—cracked me open. I had no understanding of my brother, or what he'd been through. None of it. It wasn't that I didn't want to. I did. But maybe he could try to understand what it was like to be me?

Beckett hopped a few times like he was trying to shake off our conversation. Or wake himself up.

"Come on, Caps. Seriously. Let it go. Hear my idea. I think you'll like it." He stepped toward me and bumped the coffee table. The W volume of the *Handyman Encyclopedia* he'd been reading jammed into the Zen garden. I pushed the book away and moved the sand around, pressing so hard, the miniature rake squeaked.

"Caps, listen. Even Alicia thinks it's a good idea."

I snapped up straight, dropping the rake. "You ran it by Alicia? Already?" How did he not see the problem?

He wrinkled his nose. "She was in the yard with Jenny when I drove by and—"

"You know what—never mind." Words flew from my mouth like darts. "I asked you to work on this with us. I didn't think you'd take over. But I should have. Isn't the best predictor of future behavior past behavior?" I watched the words hit. My brother's face puckered. His jaw tightened.

With his lips barely open, he shot back, "Fuck off, Caprice. Seriously. You think I care about your stupid project? Or that I want to hang out with you and your high school friends? You think I'm doing this for me?"

And then I was down too. The hit went straight into me. Because yeah. I did think he cared. I did think me, Alicia, and River were good for him. We were smart and sober and planning exciting lives. But we also made him laugh. Sometimes, at least.

I thought of the fox on that worksite so long ago. How I misread the look. How I should have run.

"You two all right?" Gramps called from the back door, gray gaze darting between us, telling us he knew we weren't.

"Yeah, fine," Beckett said, turning toward the deck. "I need a cigarette."

"Caps?" Gramps asked.

"I'm heading out for a walk, maybe I'll even run," I said.

Gramps raised his eyebrows. "Come here and give your

grandpa a hug first. Looks like you need it. Your dad home tonight?"

I shook my head. "He's headed to Canada this week. Home Wednesday." I crossed to wrap my arms around Gramps. He was tall and thin, muscled from a life of work, and for a moment I felt small and safe. He kissed my head and patted my shoulder and said, "I think I better sit for a spell with our boy. I've got those appointments at the hospital tomorrow, so see if Alicia can give you a lift to school—if it's not canceled."

"Red-flag warnings again?"

He nodded, smoothing his gray ponytail over his shoulder. "Be careful out there. Wind's coming up already. And it's getting dark."

"I will," I said.

In the front yard, Cheerio rubbed my ankles and meowed. I let her in and texted River:

> Hey—you back?

> yeah just out of the shower

A freshly showered boy would take my mind off my brother.

> Could you come get me?

> Please?

> u okay?

I paused, wondering if I should tell him. But I didn't know who he'd side with. They were friends. And when I called

Grayson after Beckett's accident, he, well . . . he never called me back. Later he texted that he couldn't deal with drama. I wrote:

> I need to get out.

> moms say yes

> see u in a few?

> Meet you on the road

It was dusk and the neighborhood was mostly quiet. A hum of insects, dirt bikes abandoned in yards, TVs flickering behind lit windows. The wind was hot and dry off the canyon, and I breathed in the scent of dry pine as I watched clumps of golden needles tumble across the road. It was dark enough that when drivers saw me walking, they clicked on their headlights. Monday evening quiet. I neared Alicia's and could hear her playing piano in the music room at the front of the house. I stopped. Since we were ten, Alicia had practiced three to four hours a day. A fact that mostly impressed, and occasionally annoyed, her parents, who'd taken to sleeping with earplugs and a sound machine because Alicia got in an hour and a half in the mornings before school. The practice paid off. I closed my eyes, letting the music carry me a step forward. I imagined going into Alicia's, lying down on the floor, and listening to her play. Her fingers flying over the keys. The notes traveling from her sheet music, through her brain, and out her fingertips. I knew it was practice, hours of hard work. But listening to her, it sounded magic. I heard an engine then and opened my eyes as River's headlights slid across me. I took a deep breath and tried to let the whole thing with my brother go. River leaned over to open the door so I could hop in.

"Where to?" he asked.

"I don't care," I said, giving him a small smile.

"Okay—I've been wanting to see that place Beckett kept talking about. The second-best spot in Sierra?" He didn't say *Impregnate Point*. I knew what he meant.

He tapped the steering wheel.

"Yeah, okay," I said, my face already hot. "Turn right."

The road wound around the side of the canyon. We passed the turn to the lake.

"Slow down—it's half-hidden." We bumped along the dirt road. When we got to the point, the sky was a pale purple that made my skin feel alive. Or maybe it was this boy. Maybe it was both. River turned off the car. My knees shook. I tucked my hands under my thighs. My elbow trembled. I didn't trust my arms. My hands wanted to touch him.

"Are you sure you're okay?" he said.

"Yeah—"

But when he turned to me, his eyes wide, I couldn't stuff down what happened. "I got mad at Beckett. Snapped."

"Because of the Cecil thing?"

"Wait—how did you know?!" Cecil. Alicia. And now River too. My brother had talked to everyone before he talked to me and then acted like I was some kind of monster for being angry.

River held up his hands. "He texted. Said he'd talked to Cecil and was excited. That's all I know. You can see—" He held up his phone.

"No, it's fine." I pushed my hands farther under my legs. Beck texting River meant he did care about my friends. His friends. We weren't just dumb high school kids. "I know it sounds awful, but it's exhausting to always be understanding about Beckett. I suck, I know."

River shook his head. "That doesn't make you suck, Caprice. I feel that way about my dad sometimes."

"You have a dad?"

River laughed. "Yeah, most of the time I avoid explaining to people that Megan's first marriage was to a roadie she met at a Phish show. I'm pretty sure I was conceived at one."

"Yikes."

He smiled. "Yeah, that's not intel I share widely. Don't tell Mitchell."

"My lips are sealed," I said.

"They were only married four months." River pulled at his fingers. "With all the moving, I got used to telling people only what they need to know. You get judged right away no matter what. Some moves I was cool, others—not at all. I got used to being in the moment."

"Oh," I said. It made my brain hurt. How different his life had been from mine. In Sierra, so much about me was known. By everyone.

"I think . . ." River said. "I think Beckett's trying to be in the moment. But everyone's judging him for who he was before. It's not easy."

"Did he say that?"

"Kinda."

I shook off the heavy feeling that Beck hadn't talked to me first, and that maybe it was my fault he hadn't. Did he notice how I'd avoided him? Was I among the everyone judging him for who he was before? I held my breath deep in my lungs and freed my hands from under my thighs. Then I put my hand over River's. He'd already unbuckled his seat belt and was angled toward me. I fumbled to unbuckle my lap belt with my free hand. And then he had both of my hands and he said, "It's silly, I know"—his eyes were on our fingers—"but this last week felt like a thousand years."

"I was going to say million."

"So can I finally kiss you?" All thoughts of my brother floated off into the sky.

"Yes," I said. "Please." Wind gusted through the windows, the scent of dry earth and pine. His head tipped down to mine and finally our mouths met. Our kiss was cricket song and slivered-moon perfection. Soft-lipped and slow. Everything, everything was suddenly okay and so right. We both pulled deeper into the kiss, my arms drawing him closer as his fingers slid into my hair, his palm cradling the back of my head. When he pulled away at last, his eyes were sleepy, heavy-lidded but smiling. He rested his forehead against mine. And the world was River—that clean mint scent mixed with sky, pine, and possibility. I breathed him in, then reached for the door.

"Come on," I said. "Stars are coming out."

The day was darkening to a purple black and the wind off the canyon was hot, fierce, dusty, and full. It whipped my hair around my face, and I held it back with one hand. "You hear they might cut the power tomorrow?" I said. "Maybe we'll get our wind day after all."

He dropped the tailgate and hopped up. I joined him, swinging my legs alongside his.

"I'm thinking I should start a side project. A wind day predictor app."

"And what would it say tonight?"

"Ninety-eight point five percent chance."

"What's your algorithm based on?"

"Hope."

"So we don't need to worry about the time?" he asked, lifting his hand to my cheek.

"Probably not," I said, and moved my mouth back to his again—my hair tangled around our faces, and the sky darkened, then blurred with stars. Nothing else in the world but us. No school. No flower shop. No app. No college. No brother. Only stars exploding inside me. *IF you finally get to kiss the boy you've wanted to kiss since you first saw him running down your street, THEN everything in the world will feel right.*

I don't know how much time passed, how many kisses filled

the night. But I do know that it all felt so right, that for once Sierra was perfect, and I was surprised by how exciting it was to think about a senior year that was about more than waiting to get out. When the wind blew too strong, we climbed back into the truck, planning to drive home, but I leaned into his lips again and we curled together in the dark as the wind rocked the truck.

OBJECT: Handyman Encyclopedias
LOCATION: 51 Plumule Way, Sierra, California
RESIDENT: Beckett Alexander

Gramps gave me the encyclopedias this summer when I moved back home. He wanted me to learn how to build anything. He got really excited with every skill I gained, even tacking down a shingle. Maybe too excited. But I didn't mind. It's nice, you know, to have someone cheering you on even if you're pretty sure you don't deserve it. He'd hate me thinking that way. He'd say, "Beckett Bear, you deserve the world. Or at least a view of this here canyon." I liked that he thought that, even if I had trouble believing it. I never met a man prouder of where he lived. He had a story about every inch of wood in his house. I swear he could name where he bought the trim and tell you how many times it'd been painted. I wanted to be a handyman. I loved the idea of that. Being handy. Useful. To be the guy people called when they needed something fixed. I mean, I'd broken enough, right? Seemed like a good plan to try and fix things.

Gramps was sure I'd be great at it. He said the books were out of date, but they'd teach me the basics, and "all that new-fangled stuff" I could figure out online. I didn't tell him that I had to YouTube every fix I did six times. The books were cool. Pictures of guys sawing and smoking a pipe at the same time. I liked spending time in those books. Reading them made me believe that I could fix anything that was broken. Build anything I needed. A car seat, a fly trap, a seesaw, a serving cart, a rowboat. Now that's handy.

SMOKE

FOUR HOURS BEFORE

And then we woke up. The truck creaked, swayed by the winds. We must have been exhausted to sleep through it. Every year, the canyon winds heralded fall as sure as pumpkin spice at Peak Coffee and giant pots of mums at Frank's. But this was different. People say the wind howls, but that morning it was an engine—a helicopter or a speed boat. A constant roar.

In the gray morning light, the two freckles on River's eyelid fluttered as he slept.

I shook him. "Hey," I said, checking my phone for a wind cancelation notification. None. Just fifty-eight texts from my mom, thirty-two from Dad, and four from Beckett. Ten calls. Five voice mails. Oh. Crap.

"We better get out of here and hope that neither one of us is grounded until graduation."

River blinked once, twice. And when he saw me, he smiled. "Hi," he said. We should have been terrified by the number of messages we'd missed when we turned off location tracking and turned on DO NOT DISTURB. But River rewired my brain, and I was calm when I said:

"Hey. I'm pretty sure neither one of us was supposed to stay out until—four seventeen on a school night."

He rolled his head back on the seat. "What? No wind day, then?"

"Nope. I better work on that algorithm."

"Too bad," he said, reaching for the keys. "Let's go."

"I'm thinking I probably have a get-out-of-jail-free card, compliments of not being my brother," I said. And then I kissed River. Once, or maybe six times, and finally he flipped on his headlights, clicked his seat belt, and started to drive. Unless he was shifting gears, we held hands, clueless that this was the beginning of the worst day of our lives.

When we got to my house, I opened the red front door, and it practically blew out of my hand. So much for being quiet on the way in. Mom was lying on the couch. The camping lantern sat on the table next to the Zen garden, and she jostled both as she stood up.

"When your dad called last night, I had to tell him I didn't know where you were. And there he was up in Tacoma."

"I—uh." What could I say? I couldn't believe my mom stayed up worrying about me. I figured it was me, so she wouldn't. Oops.

"I'm sorry," I said weakly. "I was mad, and River picked me up and then—why isn't school canceled? That wind is bad."

She arched her eyebrows and tightened her hands on her hips. "The power's on. You're going to school."

"Mom. I'm sorry."

"You should be." Her hands dropped from her waist and went to her eyes.

"Really, really sorry."

"Your brother was up half the night waiting for you. I made him go to bed after the third time he fell asleep on the couch."

Beckett? Waited up? When he was in high school and didn't come home, I'd fall asleep on the couch and wake up when Mom and Dad were trying to walk me back to bed. I'd ask, "Is he home?" And usually they'd say, "Not yet, but soon." Then I'd be asleep as soon as I settled into my pillows.

"And you turned off your phone's location tracking. You know what that means."

Mom opened her palm for my phone.

"Mom, no. Please."

"Caprice. That was in the contract. You're a good kid, but something like this—there has to be consequences. Or—" She shook her head. It meant *you'll end up like your brother.* "Hand it over."

I glanced at my phone. It lit with a message. River.

> Moms are sleeping. But their note was just a warning not to open the fridge in case they cut power.

> So I think they aren't too mad.

> You?

With every fiber of my being, I wanted to write back, but—

"Don't you even think about it," Mom said.

"I—um."

"Nope." She stepped toward me. "Don't make me pry it from your fingers."

I felt like my body was folding in on itself, like I was one of those paper-chain dolls doubling over and over. I dropped the phone into her hand.

"Thank you," she said.

"I'll call your dad, and then I'm going to try and sleep for an hour before I go to work. You should do the same."

My body vibrated. Hummed. I had never gotten in trouble like this. Never let my parents down.

"I'm really sorry, Mom," I said again.

She pocketed my phone, rubbed her eyes, and opened her arms. "I'm glad you're okay. And I hope you're using protection."

"It's not like that."

She gave me a tired look that said it was exactly like that. It wasn't. Yet. But no point in arguing. All the good feelings of the night came crashing into how bad I felt. I thought of the first time Beckett got caught drinking and Cheerio got out. I woke to the sound of my parents fighting, and I reached down to the foot of my bed, where Cheerio was usually curled, to pull her to me, and she wasn't there. After Beckett's cat, Domino, was killed by something outside, we brought Cheerio in at night. I'd crept out of my room, calling "Cheerio," over my parent's shouts as I made my way down the gray rug into the hallway, and through the living room. Cheerio wasn't curled up on the couch.

In the kitchen, Mom sat on a stool with a glass of wine. Cheerio wasn't on her lap. Dad pushed on the granite counter-top as if he might, at any moment, pop muscles like the Hulk and smash the island in two. Cheerio wasn't at her food bowl. Like me, she probably wanted nothing to do with this battle.

My parents filled the air with words sharp as broken glass, and I wondered why Beckett couldn't follow the rules. My mom and dad never fought with fists and objects or even slammed doors. Just words that cut and cut.

Mom's voice dropped as she said, "Look, I don't know what to do. We tell him one thing, he does another. We give consequences, he doesn't care. And you—" She raised her wineglass. Dad stepped back holding his hands up.

"Dad? Mom?" My voice, two questions. They turned to me, eyes wide and red-rimmed. "Cheerio isn't here."

"She's around, I'm sure. Back to bed."

"But Domino? What if . . . ?" I said. Mom shook her head, and the lump in my throat grew. I imagined finding Cheerio's body in the yard, heaped on oak leaves and soft pine needles, the way Gramps had found Domino the year before. And Alicia's family's chickens were killed, all six of them, in one night. They found parts around the yard for weeks. My friend Kim's little dog? Also eaten. Mountain lion. Bobcat. Fox. Unless there were prints, you didn't know for sure what had turned your pet into dinner.

"We'll find Cheerio, Caps. She'll be fine. Back to bed," Mom said. I could tell by the crease that appeared between her eyebrows that she wasn't going to remember my cat. So I turned away. I'd get her myself.

"Hey, Caps," Beckett said. He was slumped in the hallway

under a painting of Mount Lassen he'd made in high school.

I whispered, "Cheerio's missing."

"I told you." Mom's voice rose from the kitchen. "The research says peer group, peer group. And Mason, he's—"

"Stop." My dad's voice was a command. I froze.

"Caps," Beckett said again. "I'll help." He pulled himself up, steadying himself on the wall.

Outside, the ground was damp. Goose bumps rose on my legs as we walked through the strip of lawn to the pine needles at the edge of the yard. I called, "Cheerio," and the sound pulsed back at us from the canyon.

My brother called, "Kitty, kitty, kitty, Cheerio," and moved toward the azaleas under my window. Something rustled near the oak tree and Beckett darted into the darkness, then called, "She's here, Caps! I've got her." He slung her over his shoulder. I ran to them. Cheerio seemed to be trying to decide if she should purr or claw him to death. I hugged them both hard. I remember the oaky smell on his breath that I didn't have a name for yet—and Beckett's arms around me. He said, "Let's go inside."

And we did. The yelling hadn't stopped, but I had my cat and my brother, and I knew that was what mattered.

Now on this windy morning, my mom's disappointment and that memory made me feel like I was fizzing, like the slugs Beckett and Mason would salt along the deck rails.

"We'll talk more after school," Mom said, turning away.

In my room, I curled up on my bed, listening to the moan

of the wind, and Cheerio found me. She worked herself into a ball on my chest. I closed my eyes and tried to think of River, to imagine myself back in his truck, my body charged with the energy of a thousand stars. I drifted off.

My alarm was loud and felt like it went off seconds after I lay down. In the kitchen, a note from Mom:

After school, we'll settle when you can have your phone back and how long you are grounded.

Grounded? I shook my head. I hadn't been grounded since Alicia and I decided to take a mud bath in fifth grade. We brought actual buckets of dirt to the bathtub and then added water. Gram was supposed to be watching us. She'd figured if we were playing in the dirt, we couldn't be causing too much trouble.

I started some coffee and rummaged through Mom's underwear drawer for my phone. It wasn't there. I checked the cupboard above the sink. I tried to track it from my computer, but apparently Mom never turned location back on. I dressed in comfortable clothes because I was tired and in trouble and needed my favorite jeans and my PROGRAM OR BE PROGRAMMED T-shirt to feel better. Then I waited for Alicia at the front window, watching the oak leaves skittering down the road. Layla Montoya was out for a morning jog with her goldens; her part-timer must have been opening the shop. Someone's grocery-store plastic pot of violets rolled down the center of the street. Alicia pulled in with a honk. I hurried to the yard. The light was flat. Strange. I hoped clouds were coming on the wind, that it might rain. The pines swayed. I caught a whiff of smoke, like a fire far away. I thought, *Our power wasn't cut. We're in no danger.*

"Someone's practically trailing sparkles across the lawn from their night on the River," Alicia said. She wore a dark burgundy lipstick that she definitely applied after she said goodbye to her mother, a purple-and-black tank top, and her jeans with the tiny *Kiki's Delivery Service* patch.

"How did you—" I started, but of course, Mom and Beckett had checked with her.

She wrinkled her nose. "So Irene took your phone?" I nodded. Her eyes actually twinkled. "Was it worth it?" she asked.

My face went warm. "You do not get details about my love life when you're so cagey about yours."

"Oh," Alicia said with a grin, "so you finally understand why what happens in the make-out cabin stays in the make-out cabin."

"Maybe," I said. I reached for her elbow to give it a squeeze, but it slipped out of my hand as she swerved to avoid a cardboard box tumbling across the Ridge Road.

"At least tell me"—she glanced at me sideways—"was it rated NC-17?"

"No!" I jostled my Hole in the Dam Donuts travel mug for emphasis but only ended up spilling some coffee on my hand.

"R?"

"Ali! How would you rate the make-out cabin?"

"This is not about me!" She held up her hands. "PG-13?"

I dropped my head and groaned.

"Ah-ha!" Alicia cheered, letting go of the wheel and slapping the ceiling. "PG-13 then."

"Al, when Beck started talking app plans without me, why didn't you text me?" I sipped some coffee.

"There you go changing the subject—"

"Like you do every time I bring up Felix."

"Oh, you do know his name." Alicia jostled my arm.

"You mean it's not French Cello Man?" I smirked. Alicia waved a hand in my face. "So why didn't you text me?" I asked again. The sky darkened. The smell of smoke intensified.

"Uh, because Beck was on his way home. And I figured you would talk to him."

"Alicia, you know how he takes over."

"Is this really what you want to talk about after your dip in the River?" She doubled over the steering wheel in giggles.

"Oh. My. God! Alicia! *Please*." But by that point I was fighting myself to keep from smiling.

"Okay, okay." Alicia straightened. "Beckett's a lot sometimes. I get it. But his idea, it's good. You should listen, 'cause I can tell you're annoyed by how the boys are spending more time talking about the whole Vanagon project than they are helping with the app."

"I am?"

"Uh. Yeah." Alicia widened her eyes. The sky went dark. The wind turned up its volume. I reached for my phone to check for fire alerts, then remembered I didn't have it.

"Look, Caps. The app is your thing—and we're on your team—but we all have other stuff going on. Beck's so into the whole car conversion idea, I *thought* you'd be happy something got him into the app. I wasn't trying to rebuild the Older Siblings Club Fort or anything."

"Oh," I said. "That." When Jenny was born, Alicia stayed with us because her grandparents hadn't made it out from Chicago yet. A day into the stay, Beckett and Alicia took all the couch cushions and built a fort they called the Older Siblings Club Fort, and wouldn't let me in. I ran crying to Gram, who followed me back to our house and tore it apart. Then all three of us were crying.

It looked like all the color had drained from the day. I blinked. Maybe I was just tired. Or maybe Thor was about to descend from the heavens. The sky was purple black. There was an acrid taste at the back of my throat. I pulled up my leg and rested my chin on my knees.

"Cappi, I'm sorry—I thought if you saw how excited he was, you'd listen. The sky is weird today, isn't it?"

"Don't change the subject," I said, but at least I wasn't having some weird emotional hallucination where the weather was matching my tangled mood—upset about Beckett, annoyed at Alicia, and ecstatic about River. But now the sky was a-portal-is-about-to-open weird. The wind had gone from sounding like an engine to a league of descending demons.

"It's got to suck for him to be back here after Mason—"

"You know I think about that every single day."

"I know you do. But Cappi, it didn't just happen to you." Alicia's voice was soft.

"I know that," I said.

I pressed my palms into my eyes. I was mad, but I felt like I couldn't be mad. It wasn't supportive to be mad. I mean, if what had happened to Mason had happened to Alicia? How would I even get out of bed, let alone try to fight a disease like alcoholism? I wanted to say something that would fix everything. But I never had the words. Maybe there were no words. My eyes closed. I wanted a piece of wisdom from the families of alcoholics website I secretly checked on most days. I wanted to say something that felt glowing and pearlescent. Thoughtfully formed. But the smoke was strong now, like I was sitting on the wrong side of a campfire. All my words were snuffed out. I opened my eyes.

"Cappi, what the hell is going on with the sky?" Alicia turned into the senior parking lot.

"Um—" In the rearview mirror there was a black column. And that smell. It *was* smoke. Real smoke. "Oh no," I said.

"Fire," Alicia said.

"Like, a big fire," I said.

"So maybe no school today?" Alicia made it sound fake-cheery.

"Yeah, no." As I spoke, I felt dread pulling me down, down, down.

OBJECT: Quilt
LOCATION: 154 Highland Road, Sierra, California
RESIDENT: Layla Montoya

It wasn't the finest quilt by any stretch of the imagination. Squares sewn in blue and yellow hues. But my mother made it for me before the cancer got her. It wasn't hand quilted, and Mom thought that was a flaw. She was a perfectionist who loved to point out imperfections. I kept that quilt on the back of the couch, and once the dogs chewed a hole in it. I patched it right back up. It's not like I thought I'd be buried with the thing wrapped around me, but I do miss it. There was this one corduroy patch made from a dress I'd worn about second or third grade. I liked to rub my fingers across that when the anxious feelings were running around inside me. Something about it. You could run a fingernail along the side of it and it would make that tut-tut-tut sound that was part ocean and part running fast on the playground. I led Sierra High to state for track back in '82 and no girl's broke my record yet, even though athletes these days are all vitamin fed and tech trained. I don't know if the trophies were in the part of the school that burnt or not. I should find out. I'm still quick. I went for a run that morning because Haven was opening the shop for me, and by the time I got home, well—there was just enough time to load up the car. I got trapped behind a power line and could feel the heat behind me. I took the dogs, and we ran down Highland all the way to the intersection of Hawkins Road—it was somewhere in there one of the dogs got away, just tugged my arm so hard he ran off leash and all. Then Keenan Treadwell's boy, Ocean, or Frost, or some such name I can never remember—anyway, real sweet kid—he picked me up and we got out, but I didn't have the quilt or nothing I packed up in my car. They found that burnt up where I left it. Someone picked up the dog, though, somewhere along the Ridge Road. So I've still got both of them. That's good, because everything else in this quarter acre of bent metal and dust they tell me has got to be cleared. The shop didn't fare much better, but I'm thinking we could do well with a food truck. I'm going to see if we can get it to run on cooking oil.

FIRE

Everything that happened next was fast. Alicia's phone rang. I grabbed it for her and answered on speaker. Mariana's voice came through clear and commanding: "There's a fire. Where are you?"

"School?" Alicia said. Like it was a question. Like she was no longer actually sure.

"Good. Pull right out of there and get your sister. It's—bad. I'm evacuating the hospital. Meet us at Willow Springs General, the north parking lot."

"Okay," she said.

My mouth tasted like tin. My pulse was all over my skin. I released my knees and leaned forward, peering through the windshield. The sky had gone deep gray.

I knew people who'd lost everything in other fires, in other towns. I knew evacuating the hospital was only done if it had to be.

"Be safe and drive like hell, baby. I love ya," Mariana said. And then the call dropped.

"Mom?" Alicia said. But she was gone.

The parking lot was all horns and whistles as the teachers ordered everyone to leave.

Alicia was about to yank the car into reverse when I reached out my hand, stopping hers on the gear shaft.

"Beckett's sleeping," I said. Because he was up half the night waiting for me to get home. "Dad's on the road, and Gramps is at the hospital for his appointments—he's alone. Beck's alone."

"Call him! Tell him to get moving. We've got to get Jenny."

"No phone," I said.

She tossed me hers, starting to maneuver the car through the lot of teachers shouting "Go on! Be safe!" while kids scattered back to their vehicles. I pressed CALL on Beckett's number over and over. "He's not picking up. And Ali—the Vanagon still isn't running."

Out of the corner of my eye I saw the green of River's truck.

"River," I said. I thought of that calm excitement of the night before—*how was that just hours ago?*—and the feeling that things were going to be okay. I wanted that. "He'll take me. He's the reason Beckett doesn't have a car."

"Okay—but—"

"This will be quicker. And River agreed to be Beck's low-carbon chauffeur."

"If you say so." She shook her head. "I love you, Capybara. Be safe."

"Love you too, Alicia Bea," I said. Then I wove through the already ashy air and gridlock toward River.

"Caprice—" River said as I opened the passenger door. "Where did you—"

"I was with Alicia." I slid onto the bench seat next to him. "She's back there. I saw you and—" What could I say? I pecked his cheek, his skin warm, damp. I didn't feel better.

"Let's go," he said, all business.

"We need to get Beckett. He's home. Asleep. He's—" I hugged my backpack onto my lap.

"Can't your gramps get him?" He was starting to sweat. Beads above his eyes. I blinked.

"He's at the hospital for an appointment. He left before me."

River gripped the wheel. "Isn't that"—he pointed to the smoke—"the direction of your house?"

"Yeah, but we can't leave him," I said.

"Caprice, I—we—we can't drive into that."

"If I don't—" My throat tensed up. I couldn't say the rest. *If I don't get my brother—IF, IF, IF, IF, IF.* River put the truck in gear. It rolled forward. He stopped short, almost plowing into the bumper of Violet Homesteader's van.

"Someone will get Beck—your gramps or your mom. Let's go to Megan's shop and wait." I thought of him at the lookout. Everything a question, how I met him with soft assurance. But now there were no questions. Just commands. All my muscles tensed. The sky blackened. But inside, the truck was Technicolor bright: River in his green-and-gold hoodie, the faint hair on his knuckles as he clutched the wheel.

"Beckett's car's broken because of you." The words were hard. "He's stuck at home in this"—I pointed to the smoke—"because of you."

River dropped his head to the steering wheel. The radio station blared Kelly Clarkson, national, unaware. "Caprice, please." He wasn't looking at me. He was rolling his forehead back and forth. "We've got to go."

"No," I said, opening the car door even though the truck was in a slow roll. "*You*'ve got to go. Alicia'll take me."

River braked, but he kept his hands on the wheel.

I turned and, without looking back, dropped into the chaos of the parking lot, running back to where I'd left Alicia. River shouted into the wind after me, "Caprice, come back!"

My eyes stung. I told myself it was from smoke.

Alicia's wipers clicked on, clearing ash spots from the windshield. She reached across the seat and opened the door for me. "So, he's not a martyr?" She was trying to smile, but the words were sharp.

Oh. I should've realized she hadn't wanted me to leave her. I didn't even ask if she'd be okay alone. Ugh. I pressed my palms into my eyes. I was tired. Brain scrambled on a boy and now this. "Oh Al, I should've stayed with you."

"Whatever, abandon your bestie in hell."

"Sorry. I'm the worst."

"Maybe."

"My mom will probably be at the elementary school. When we get Jenny, she'll want me to stay with her. I wish I had my phone so I could see everyone's location."

Alicia pulled onto the main road, turning toward the elementary school. "Caps"—she shook my elbow—"we can check in with your mom but we should stay together. You know I'd go back for Beckett even if you wouldn't."

"You would?"

"Well, yeah—we're not going to lose him again."

"No," I said. "We're not."

"Plus, we need to get Jenny's rabbit, so we're going by your house anyway. If you'd stayed with me, I could have told you all that."

"Sorry, sorry, sorry," I said.

"It's fine. You were blinded by that starry night on the River."

"Stop!" We almost sounded normal. The words were. But behind everything was this humming. The wind? Or maybe the noise was inside my head. I couldn't feel my hands. I kept thinking *Get-us-to-Beckett-please, get-us-to-Beckett-please,* on a loop. I don't know if that was happening to Alicia too. I couldn't ask. It helped that she looked normal. Maybe I did too.

She cleared her throat and squinted at me, adjusting invisible spectacles, cueing her dad impersonation. "Your decision-making skills"—her voice was low—"are worsened by your lack of sleep due to a PG-13 evening with one running boy."

"Thanks, Dr. Johnson. I know it's those R-rated evenings in the make-out cabin that inform your assessment."

Alicia opened her mouth to quip something back, but the car rounded one of those hairpin turns, and suddenly the houses on both sides of the road were on fire. That stopped our words in our throats.

We drove. Traffic thickened. The world darkened. I tried to call Beckett with Alicia's phone. Then my dad. Mom. Gramps. I pressed CALL. CALL. CALL. CALL. The phone rang and rang and rang.

Alicia played steering wheel piano to the *Totoro* soundtrack. I gave up and focused on the pavement, that black expanse in front of us, and tried to separate the wind roaring behind the radio from the little chant in my brain: *Get-us-to-Beckett-please, get-us-to-Beckett-please, get-us-to-Beckett-please, get-us-to-Beckett-please.* I tried to think of my breathing like they taught us in yoga, but even my breath felt outside myself. *Get-us-to-Beckett-please, get-us-to-Beckett-please, get-us-to-Beckett-please, get-us-to-Beckett-please,* then *Maybe if I talk I'll be back in my body.*

"Doesn't the sky look kinda like those videos of time-lapse bruises your dad made us watch?" I said.

Alicia's hands stilled. "Usually they go red, blue, green, then yellow and brown."

"Hemoglobin breakdown," I said. My eyes ached like I'd opened them in chlorine. But I remembered this.

Alicia's shoulders tightened. "How are we even talking right now?"

"I have no idea." I turned her phone over. I tried my calls again. Beckett. Mom. Dad. But now it wasn't that no one picked up. It was that the air was dead. I tried texting. Nothing sent.

By the time we reached the Sierra Central parking lot, there was only one bus left, and a swarm of children and teachers around it. Alicia ran into the crowd. I followed, my legs supercharged, my lungs heavy. Wind, adrenaline, and smoke fast-forwarded time.

My mom stood near the SIERRA CENTRAL sign, holding the hand of a little girl. When she saw us, the clipboard in her hand fell to the ground.

"Oh God thank God!" She put an arm around me and shouted against the wind, "Jenny's on the bus." Mom kept the hand of the girl—a kindergartener? One of the preK kids?—as she hugged me tight with one arm. She kissed my forehead. Her lipstick left a residue. "When the kids are gone, we'll get your brother." The birds inside my chest beat their wings. I wanted to tell her to leave. Just go. But I knew she would wait until the last kid was safe.

"Alicia's getting Jenny's rabbit. They'll take me with them

to get Beck. It'll be faster. Cheerio ran out this morning—we'll get her too."

She squeezed me tight. "But I don't want you to go."

"I know. This'll be faster."

"Well," she yelled over the wind, one arm still around me, "I need to make sure Kayla here gets to her daddy safe." She shook her other hand—laced through the little girl's, Kayla's.

"This is safer," I shouted back, and felt her nod against my shoulder. She held me with one arm until Jenny and Alicia were back.

As we parted, a propane tank in a yard that bordered the playground exploded. The sound reverberated like a bomb. We froze, and then Mom pushed my shoulder. "Go. Be safe! Hurry! Alicia, thank you! I love you! I love all of you!" We were running when she took a few steps toward us and called, "Grab the go-bag—in the hall closet—that Mickey Mouse backpack!"

I nodded as we ran, dragging Jenny along, her violin case bumping between us.

"Dammit," I said as Alicia drove, "I forgot to ask her where she hid my phone."

Alicia pointed to hers. "Try calling again."

I did. And nothing. Dead air.

"And text."

"Just sends errors."

I watched the traffic move down the Ridge Road in the direction of our houses. I thought of how Gramps once told me about a town where a molasses factory exploded, and the streets filled with a sticky flood. I imagined this was like that, our cars trapped in molasses, so many trying to leave on so few roads. The smoke everywhere. Fire breaking out in patches all around us. I prayed we would not get stuck.

I sat with my hands under my knees. Glowing embers crossed the windshield. We passed my old friend Luisa's house, its roof already smoldering, and somewhere before the turn to Mitchell's, my sight disappeared.

It clicked off like a light switch.

The world went blank. I couldn't see the rows of slow-moving cars. Or the houses on fire. Houses my gramps built. Houses my friends lived in. Houses I wasn't sure were empty and couldn't stop to check. People's homes. People's lives. I couldn't take it. I stopped seeing.

An automatic program ran. *IF what you are seeing is too horrible to witness THEN don't see.*

"Why are we going so slow?" Jenny asked. "And everyone in the same direction—what if someone needs to go the other way?"

"No one's going the other way," Alicia said. "We're using both lanes. It's faster."

"Then why are we barely moving?" Jenny asked. Alicia grunted. I touched her arm, counted my breaths.

I don't know how long my vision short-circuited. All I know is when it came back, it came back slowly. First, it was like squinting through a pinhole camera. Then a telescope, then a camera's viewfinder, a wide-angle lens. Finally, my whole field of vision returned, and out the windshield I saw all the smoke and surreal orange light. Sierra transformed.

We were nearly at the turn to our houses when we saw the first firetruck, pulled to the side of the road, lights flashing.

"Are they putting out the fire?" Jenny asked. Her voice was small and hopeful. One firefighter motioned the cars to keep driving. Another sprayed water around the parking lot of The Last Dam Stop, the gas station we used to walk to for candy. Alicia put on her blinker.

Smoke filled our noses, scratched our throats.

A firefighter stepped in front of us, waving his arms. "You can't go that way." I blinked. It was Mike Solano; his wife, Ana, was Adrienne's best friend in high school. They were practically family.

I screamed, "My brother is in there. Beckett's in there."

"Go," he said, stepping out of our way. "Hurry."

Alicia careened around the final turn to my house. The smoke thickened to a gray black. I closed my eyes because *what if, what if, what if* my brother was lost again? What if we were too late?

The world was a rush of wind, heat, and acrid smoke. It burned.

"We're here," Alicia said.

I ran to the red door and thrust my key into the lock, calling, "Cheerio! Beckett!" The wind swallowed my voice. I slammed the door against it, but still it howled. I jogged down the hallway to Beckett's room. I didn't notice when I crossed the white rug with the black circles, or past the picture of Beckett and me with Cheerio and Domino the day we got them. I didn't look at Beckett's painting of Mount Lassen. I didn't see anything. I didn't take anything. I didn't think to. I only thought: *Beckett.*

I twisted the L-shaped doorknob and tumbled into my brother's room.

He slept under a white-and-gray duvet. Gramps had built his bed, the walnut headboard carved with a forest scene—pine trees and a deer grazing. I grabbed his shoulder and shook.

"Beckett. Beckett! Fire."

"Huh?" He grunted and pulled a pillow over his head.

"Beck! Come on! Move!" I took both his shoulders in my hands. The clock next to his bed flashed 9:15. How had almost two hours passed since we got to school? "Beckett! Move!"

He sat up. Eyes half-open. "Cappi? What the—?" He wiped his eyes, the lashes crusted with sleep.

"FIRE!" My voice cracked. Maybe he smelled smoke then, because his eyes widened. Then the house shuddered with the sound of an explosion.

"Come on," I said, quieter now, pulling him up by the hand. Beckett stood and searched the floor for clothes. I grabbed the half glass of water from his bedside table and swallowed it in one big gulp. Beckett pulled on a pair of jeans crumpled by his bed, pocketed his phone.

Another explosion rattled the house.

"Gas tanks," I said, trying to stay on my feet. I set the glass on the table next to whatever book Beck had been reading and said, "Hurry!"

"It sounds bad." His voice was gritty with sleep.

"It is. Your shoes are by the door."

"Gramps?"

"At the hospital. They're evacuating."

"Cheerio?"

"She got out this morning. I called for her—but Alicia's waiting."

"Alicia's here?" He turned in a circle as if looking for something.

"Let's go." I tugged his arm. He followed. I didn't grab pictures or clothes or anything.

We walked right by the front hall closet. I didn't even think to reach in and grab the go-bag. I forgot everything. I ran out the door, holding my brother's arm.

Outside, embers slid through the dark like tiny orange and red comets. I called, "Cheerio!" Closed my eyes. Opened them. I couldn't see. Then could. Somehow the world was both running at high speed and suspended like those dreams of falling and falling and falling.

"Cheerio!" I called as the wind tore my words apart. "Cheerio!"

"Let's go!" Beckett said, tugging my arm.

I called "Cheerio! Cheerio!" scanning the yard and road. A truck—round headlights—

"Gramps!" I shouted. He pulled into his driveway, and I strained against the wind.

"You need to leave," Gramps shouted as we pushed toward him. He jumped out of his truck. "Go on!"

"I'll stay with you," Beckett said.

"No!" Gramps shook his head and a lacy piece of ash floated between us, then in a gust of wind, it was blown to bits. Gramps

cleared his throat. He pointed to Beckett. "Stay with the girls."
Beckett stepped toward him.

"Gramps, we're not leaving without you," I said.

"You're leaving *ahead* of me. Now git. I'll see you in Willow
Springs."

Beckett grabbed my elbow, pulling me to Alicia's car, but I
leaned toward Gramps, straining against my brother and the
wind. "We'll help you. It'll be quicker—you know it will," I
said. I knew his house as well as my own—where he stashed
money in the bottom of the mantel clock, where Gram's diaries
were kept, the file of birth certificates and legal documents. The
meds. Whatever he needed, I could find.

"No." Gramps put a hand on my shoulder. "Get on out of
here, Caprice." He was commanding. And calm. So I listened,
and when he put his hand on my shoulder, I didn't even look at
it. I didn't see the tarnished gold of his wedding band. I didn't
reach up and hold on. I didn't say there's no chance in hell we
are leaving without you. I didn't demand that he stay with us. I
didn't run ahead to grab whatever he needed twice as fast as he
could. I didn't. "Go on now." He pushed me. His voice losing
its calm. "You got the cat?" I shook my head. "I'll try. Now git.
Roads are full up."

I didn't say *You're not following your own advice,* or *What would
we do without you?* I didn't refuse to leave.

I said, "Okay." No hug.

He nodded, sucked in his bottom lip. "I love you. Both of

you," he said. Then Gramps turned and hurried toward the garage, calling "Cheerio!" as he went. I didn't glance back at my house, at the picture window, the oak and pine trees, the flower beds between our yard and Gramps's. I ran with my brother to Alicia's car, and when I got there, she was in the back seat with her arms around Jenny, who rocked back and forth.

"Ali?" I said.

"Caps? Can you drive?" she asked. "Please?"

Could I? My vision glitched in and out. But there wasn't time to think about that. I threw open the door and climbed in.

IF I tell you what happens next **THEN** I will see it all again.

IF I don't tell you what happens next **THEN** I will see it all again.

IF I try to close my eyes **THEN** the red flashes in my head.

IF I sleep **THEN** I will dream, the roads dark, smoke denser than whiteout fog, people, dogs, horses, deer running by our window, disappearing alongside us as roofs ignite one after another like a Rube Goldberg machine gone wrong, a chain reaction you never want to see.

IF I tell you **THEN** it will hurt like blue flame dancing across skin.

IF I speak what I said, and did, **OR**—

IF I speak what I didn't say **OR** what I didn't do, I will *IF FIRE.*

AFTER

OBJECT: Rosewood Body Lotion
LOCATION: 4 Arborage Road, Sierra, California
RESIDENT: Megan Parker

. . . .

Yeah, I know what you're thinking. Rosewood Lotion is completely replaceable and not at all unique to Sierra. It's true. I got a new bottle three days after the fire. But the thing is, when I was going to bed that night, the skin on my legs was dry and everything smelled like smoke, and I wanted nothing more than to drench myself in that lotion, to rub it down my calf muscles, across my stomach, up my arms. I used to keep some at the shop. I'm a potter. My hands get dry. But I had run out the week before, so I was using my backup cheap unscented stuff at the shop. Sure there was other stuff I cared more about—pictures, especially the ones from our wedding, and Riv as a baby. Pretty much everything in the house. The house itself—it was our dream. We finally owned a home! We didn't get insurance right away—because the shop's rent had gone up, and its insurance too. And we'd inherited the house. We needed to make expensive upgrades to make the insurance affordable, and our plan was to save for the fixes, make sure River's scholarship continued for a second year of college, and then get all that done. We thought: What are the odds? That's ironic, I guess. After a life of moving, we finally had a place to call our own. Our little haven in the trees.

And then—poof. I don't know, I guess what I can hold on to is how it all comes and goes, you know? I can have my lotion now, and I can buy more when it runs out. It's comforting how some things are replaceable because so much isn't. And that's out of our hands too. Stuff disappears. I knew that as a potter. Things break. And you replace them. Build them again. You think your dreams are finally all coming true and then—nope. I try to tell myself it's not that bad. I have to. Otherwise, what am I showing River? River, who's got to become a man in this world on fire. I have to have hope for him. That's why I focus on the things I still have and love: Kate, River, Spock. And beyond them, what matters is things that are useful and can be used. That's why I make plates. Cups. Bowls. When they break, I make more. Stuff comes and goes. And you can expect that of a bottle of lotion, right?

ONE HOUR AFTER

The bathroom in River's moms' paint-your-own ceramics shop had two light fixtures: one square in the center of the ceiling, and one rectangular over the mirror. Also, a cement floor, a toilet, sink, and cleaning supplies stuffed in a bucket. The square light hummed, and the rectangle light flickered. In the mirror I saw a girl with messy, shoulder-length hair and smudged makeup. Flicker. I splashed water on my face, closing my eyes against the light. I splashed more. Opened them. Flicker. Somewhere in my head I knew it wasn't flames. We were in Willow Springs. The fire didn't make it this far. Wouldn't.

There'd been a row of firetrucks at the entrance to Willow Springs. And even the evacuation warnings into the east edge of town didn't come this far. But I knew, after what we saw, that it was possible for the fire to reach us here. Warnings might not come. Warnings could be wrong. Fire moved fast. I shook. I held my breath. Flicker. I knew it wasn't fire. But my body saw fire. I put my forehead on the cool mirror. The room tilted. My mascara was still smudged under my eyes, but when I tried to splash more water, the light pulsed, and a dizzy wave rolled through me. I charged out the door, stopping in front of a shelf of pink ballerina figurines and anniversary plates waiting for the kiln. I held the edge of the shelf and thought about my feet on the ground. I saw them on the sealed concrete floor, but I couldn't feel them. My right sneaker was singed, the edging gray with ash. I held on. I tried to feel weight in my toes, on my heels. I tried to feel my feet at all. But even though I knew they were there, I couldn't feel them. My default program ran. It kept me upright.

I thought of our road. The turn home by The Last Dam Stop, the three pine trees, the neighbors' houses—our house. Our red door. The collection of shells on the bookshelf from trips to Monterey and Santa Cruz. The Zen garden on the coffee table. A picture of Beckett and me when we were little, holding our cats. The plaster print of Domino's paw. I swayed on my feet. Cheerio. Gramps. I hoped they were together. I hoped they were almost out.

I told myself *I will be okay. I will be okay. I will be okay.* I ran the sentence on a loop. As if saying it enough would make me believe it. *IF your town is destroyed by wildfire THEN you will be okay. You will be okay.* I will be okay. I will be okay. I will be okay. I will be okay. I will be okay. I will be okay. I will be okay. I will be okay. I will be okay. I will be okay. I will be okay. I will be okay. I will be okay. I will be okay. I will be okay. I will be okay. I will be okay. I will.

It was a shit program. Untrue and impossible to follow. But numb as I was, I stepped forward.

IF the house is still standing—

IF Gramps's house is—

IF Frank's—

IF we find a place in Willow Springs for Gram—

IF Cheerio—

IF the fire's controlled—

IF the rains come—

IF schools reopen—

IF we can get back to town—

IF River and I—

IF college—

IF Beckett—

IF Gramps—IF Gramps—IF Gramps—IF Gramps—IF—

TWELVE HOURS AFTER

I woke to a whole shelf of unpainted garden gnomes staring at me. White moon faces matching the pale mushroom at their feet.

When I'd lain down, I thought sleep would be impossible, but eventually exhaustion won, and I fell into an empty dark.

The moment light appeared behind my closed eyes, I wished I could reenter the void of heavy sleep. Or maybe seal myself in a cask underground and never have to see the light or look at this world-turned-over again. But there I was, waking up. In a ceramic shop.

Beckett's cot groaned. I sat up.

"I'm coming with you," I whispered.

"To the bathroom?" He threw his pillow at me. His Willow Springs friends had been texting him. I didn't know who they were, what they were up to, if he wanted to go off with them, and if he did, if he'd be safe, if they drank, or did drugs, or if they'd be near fire.

"No, wherever else you're going." I didn't want him out of my sight. Maybe ever again.

"I'm going somewhere else?"

I pulled my legs up to my chest. "I don't know. Are you?"

"Nope. What are you still doing here? I figured you'd have snuck off with your boyfriend by now." River and his moms were upstairs in Megan's private office. Probably still sleeping. My brother stood.

"Oh come on, I wouldn't—"

"Why not? You should hold on to whatever good you can in this shit-show."

I opened my mouth to say something back, but what? I wasn't sure I'd want to sneak off with River, and Beckett was already halfway to the bathroom. Fine. Better not to raise my voice anyway. My parents were sleeping. It was a lot that his moms had offered us to stay at the shop. We'd had nowhere else to go. All our family lived in Sierra. Most of our friends too. I felt full of shattered glass, like if I ran my fingers down my arms, I'd get cut. My lungs ached. But River. How was it that our night at the point was followed by this day of fire? After it, were we still good? He'd asked us to come, to stay here. So maybe he was my one good thing.

I took my computer from my school bag. It was lucky I had it with me, especially without my phone. A quick check of social sites showed videos: all fire. Mo had footage of Main Street: Frank's on fire, then Hole in the Dam Donuts, outbuildings at school. Kim had a video from the north edge of town: fire, fire, fire. I closed my eyes. I knew who lived in those flaming houses. I remembered my gramps building them. Still, I scrolled. This was how I found where everyone was: the Walmart parking lot, the fairgrounds emergency shelter, churches in Willow Springs that opened their doors for Sierra, people already gone to family in Sacramento or the Bay Area. Selfies that said *I'm alive!* Everyone was waiting. Waiting to know what had happened to their friends, family, houses, pets, wanting to know if—or when—we could go home.

I swallowed. Dizzy. We were lucky. Alive. Together. But sleeping in Megan's shop, under the watchful eye of my parents, River's parents, and a shelf of terrifying garden gnomes, was not where I wanted to be. But what I wanted wasn't possible— to pull up my orange-and-white duvet, snuggle with my cat, and wake to a familiar world.

I clicked away from social to scan news. The fire was out of control but burning up into the mountains, away from Willow Springs. Sierra was 90 percent gone. Nine out of ten buildings. People were missing. Hundreds. Two confirmed dead. I closed my eyes. My ears rang. My stomach ached.

If 90 percent of buildings were destroyed, then how many people really died?

Not a program. A question. One no one had the answer to. My computer quaked where it sat on my knees. My hands shook. But I couldn't feel them. My body was one giant tremble. Somehow I managed to slip my laptop into my backpack without dropping it on the polished concrete floor.

The bathroom door squeaked open, and Beckett appeared,

hair wet and dripping. I thought, new program: *If Beckett is here THEN Caprice is also here.*

"If we're going somewhere, I'm ready. I don't even need to get dressed," I said.

"Look at you, pointing out the perks already." He dropped next to me. "I'm not going anywhere."

Good. If the wind changed and I didn't know where he was? If the fire came back? And if we were apart again? If, if, if, if, if—

Beckett's nose twitched. "Even after I scrubbed my hair in the sink with that lemon hand soap, all I can smell is smoke. Somehow the water tastes like fire pit."

I exhaled. "Should we make a new blend of coffee? We could call it California and flavor it with ashes?"

Beckett made a sound that might've been a laugh if any of us could laugh.

"Where's the coffee?" Mom said. The words sounded like they scraped their way out of her throat. I peered around the shelf to see my parents and saw Dad was awake, his phone to his ear. I knew without asking that he was calling Gramps. When news of the fire had reached my dad, he got someone to finish his haul up to Canada. Then stopped and bought cots, sleeping bags, and other camping supplies somewhere in Oregon. He'd helped truck goods to other communities after fires and knew the local stores would sell out. After Dad set us up in the shop, he gave the rest of his haul to Adrienne, who was helping transform a Willow Springs church, where her friend was pastor, into a shelter.

Dad's face was a worried point. He held his phone to his ear. Gramps, wherever he was, was not picking up.

"Coffee's at the coffee shop," I said as Mom sat up. "And I have a Dam good mug to put it in." I held up my insulated cup from Hole in the Dam Donuts. I thought, *This cup and the contents of my backpack might be all I own*. I wondered if Mom was thinking that too. All she said was:

"Please, please, pretty please go get some?"

Dad hung up his phone. "Don't the gnomes make us coffee?"

"Apparently they're not helpful gnomes," I said.

"I bet they help Cappi have nightmares." Beckett picked one up by its hat.

"Actually, they're helping with my impulse control. Somehow I've managed to not murder them all despite waking to their homicidal faces."

"Since when have you had problems with impulse control? That's my role in the family," Beckett said with a bow.

"Beckett," Dad warned, but his voice was tired.

"I suppose you could include Mom, or Gramps. Both have had times when they were perma high. But they managed to keep up appearances. And appearances are what matter, right?"

Mom cradled her head in her hands, and Dad looked like he was about to be hit by an oncoming train. "Beck." I reached out to touch his arm.

"Yeah, right. Sorry. I'm a little—you know, off today."

"Witnessing a fire-pocalypse can do that to a person," I said.

Beckett pressed his hands into his eyes and said, "Really though, Gramps?"

Mom and Dad exchanged a look and shook their heads. Then Mom plastered on her cheer-up face and said, "We'll hear something soon, I'm sure."

"Gram's fine," Dad said. "I'm going over to Willow Springs General later. We're looking for a care facility close by. We can't keep her in the hospital forever."

"Yeah," Beckett said. "Okay."

But it wasn't okay. He wasn't okay. He wasn't humming or singing. He looked exhausted. Had he even slept? The only person who was probably okay was Gram, and that was because she had no idea what had happened. Or at least probably not. No memory of it anyway. I was almost jealous.

"I don't know about you, Caps, but I really need to do some yoga. Maybe I'll pick up some mats when I run out for toothbrushes and underwear after you get us coffee," Mom said. Then she peered out at the thick gray smoke and frowned. "If anything is open."

"Sure?" Because yeah, we needed to find Gramps, and we needed, well, everything. "What about a phone? I don't have one."

"We'll see what we can do," Mom said. "Do you want a yoga mat, Beckett?"

"Why not? I can store it under my cot." I'm not sure Mom heard the sarcasm. "Come on, Caps," he said. "Let's see if we can find someplace to get that coffee. I need to buy some cigarettes too. You were wanting to go somewhere with me, right?" He cupped his hand on my shoulder.

I stood. I couldn't feel my feet. There was a buzzy feeling in my head. Did smoke inhalation cause that? "You really want to smoke?" I asked.

"Trust me, it's the healthier choice."

My stomach turned. A sick wave passed through me. Had I been run through a pasta machine? If Beckett was feeling how I was feeling—he could relapse. Maybe *would* relapse. I reminded myself of what I'd read on all those websites about trust and support. Trust, trust, trust, trust, trust. I said it to myself. But the words were puffs of smoke. I had no idea how to run a trust program. My concern was all over my face. Beckett shook my shoulder.

"Caps, come on. Don't look like that. Seriously. You know I'm— It's one day at a time. Okay? And we had a really shitty day, so maybe it's one minute at a time and the minutes are long. Hell, the seconds are long. But it's one at a time, and I've already gotten through like twelve of them today. Let's call that a win, okay?"

I nodded.

"We love you," Mom said. Her mascara had seeped into the lines around her eyes.

"We're here for you," Dad said. "Anything you need." But there was no way he could get us what we needed. I guess that's why he kept his eyes on his phone as he spoke. Maybe our parents wanted to be there for Beckett, for me. But they sure didn't look like they could help with much.

I followed my brother out the door, shop bells ringing behind us. I wished I could crawl into a shell like a turtle or mollusk or snail. I wanted to pull my arms inside myself and be home safe. And I wished my gramps was safe. I wished we knew for sure that he was safe. And I wished I could keep my brother safe. That we could all be home safe. But we didn't even know if we had a home. How could we be safe?

Program for Creating Social Media Posts to Find Your Grandpa After a Fire

PICK a recent picture stored in the cloud.

Example: Gramps in an Even Frank Wants Flowers T-shirt on his birthday. His ponytail flopped over his shoulder. The cupcake in his hand decorated with a Grateful Dead bear, one red candle.

ADD CAPTION. Include: Grandpa's full name. Home address. Where and when he was last seen.

Example: MISSING: Glenn Alexander. My Gramps. Last seen at 53 Plumule Way about 9:15 a.m. morning of the fire. #SierraFire #SierraStrong #ThisDamTown

THEN POST. Turn on notifications. Do not reload every second. Wait.
[Repeat]

18 HOURS AFTER

River stood in the shop's backyard while Spock sniffed a rusty folding chair. The air stung our eyes and scratched our swollen throats. The ground was ash-speckled and the sky a sick brown gray. We weren't supposed to be outside, but it was the only way to be alone, so we'd slipped out with Spock jangling at our heels. On the other side of the metal fence was an abandoned henhouse with a wall missing and hay still inside. If Gramps were here, he'd fix it for them. He hated looking at something falling apart. I pressed my fingers into my eyes. Gramps. We'd left him. Alone.

"Yesterday—Caps—I—" River started. I could tell this was about the school parking lot, how I came to his truck, why I'd left.

"Look, it's okay." I dropped my hands from my eyes. "We both made it."

"But Caprice, I—"

"We're here. That's what matters." I stuffed my hands in my pockets. I meant it.

River rolled his foot back and forth on a stick. "I know, but that night, and then yesterday—You know I didn't want to go back because I was scared, and my moms—I'm their only—"

"Riv, stop." My throat tightened. "Please. I get it. You had to get to your family. I had to get to mine—I really don't want to talk more about it. Please." Was I mad? It was hard to tell how I felt, other than that there was a hard ball in my abdomen and my head pulsed. I didn't think I blamed River for his choice. There were no good choices. Wasn't that the whole problem? The only thing I wanted was my world before. And there was not one thing I could do about the fact that I couldn't have it.

River put his arms around me, put his chin on my head. He spoke softly. "You know, our house—it didn't have insurance, and so if—"

"Oh shit," I said. All I knew about insurance is if you don't have it and something like this happens, you're pretty much screwed. "Riv, I'm so sorry."

He pulled away, shut his eyes. "We'll see what's happened. Probably it's gone. But still, there's a chance." He shook out his arms, rocked to his toes. Looked like he wanted to run far away. "The thing is"—his voice had a fierceness I'd never heard before, like it was about to crack—"even with all that I—I can't stop thinking—" I stretched my hand out to him, but he was pacing now. Out of reach. He stopped and turned to me. "Caprice, if we couldn't find you today—" He practically choked on the words. I knew he was feeling it—the program he didn't run. I stepped toward him, tugged on his T-shirt. I wanted to offer comfort, but when I opened my mouth, there were no words. Instead I felt like I was back in that black cloud of smoke and fire. What I did. What I didn't do. Caught in if, if, if, if, if, if.

But his voice was firm above the wind. It found me through the smoke. "I just—I want you to know, yesterday—"

"River, stop." It was too much. My feelings mixed and boiled. I wished I could dump the entire memory from my brain. Blot it out. Be Gram. Because if River told me his ifs, then I might tell mine. But how could I admit the things I did and didn't do? If I kept those thoughts still, maybe we could have back what we'd had at the point. All that sweet softness. That was what I needed. That was who I needed. How else was I going to stand when I couldn't feel my feet?

"Riv, please. If I think about yesterday, my hands and feet go numb."

"That sucks." He cocked his head to the side. "But is it even possible to not think about it?"

"Seems worth a try. Because my hands are like those rubber Halloween hands. Not even attached. I'd flinch if you tried to put a knife through them—because reflexes—but I'm not sure I'd feel anything."

His nose crinkled. He took a step closer and took my fingers in his. "They're numb? All the time?"

"I'm trying to think of it as a positive. I mean, I don't need to worry about anything hurting if I can't feel my body."

"Huh." He pulled our interlaced hands up to his eyes as if examining them.

"Yeah. If a space rock fell out of the sky and landed on my fingers, I'd be fine."

"Really?" he said, and I felt his breath across my knuckles, then he leaned closer and kissed them. His lips were warm and dry. "You can't feel that?"

The nestlings in my belly were back. Huh. I thought they might have died in the fire. "I can," I said, slipping my free hand around his back. "Perhaps I'm cured."

"Good, because"—his voice went soft as he let go—"you not feeling your body would be catastrophe squared." He slid his arms around me, under my T-shirt, along my back. I shivered.

"Maybe it's just my feet?" I said. Because when River touched me, I could feel again. And everything that happened the day before—all the horror of it—despite all that, somehow we were both here. He was here. That was all that mattered.

I didn't want him to feel bad about not coming with me. Who knows what would have happened—if we'd gone for Beckett alone, if I'd left Alicia. My hands tingled. Anyway, I was the one who'd made the biggest mistake. The worst mistake. But that was after he left. That was something he didn't know about. Something I wouldn't tell him. I leaned into him. My breath lifted ash off his shoulders.

"Careful," he said, leaning so his lips almost touched mine. "I get pretty antsy when I can't run—lots of pent-up energy."

"I'll risk it," I said, and kissed him, and even with the smoke and ash around us—we were sucked under. I pulled up his T-shirt to feel skin-on-skin, leaning into our kiss, deepening it. I felt my pulse all over my body. *I could disappear into this,* I thought—

"*River!*" Kate called from the back door, and we jumped apart. She wore some too-small clothes that Megan kept at the shop. Her hair was pulled tight in a ponytail and her voice was commanding. "Breathing this air is worse than putting your mouth on the tailpipe of a car from Arkansas. Seriously, come inside. You two are going to need to figure out how to keep your hormones in check." She paused, looking at each of us. "And there'll be no more of that staying out all night stuff either."

River's mouth quirked. "Some people probably have electric cars in Arkansas, Mom."

"Inside," she said, unsmiling, as we slipped through the door.

"But if you're assuming cars in Arkansas are spewing tons of CO_2 'cause their old, you should really call out all twenty states that don't have emissions testing. Montana, Iowa, Michigan—" River said, holding up his fingers as if he were going to list them all.

Kate cuffed his shoulder and he stopped. When she looked at me, her mouth turned down.

"Uh . . ." It felt like I should apologize, but I couldn't find the words. I examined my numb but somehow functioning feet.

Then Megan was there too. She touched my arm. "She's not mad. You're young! You should be kissing. It's this— It's—"

She gestured to the air, and I thought she meant *The world is on fire, I've probably lost my house, and strangers are living in my shop.* But she said, "With River's asthma and running scholarship, he just really can't. If anything was open, I'd say you should go out to the movies, but practically everything but the grocery store, a few restaurants and coffee places are shut down from the smoke, and they're packed with people from Sierra, so . . ."

River and I exchanged a look. Was she suggesting we make out in public?

"Look, I know," he said. "I'll stay inside. I don't want hives."

"You get hives?"

"I have an EpiPen," he said.

"He hasn't used it in years," Kate said. "But when the AQI's bad, we worry."

Huh. River's environmentalism sometimes felt extra intense. But maybe it wasn't. Hives from air? An EpiPen for smoke inhalation? Our town on the list of towns destroyed by fire. The hottest summer on record following the hottest summer on record. The tiny burns on my arms. No rain.

I pressed my hands to my stomach and felt nothing but tightness. No stretching wings, no restless rustling. Nothing. The kissing feelings didn't hold. Maybe I was the shell now. A thing for the wind to roll through. Maybe River was the wind, and together we sounded like the ocean, but we weren't. We were just air and calcite. The thought made me dizzy. I laced my fingers through his and pushed it all away.

I needed something to hold on to.

OBJECT: Box of High School Memorabilia
LOCATION: 4 Arborage Road, Sierra, California
RESIDENT: Kate Holt

· ·

People are always surprised to learn that Megan and I knew each other in high school. I was in love with her even then, but she sure wasn't. She had eyes for everyone. She was an incorrigible flirt, a daredevil, the first one at any party and the last one to leave if she left at all. I was pulled toward her like a magnet. In the summers, we were every night back and forth at each other's houses—depending on whose parents were paying less attention to where we were going. I don't know why I kept the lists we made, concert ticket scraps, the comics we drew in each other's notebooks in the chemistry lab we both failed. But I did. It was at my mom's house. She was downsizing. That's when I found it all again. By then, Megan had come back into my life with River, and I knew we were it. Maybe I always knew. Or maybe that's what I tell myself now.

Anyway, I brought the box home, and I showed her. River toddled around as we laughed and laughed about how I'd kept the cigar butt from that night we got drunk at Heidi Garcia's seventeenth birthday party and smoked a whole blunt with Kevin Mills. The night ended with me holding Megan's hair as she puked into the rhododendrons. She didn't remember that we kissed then, quickly and then feverishly in the dark—because that was before the puking. I kept the stub of the blunt in my pocket and put it in the box the next day, a charred bit of hope, a little reminder. I don't need that anymore. I've got her and Riv. I guess it's fine that the rest is gone.

21 HOURS AFTER

"I don't need to text before showing up anymore, right? Because I don't have a phone charger," Alicia said as she entered the shop, Jenny on her heels.

"Welcome to the pottery shop and power bar." River made a sweeping gesture.

"Since Mom decided to take my phone away on the worst possible day imaginable, I don't even have one, so please—charge away." I pointed to the charger setup in a back corner. Thankfully my parents each had one in their cars.

"I'm never going to live that one down, am I?" Mom said to Dad.

"Nope."

"The phone store was one of the few places open yesterday, but the line! There was no way I could handle it," Mom said.

"Probably won't be any better today." Dad unplugged his phone and offered the charging cable to Alicia. "In the meantime, dropping in is back in."

"We could go back to carrier pigeons," Alicia said. "That always seemed cool."

"It'd be cruel to send one in this smoke," I said, because apparently even if you feel like you're floating three feet above your head and you're sure your abdomen is full of holes, it's still possible to stand, look normal, and banter.

Jenny spidered up my back and said, "Last night, Alicia said she wished she died in the fire because Mom said the house is probably gone and that means Alicia's piano too. I think she's jealous because my violin was with me at school, and it's so small, we would've grabbed it when we got Rowdy even if it wasn't with me—like how Beckett got Alicia's piano music but couldn't get the piano because it's bigger than a car and you need special movers for a piano, but it's not okay to joke about wanting to die, so when Daddy heard Alicia say that, he drank so much beer, he fell through the glass coffee table at the Williamses' guest house, and now Mom says Alicia needs to go to therapy and we need to pay for Williamses' new table too."

"Dad got drunk because our town burned down," Alicia said, standing before us now. "Not because of me. No way the Williamses' will take our money for a table. And we all need therapy."

"True." I bounced Jenny on my back and wondered if Alicia could tell by looking at me that my limbs were made of plastic. "But seriously—your dad, Doc Johnson, ultimate model for moderation in all things, really drank so much he broke a table?"

Alicia widened her eyes. "It was pretty epic. Thank God

you were spared the lesson about stress's relationship to poor choices we had this morning."

"I can imagine," I said. More than once, I'd sat on the couch between Alicia and Jenny as her dad lectured us about how developing good habits, dict, and stress management, alongside strong friendships, would not only help us get decent jobs and keep them, but would do wonders to reduce our chances of landing in the ER. I thought of the air and River's hives. And I wondered why Jake never talked about all the things we couldn't control that might send us to the hospital, like breathing. Thinking about it made me feel like a ghost, floaty and made of gauze. Or maybe it was that my feet had disappeared.

But somehow, I held Jenny on my back and heard her say in her deepest voice, "Now's not the time to neglect self-care, girls."

"It's true. Breathing this air will make you grow a third eye."

"No park or shop yard for any of us," Beckett said. His eyes flashed between me and River. I didn't even attempt a comeback.

"That means we should go for ice cream." I knew Jenny's pleading voice well, but some spark was gone. She was a paper version of herself. Was I too? Were we all? I spun around, whirling Jenny with me.

"Uh, careful," River said, putting a hand on my shoulder to stop us. "Lots of breakables—remember?" he said, indicating the shop.

"I'm impressed I haven't destroyed anything yet."

"Cappi has a vendetta against the gnomes," Beckett said. "But so far her frontal lobe's keeping her in check."

"I'm a model of self-discipline," I said. "I bet we can find you some ice cream at the grocery store, Jenny. We have to go anyway, so how about we do that when Ali's phone is charged?" I peeled her off my neck.

"What am I supposed to do till then?"

"Want to pick something to paint?" River asked. "The coolest stuff's back here." He took a step toward the back wall. Jenny slumped but followed.

"Hey," Beckett said to Alicia. "I'm really, really sorry about your piano. I'd have rolled it into the car if I could've." He opened his arms and Alicia stepped into them. They hugged for a long time. Beckett's hand stayed on her arm as they stepped apart. Alicia glanced at it, then he stuck it in his back pocket and leaned away, his neck pink. Huh.

River's moms were setting up a small TV in the corner of the shop. Local news. All fire and smoke. The number of confirmed dead: 4. The number of missing: 489. An interview of Layla Montoya showing a picture of her dogs. Aerial views of what they said was Sierra but what looked like a warscape: whole neighborhoods just gone; streets with nothing but buildings turned to brick piles; trees smoldering. Everything gray and black. Willow Springs parking lots crowded with people. My stomach ached with a deep weight. I let my breath out slow. It didn't relieve any pain. I told myself I wasn't going to think about the fire. Not anymore. Not if I could avoid it. The past was gone. Like everything else. Better to find the next plan.

Make the next program. Which would be great, but I couldn't think beyond *IF. IF. IF. IF. IF. IF.*

Beckett rocked from toe to heel—back and forth. Could he feel his feet? I didn't ask. "I need a cigarette," he said.

"Not smoky enough for you?" Alicia asked.

His arms went loose. "Addiction sucks, kids," he said with a bow, and the shop doors jingled behind him.

"Why's he such a loveable ass?" I wondered.

"I wish I knew," Alicia said as we stepped into a little corner at the front of the store. "You hear from anyone?"

"On social I saw Luisa at her sister's apartment somewhere down here, Kim and Violet are with their families, camped out at the Walmart parking lot. I messaged them but only got a heart response."

"Yeah, I drove by there. It's—" Alicia nodded toward the TV, and my brain filled in possible endings to her sentence. Apocalyptic. The stuff of nightmares. Worse than watching the baby birds Cheerio brought in die.

Alicia bit her lip, gazed out the window to where Beckett was smoking in the brown air. You couldn't tell what time of day it was. The sky was the shade watercolors turn when kids mix everything together. The sun—when you could find it at all—was a dull hazy circle glowing far away.

"I'm worried about him," I said.

"Beck?" Alicia nodded. "Of course you are." Outside, Beckett brought his cigarette to his lips.

"I don't understand wanting to touch anything that burns."

"Everything burns." Alicia hugged her arms around herself as she stepped closer to me. I wished she was wrong and feared she was right. Apparently, your world can be incinerated and somehow it's still possible to stand. Alicia lowered her voice. "Are you and River okay? I mean after—"

"Yeah," I said, leaning close. "I mean, other than how weird it is to be staying with him— But you know how it is. We got out. That's all that matters."

Alicia breathed in, watching my face. "I know." She smiled and I felt a rush of happy like the day before when we'd turned a corner and the sky cleared and we realized we made it out. We'd escaped the fire. We'd lived. Then our eyes met, and the surge of joy cracked. Alicia's dark eyes were watery and wide. I could feel how we were both wondering about Gramps.

I felt heat behind my eyes and blinked hard.

Alicia cocked her head toward River and said, "So, you going to reenact that scene from *Ghost*? The pottery wheel, the—"

"Please! Alicia. No."

"Really? Why not?"

"Look, it's— His moms were trying to get us to go to the movies to make out—"

"Not a bad idea," Alicia said. "But they're closed."

"Ali!"

She smiled but then pulled on my arm, dragging me closer to her. "I do need to tell you something." She lowered her voice. "I broke up with Felix."

"You what? Why? Weren't you just saying—I mean, don't

you need some long-distance cello love now more than ever?"

She pressed her hands into her eyes. "No."

"Alicia, seriously. You said you wanted to die, and you broke up with Felix. How worried do I need to be right now?"

"I don't know. I think— " She dropped her hands to her sides, drumming her fingers. "I'm not a danger to myself."

"You'd tell me if you were?"

Alicia clutched her hands together. "Yeah. I would. And I know it's weird. But once we were on national news, Felix kept calling—over and over. And he sent like a thousand texts— people really needed to reach each other—he didn't get it. He was clogging the network. I messaged saying I was okay but— it was—" She looked at the ground, at me, then at her sister, painting a rabbit-shaped coffee mug, two floppy ears for handles. She frowned. "It wasn't going to work anyway. Not unless we ended up at the same conservatory, which you know—"

"College or conservatory? Once your biggest problem." I smiled.

Alicia chuckled. No heart in it. "Like how *your* biggest problem was figuring out how to work with Cecil on the app?" I traced a crack in the cement floor.

"Ali," I said, "I forgot about the app until right this second."

"Well—yeah." She shuffled closer. "Of course you did. I mean—we could have died. And now, all that matters is we're alive."

And if Gramps is, I thought, but said, "Beck says shock can do all sorts of weird stuff."

"Maybe. But I don't think my Felix thing was shock, I figure if you go through that and don't want to talk to the person you're with, that means something. So I told him I have way too much going on and I can't communicate with him anymore. Then I blocked him."

"You blocked him?" I felt cold. *Was* Alicia okay? Could this be the shutting down people do before they get really, really depressed? And then this little selfish part of me thought, *Well, it must be a good sign that I still want to kiss River.* That kissing him still felt so good.

"Seemed like a good time for a clean break."

"Good for you." I put my arm around her back. "Something tells me the universe is calling us to consider new beginnings."

Her eyes darted to Beckett. "Please tell me your mom did not say that."

"Oh, she did," I said. "Then she blamed the fire on Mercury being in retrograde and ran out to complete important errands for floss, toothbrushes, yoga mats, underwear, and a supersized box of gummies from the Cannabis Café."

"Well"—Alicia crossed her arms—"at least the Cannabis Café didn't close because of the smoke."

"How else would the adults be okay?" I said, but thought, *How will I?*

"The app," Alicia said. "It was your life, Cap."

"I know, but now—" I looked out the window again, into the smoke. An obliterated town did not need a tourist app. Maybe it never did. I didn't know what not finishing it meant, not really. Except I'd have to get the money back to Cecil. I couldn't imagine focusing on code when there was this sound in my head, like the tone only people under twenty-one can hear—only no one was hearing it but me.

And if I didn't feel full of that sound, I was starting to loop on questions: Was Gramps alive? Cheerio? What happens now? Where will we live? What about school? Will I be able to focus on my AP online comp sci class I had already missed an assignment for because it was not stopping for this? But I didn't say any of that to Alicia. I said, "The app was my way out. And look! We're out!"

"Funny." She laced her arm through mine.

"IF no town THEN no tourist app. I don't know much else, but I know that." There I was sounding like myself. I was aware, vaguely, that I probably should be sad about the app, or at least worried about what it meant for college. But college too seemed this far-off thing. There was so much to be sad about, so much to worry about—everything sounded like static.

"Caps?" Alicia said. "You still here?"

"Maybe?" I said, steadying myself with her elbow. Out the window, Beckett spit on the ground, extinguished his cigarette in it, then touched the butt before tossing it into the trash can. He looked at us, or maybe past us. Maybe through us. I had no idea. I leaned my head against hers. "You know, I never liked Felix anyway," I said.

"You never met him!" Alicia pushed against me.

"Exactly." I pulled open the door for my brother to come in. "It was a serious flaw. A mistake I hope you never make again."

Alicia smiled and followed my brother back to the table where Jenny was working. He sat down on the empty bench seat across from Jenny.

"I'm painting a Rowdy Rabbit mug," Jenny said. "If he was purple with pink spots."

"I like the color change," Alicia said.

"Me too," Beckett agreed. I watched their eyes catch. Hold. Release.

The day before, I might have thought Alicia was too good for my brother. Because sure, he'd been trouble. But nothing was the same anymore. And maybe in this upside-down world, Alicia and Beckett would make sense. I knew Beckett had lied when he said he didn't want to hang out with me and my high school friends. He'd always liked Alicia. All the way back to the Older Siblings Club Fort. Beckett scooted over on the bench seat. Alicia sat down.

48 HOURS AFTER

"Is Alicia coming with us?" Beckett tossed a paintbrush in the air.

"I didn't ask," I said as Beckett launched a second brush, caught the first, threw it and a third, then dropped all three.

"You're losing your skills." He made a face that probably meant *Don't judge, you can't even feel your hands.* He tried again; this time he kept all three in the air. Then caught the brushes and put one in his mouth like a cigarette. I grabbed it. "Customers use these."

"You mean like they use the gnomes you almost took out with your yoga last night?"

"I would've been doing us all a favor if I took those gnomes out." But I thought, *If you can't feel your feet, don't try to balance on only one of them.*

Beckett dropped his head. Was he trying to knock out a buzzing sound, or shake an invisible vise off his forehead, or figure out if his limbs were still attached?

"I need a cigarette," he said. "Then we'll go. Tell Alicia to meet us there."

"You can! I have no phone, remember?"

"Right." Beckett wiped his hands on his jeans before pulling his phone from his back pocket. "Yeah, okay. I have her number." I almost smiled. Maybe I could read my brother after all, at least about some things.

"Cappi? You ready?" River called from the back of the shop. I wanted to reach for him, even though his hair was greasy, and his eyes looked flat. If I felt him unwind under my hands again like yesterday in the yard, I might forget what I'd done, at least for a minute. Maybe I'd even forget that River's family was letting us stay here, sharing their space even though we had insurance and . . . maybe I could forget we were going to look for Gramps. Maybe I could feel more than full of static. "Cappi?"

I blinked. River stood in front of me now. If I reached out, I could touch his T-shirt, so I did. Just a little tug. He smiled weakly. How much time had passed? I hadn't seen him cross the room. Five seconds? Fifty seconds? Three minutes? "Yeah. Okay—yeah. Let's do this." I clapped my hands. Did I look hopeful? Together?

"I'm more excited than I would be for an appendectomy," Beckett said.

"That's the spirit!" I cuffed my brother on the shoulder.

"You can count on me to see the light at the end of the tunnel. Especially when it's a train."

"I never said you were good for nothing."

"You sure about that?"

I wasn't. I took the car keys from my mom and tossed them to him. "You know Willow Springs better than I do," I said.

"Mom, Dad, did you hear that? Caprice admitted I knew more about something than she does!" Dad lowered the phone from his ear and nodded. Mom raised her hand off her tablet and waved.

"Hey, come on, you know more about meth labs than I do—like how they smell?" I bit my tongue. The barb was thoughtless and unfair. My parents were so zombified, they didn't even hear.

"That's right," Beckett said. "And that smell is better than the world right now. Let's go. Riv gets shotgun." He chuckled. I hoped he wasn't mad. He seemed annoyed. But he was still coming with us. I could still see him. He wasn't running away, or drinking, or breaking in a way that would make everything worse. If I could keep him in my sight . . . *IF Beckett is here THEN Caprice is also here.*

The Walmart parking lot was cars and smoke and campers and people handing out masks. Water bottles. A Red Cross table with a long line. Mobile FEMA unit. Dogs barking. Babies crying. Folding chairs. Sleeping bags. Tents. Tarps. People we knew. People we didn't. Coughing. Food trucks giving out meals. Someone screaming. Laughter. People hugging. People slipping quietly by. People finding each other in the crowd, people kissing. People with eyes red and wide and sleepless. People under the sick brown sky. People breathing the bad air.

Alicia stood at the edge of it all, waiting for us in her purple-and-black tank top and *Kiki's*-patched jeans, an N-95 mask over her face, and a stack of papers in her hand. "The people we were staying with let me use their printer," she said, holding up my social media post-turned-flyer.

"Thanks."

"Let's split up," Beckett said.

My throat closed and I shook my head. The buzzing got loud. Alicia said, "Good idea, I'll come with you."

"Okay, yeah." My throat loosened, and my head quieted. Beckett and Alicia. She didn't want to lose him either. Not again. After everything, maybe they could make sense. Maybe her blocking Cello Man had less to do with Cello Man and more to do with Beckett. "You guys take everything to the left of the camper—that one with the airbrushed bear on the back. And River and I will take everything to the right." I almost cheered for myself, I sounded so normal.

Alicia brushed Beckett's arm. "Come on," she said, turning to him. "Let's do this."

"Good luck," River said as they walked away, and then he laced his fingers through mine. His survival cord bracelet rubbed my wrist. I wanted to stop there in the parking lot and lose myself in kisses, but there were too many people around. And we were there for a reason. So we called out, "Glenn Alexander? Anyone seen Glenn?" We thrust our little pieces of paper into the parking lot's bustle, and people took them and wished us luck and promised to look out and get it touch if they heard anything. "Glenn Alexander? Anyone seen Glenn?" My feet touched the ground but didn't feel it.

"Glenn Alexander? Anyone seen Glenn?" we called. But he was nowhere. Not there. I tried to swallow the memory that told me I knew why. Gramps in the driveway—Gramps telling us to go on ahead—he'd see us here, in Willow Springs. He'd be here. That was the plan. He would be here. He had to be here. He must be somewhere. He had to be waiting for us. He must have been helping someone during the fire, maybe getting a friend settled somewhere. But now he had to be looking for us. Maybe even here. In this parking lot. I told this to myself again and again as I floated through the people. And my throat ached and ached. And my brain looped on if, if, if, if, if, if, if, if, if, if, if, if, if if, if, if, if, if, if, if, if, if, if, if, if, if, if, if, if, if, if, if, if, if, if, if, if, if, if, if, if Gramps was here somewhere, somewhere, some-where, somewhere, somewhere, some—where, some—where, some—where, so—me—where, so—me—where, show—me—where, show me where, show me where, show me where, show me where, show me where, show me where, show me where, show me where, show me where, because *IF someone had seen him THEN all of this would be okay OR better OR possible.*

But we didn't find him. Or anyone who had seen him. Or anyone who could show me where he was. And Beckett and Alicia didn't either. And my parents didn't find him. And Adrienne didn't find him. We looked and we looked and we looked and we looked and we looked and we looked and we looked and we looked and we looked and we looked and we looked and we—

Program for Living as an Evacuee in a Ceramics Shop with Your Family and Your New Boyfriend's Family

IF you managed to sleep *THEN* wake up.

IF you did not sleep *AND* the light is coming through the sheets hung over the shop windows *AND* you can hear people moving around *THEN* open your eyes *AND* sit up; you are not going back to sleep now.

IF awake *THEN* look at phone *AND* check all social accounts for:

A. Information on missing grandpa

B. If there is news about when town will reopen (you don't want to go, but you want to know)

C. If there is news about when school will reopen (you want to go, to see friends)

D. Anyone already announcing they're moving away

THEN:

Repost call for information on missing grandpa to all social channels.

AND read the updated list of missing people *AND* notice how not all names that disappear off the list join the names of the dead.

AND be thankful for the rain even if it is slowing the search for the missing. It clears the air and slows fire.

IF bathroom is free *THEN* wash face *AND* brush teeth before the flickering light makes your head fill with static.

IF bathroom is occupied *THEN* wait while considering ways you could smash the gnomes.

IF no one has gone out for coffee **THEN** get coffee **AND** pastries **AND** save receipts for insurance company.

IF someone has gone for coffee **THEN** drink coffee **AND** eat pastries.

IF at any point it seems like flames are appearing out of the walls, **OR** like you are slipping backward away from your body **THEN** hold on to a bookshelf **OR** brother **OR** boyfriend **OR** chair **AND** try to feel your feet pressing into the ground **AND** fill your lungs from the bottom up.

Work on college essays because even though it feels impossible to imagine college like you once did, you'll want the option. You can't finish any applications. You'll need your social security number, and no one remembers this. Everywhere it was written has burnt. You'll get it back eventually, after your parents fill out more forms at the "resilience center," a group of trailers deposited by the government and other relief organizations at the fairgrounds sometime after the fire. A week? Two? You lost track. Be thankful you aren't old enough to have to go there. Adults call it "going into the belly of the beast."

IF working on scholarship applications **THEN** submit only those that don't yet require your social security number.

Keep your brother, your mother, your father, and everyone else important to you in very close range. When someone is missing, the world begins to tilt too far to the left or the right and you feel like you're about to drift off.

Text your friends. Invite them over.

OR meet them somewhere for smoothies.

OR meet them at the movies.

DO NOT meet them at the mall **OR** any store. Stores are full of too many things. Things that you used to have but no longer do. Things that, because you need them and once had them, but they are not yours, you will resent.

Encourage your brother and best friend to hang out without you **THEN** find ways to leave the two of them alone together. **DON'T** let your parents know this plan. They will worry. She's newly eighteen and he's usually trouble. But you know she can handle him. She always could. And he means well. Watch how his attention moves like a compass toward her.

THEN check animal shelters for your cat. See wrapped paws and singed ears. Leave your name. Leave your number. Your address and a description. Tell them yes, she had a microchip but no, you don't have the number. It was on a paper that burned in your house. Yes, your vet had a record, but their offices burned too.

DO NOT think about all you lost.

BUT IF you do think about objects **THEN** list them. Slide the list over to your parents for the insurance claim.

DO NOT talk about insurance. Your boyfriend's family doesn't have it. Lots of other people don't have it. The inequality of the loss is unsettling and everywhere. It's inescapable. You want the town, the state, the government, the power company that's probably responsible to do more, but what can anyone do? Your town is homeless.

IF somehow alone with your boyfriend, even for a moment behind a shelf, kiss. Kiss until your lips go numb and you forget that your world imploded, your grandpa is missing, your app is irrelevant.

IF you start thinking about that day—kiss.

IF you are in the yard **THEN** kiss.

IF your brother follows you to the yard **THEN** return inside.

IF you can't find a place to kiss **THEN** run errands for your parents. Kissing can always be done at stoplights.

Attempt to eat. Chew each bite fifty-four times. Swallow.

IF this fails **THEN** buy a smoothie.

DO NOT criticize your mom for popping THC gummies like candy.

DO NOT criticize anyone.

DO everything you can to be helpful.

Make jokes. No subject is too bleak. Anything that can help you laugh is worth a risk.

At night, lay down on your cot.

    Close your eyes.

        Try to sleep.

        IF you sleep, hope the nightmares are not bad.

        IF you do not sleep, be still and think about your breathing.

AND the fire tornado will spin around your brain until morning.

    Burning and burning and burning.

Repeat.

(Currently running three weeks and counting).

The Flaw in the Program

You can try, but really you can't write a program, or make a sim-
ple plan, when nothing is going on, and you aren't in control
of anything anyway, because even though you are almost
eighteen, you aren't really a grown-up, and everything you
planned to do before is on pause or useless, and your cat is
missing and your gramps is missing and no one can find them
so your life is only IF IF IF IF IF IF IF IF IF IF IF IF IF IF IF IF IF
IF IF IF IF IF IF IF IF IF IF IF IF IF IF IF IF IF IF IF IF IF IF IF IF
IF IF IF IF IF IF IF IF IF IF IF IF IF IF IF IF IF IF IF IF IF IF IF IF
IF IF IF IF IF IF IF IF IF IF IF IF IF IF IF IF IF IF IF IF IF IF IF IF
IF IF IF IF IF IF IF IF IF IF IF IF IF IF IF IF IF IF IF IF IF IF IF IF
IF IF IF IF IF IF IF IF IF IF IF IF IF IF IF IF IF IF IF IF IF IF IF IF
IF IF IF IF IF IF IF IF IF IF IF IF IF IF IF IF IF IF IF IF IF IF IF IF
IF IF IF IF IF IF IF IF IF IF IF IF IF IF IF IF IF IF IF IF IF IF IF IF
IF IF IF IF IF IF IF IF IF IF IF IF IF IF IF IF IF IF IF IF IF IF IF IF
IF IF IF IF IF IF IF IF IF IF IF IF IF IF IF IF IF IF IF IF IF IF IF IF
IF IF IF IF IF IF IF IF IF IF IF IF IF IF IF IF IF IF IF IF IF IF IF IF
IF IF IF IF IF IF IF IF IF IF IF IF IF IF IF IF IF IF IF IF IF IF IF IF
IF IF IF IF IF IF IF IF IF IF IF IF IF IF IF IF IF IF IF IF IF IF IF IF
IF IF IF IF IF IF IF IF IF IF IF IF IF IF IF IF IF IF IF IF IF IF IF IF
IF IF IF IF IF IF IF IF IF IF IF IF IF IF IF IF IF IF IF IF IF IF IF IF
IF IF IF IF IF IF IF IF IF IF IF IF IF IF IF IF IF IF IF IF IF IF IF IF
IF IF IF IF IF IF IF IF IF IF IF IF IF IF IF IF IF IF IF IF IF IF IF IF
IF IF IF IF IF IF IF IF IF IF IF IF IF IF IF IF IF IF IF IF IF IF IF IF
IF IF IF IF IF IF IF IF IF IF IF IF IF IF IF IF IF IF IF IF IF IF IF IF

THREE WEEKS AFTER

The marquee of the old movie theater read: WELCOME BACK SIERRA HIGH! #SIERRASTRONG.

"Well," I said, "I'm not sure I want to return to statistics, but at least we have something to do other than wonder if my mom is getting into the special gummies before she leaves for work and make sure Beckett isn't."

"Caps," River said as we walked across the parking lot dodging the Channel 4 cameras set up to document our surreal return to school. "Beck's going to be okay. School's only six hours. And that was never his thing."

"Or so he says." It was cool, and since the rains had returned, the air was breathable. I crossed my arms over my chest.

"Trust him. He'll be okay."

"I'm beginning to think *okay* is the worst word in the English language."

"Fair. But, still, you know what I mean."

I did? Didn't River understand how much could happen in six hours? *If fire, if alcohol, if you can't see, if, if, if—*

It was easy for River to assume that Beckett would be "okay." He'd only known him as okay. River had never seen the difference between Beckett going to school in the morning and how we found him after school, slurring, red-eyed, pissing in the garden. If, that is, we found him at all.

He was so optimistic. I wished I could be. I mean, we were alive. Together. I knew it was all that mattered, but I didn't feel that way.

We pushed through the glass doors. "Whoa. Did I trip halfway through the looking glass? How does it still smell like popcorn and Red Vines? The theater's been closed for seven years." The multiplex shut down soon after my parents dropped Beckett, Mason, Alicia, and me off to see a Pixar movie—I don't remember which one because we never saw it. The boys got us settled in seats and then disappeared into another theater. We followed them and didn't realize it was a horror movie until we were too scared to leave. I still don't know if I was more scared by what was happening on-screen, or by seeing my brother and Mason sipping from a flask. Still, Alicia and I said the nightmares were worth it for the look on their faces when they realized we were the annoying kids kicking their seats.

"Wow. There's actually popcorn." River pointed to Ms. Moon wheeling a popcorn cart across the room. Her lipstick was smeared, and I thought maybe she was having trouble fitting back into the lines of herself. I wondered if I should tell her in case any of the journalists came to interview her and, sometime tonight, she'd discover that everyone in the north state viewing area had seen her sketchy makeup job— "Caps." River's voice was soft. Oh. I'd stopped walking and was staring at Ms. Moon. I guess my feet had gone missing again. "You okay?"

I flashed him a look that said *You really used that word?*

"Sorry. What should I say?"

God. He was so nice. I tried to smile. "I'm fine." I focused on the warmth of his hand on my back. I could be in control. Together. At least I could look like it.

"I'm beginning to think *fine* is the worst word in the English language," River said.

I shook my head. The buzzing was loud. "Nope. It's definitely *okay*."

"Beckett's fine—I mean okay—" River rolled his hands. "You know what I mean. Without you. He's—"

I unfolded my arms, wrapped them around River, and kissed him in a way you probably shouldn't when you're standing in front of a teacher. But it stopped River from talking, and that stopped me thinking about Beckett, how I shouldn't try to save him, how trying could make things worse—there was only kissing River. Kissing kissing kissing in a movie theater. Kissing, like a drug. Kissing and more kissing—

"Okey dokey, it *is* exciting being back together—but move it on. Assembly in theater three!" Ms. Moon's voice crackled. I broke away from River in time to see her shake her head and roll the popcorn machine through the lobby toward the theater.

"Look!" I said, feeling revived by the jolt of River. I tugged him by the arm. "Empty *Coming Soon* frames! Perfect reminder of our blank futures."

River cocked his head. "I think it's supposed to be inspirational, like *Imagine your future here!*"

"Huh. I do feel like I'm watching a movie of myself. *Enter: Caprice and River. Trying to be a normal teenage couple after their world was incinerated.*" We turned into theater three.

"At least everyone feels the same way."

"I know, right? Everyone's always trying to be a couple. Take Alicia here—" Alicia sat at the end of a row with her I'M HERE FOR THE FUN bag across her lap, like a seat cushion flotation device in a water landing. "I think she's made some progress wooing my brother. They were in the shop yard for a looong time yesterday thanks to our stabilized air quality."

"Aw, the shop yard," River said, and smiled. The AQI had lowered to non-hive-inducing once the rain started; we'd spent lots of time there ourselves between downpours kissing and kissing in a corner of the patio, or behind the oak tree. Thinking about it made the nestlings inside me open their hungry mouths.

"He's going to be fine, Caps," Alicia said.

"Nice way to change the subject." I crossed my arms and slumped into the empty seat next to her.

"That's what I said," River agreed. Alicia glared. "About Beckett. Not the subject." She nodded in a way that meant *Thank you.*

"Uh, no. You said *fine* was your least favorite word."

Alicia's look asked if we were actually fighting. I didn't think so, but I wasn't sure, so I attempted a smile. She wore a new cardigan over her purple-and-black tank top. Her same *Kiki's*-patched jeans.

"Nice outfit," I said. Like me, she'd rarely worn anything else but the clothes she'd had on that day.

"I could say the same to you, but I'm getting a little tired of seeing you in the PROGRAM OR BE PROGRAMMED T-shirt, since you're not actually programming."

My feet bounced. Alicia was one to talk. She'd given up both piano and Cello Man, cold turkey. Maybe I was fine about Cello Man. But piano? If you knew anything about Alicia, it was that she played. I gripped my notebook with one hand and clutched a gel pen in the other. "What are you talking about," I said. "I'm programming all the time, see—"

On the pad I'd scrawled: *Program for Attending School in an Abandoned Movie Plex.*

Alicia huffed, but took the notepad and wrote:

IF stale popcorn smell is more powerful than Axe body spray THEN you are in confirmed hell.

"Cheer up. It's not that bad. There's *fresh* popcorn too," I said as she passed the notebook back to me.

"So does this mean we get to watch *actual* movies?"

"Probably not."

She pointed to the words *confirmed hell* and said, "I rest my case."

I wrote on the line below hers:

IF you are in confirmed hell THEN pray.

Alicia took the notepad back and wrote:

IF praying THEN gloat that you have finally saved the soul of your dearest friend.

"Ha ha," I said.

"You brought it up," Alicia said. "How many people do you think will come?"

"No idea."

Next to us, Mitchell said, "Nice space-cats shirt, Riv." River puffed out his chest to show how a calico with a purple laser sword was defending the galaxy. His new wardrobe was 100 percent found at the random donation sites popping up all over town. It seemed the whole state was off-loading their unwanted crap on the now homeless former residents of Sierra, and River had gone all out.

"It's so good to see you all!" Mr. Ruiz, the guidance counselor, boomed into a mic at the front of the theater. "Please take a seat, and I promise today we'll have lots of time for catching up." After that, all I heard was, "Something-something-community" and "something-something-buzz-buzz-buzz-resilience" and "something-something-buzz-sticking together."

"Uh, Mr. Ruiz." Mitchell his hand up and I could hear again. "Is it an excused absence if we go back to town when it opens? Because my grandma wants to go right away and—"

"I think all absences are excused from now on," Kim called from the row behind us.

Mr. Ruiz held up his hand. "As always, please have your

parents call or email the attendance office. But it'll be fine."

"The attendance office still exists?" Grayson called out.

"It's a phone number, dumbass," Kim said loudly.

"Okay—okay, none of that. We are here to support you as best we can when town opens . . ." The buzzing was loud. I hugged my arms to my chest. Alicia tapped her pen and wrote across the notebook in a barely legible sideways scrawl:

IF your section of town opens up THEN you should go even if it's worse than high school in confirmed hell.

I shook my head. When a section of Sierra opened, it meant forensics already checked it for remains. It meant Gramps wasn't there. I was trying not to pay attention to the news about that, but it was everywhere. The forensics searching was slowed by the rain, but the count changed day to day. Fifty-five confirmed dead. Thirty-eight missing. When I closed my eyes, I saw the map of Sierra in my head. That triangle divided into smaller and smaller bits. Places where they might find Gramps, if he'd died, if he wasn't hiding out helping one of his old friends rescuing dogs or something. I told myself that was possible. Dad had a friend on the police force who said it was chaos up there, and the few who'd stayed through the fire and lived were refusing to leave. There was one guy on the news who went out every day looking for animals. Maybe if Gramps had hit his head and forgotten all about us, and if he was in a hospital somewhere the doctors hadn't put it all together yet, if, if, if, if.

Alicia tapped her arm and then the notebook. Right. I was supposed to write something. Program or Be Programmed.

I wrote *IF*, and then my brain was loading and loading and loading. IF. IF. IF. IF. IF. And not a single THEN. Alicia gave me a questioning look.

Principal Wilson led us in a moment of silence for those lost and still missing. Then he introduced some local politician and someone from the state board of education. And my head filled with noise. I stretched my jaw to pop my ears. It didn't help. In my head a symphony tuned their instruments. My ribs pulled tight, my feet went numb, my vision fuzzed. Alicia played her leg like a piano. River pressed his arm into mine, and it brought me back to the room.

I wrote, *IF your hands anxiously play the piano even though you have sworn off music as quickly as you swore off Cello Man THEN play the piano.*

Alicia wrote, *IF you avoid talking about the fire or going back to town THEN you need professional help.*

"Yeah. Probably. But how is that part of the program?" I whispered, pointing to the title. "It has nothing to do with school. And your mom said it's impossible to find a therapist right now."

Alicia wrote, *IF you can't find a therapist THEN talk to Mr. Ruiz.*

I wrote, *IF you think a traumatized school counselor is going to be help THEN get a lobotomy.*

"Caps," Alicia said. "He's a good guy."

"I'm sure he is." I wondered why, if the fire was all anyone talked about, I should talk about it too. What was there to add? I wasn't about to tell anyone about my if, if, if, if, if, if, if, if, if, ifing, my brain that kept freezing, my numb hands and feet. "But I don't think—"

"Caprice, Alicia." Principal Wilson was back at the mic and smiling. "I know we all have lots to talk about, but I don't want you to miss my joke about how this is a historic day, because never before has a room full of public educators all been wearing brand-new clothes." He tried to smile. No one laughed.

"You know, because teachers usually can't afford—"

"To waste time on shopping," Ms. Moon offered, taking the mic.

Silas Brant, the new art teacher, said, "I don't even have any paint on my jeans." There were a few forced laughs.

I wrote, *IF the choir needs you to play THEN play.*

Alicia wrote, *IF school is being held in an abandoned movie plex THEN there is no piano AND choir must sing à capella.*

I wrote, *IF,* and jammed up again. Alicia took the pen and finished the program for me:

IF your town burns down THEN piano AND piano contests don't matter.

I took the pen and wrote, *OR doing something you loved before could feel good.*

She took the pen and crossed it out. "You're writing impossible programs," she whispered.

But our programs were always impossible. That's why they were fun. But when everything felt impossible?

Maybe she had a point.

OBJECT: Vase
LOCATION: 51 Plumule Way, Sierra, California
RESIDENT: Irene Alexander

. . . .

We kept the vase in the big picture window in the dining room. My kids teased me that it distracted from the canyon view, but I called it my retirement plan. That was a joke too. I would never have gotten rid of it by choice; it was made for me by Henna Krysalys. Yes, the Henna. We were college roommates. She made us the one-of-a-kind piece for our wedding, and four plates too, but those broke years ago. It was a thoughtful gift, considering how she questioned if I was throwing my whole future away by getting married in the first place. Especially to some small-town construction worker who read Derrida for fun but didn't see the use in formal education. You would think an artist would be okay with anything. Now I think maybe her judgment bothered me because I was judging myself too.

But Dylan Alexander had a smile so bright it made you want to follow him anywhere, and he could build anything. The first time I met him, I was in Willow Springs at one of those late-night diners, and he assembled this whole Rube Goldberg machine out of plastic cups, straws, silverware, and little containers of jelly. The waitress was annoyed until he had a jelly container car roll up to her and deliver a large tip. By the time we left that place, I think she was half in love with him. I know I was. I grabbed his hand and he smiled. And that smile. I was on a spring break trip to visit a friend at Willow Springs State, but I didn't let go. And neither did he. After that, he'd come down and stay in my dorm at Berkeley, tease me about my fancy friends. I'd blow my money taking him out to nice restaurants, and he'd complain that the table had nothing good on it to build with, but he always loved the food. When I graduated and started working those long tech hours, I found him a job too. We were happy. He liked it down there but there was always this restlessness about him. There weren't enough trees. We'd agreed to go back to Sierra every month, but the traffic made those drives longer each year. It was tiring.

After Beckett, Dylan said in Sierra he would work for his dad, and if that didn't work out, one of his friends was starting a logistics company that had benefits. Trucking would mean he had to be away some, but he'd have flexibility. Choice. And whatever he did, we'd have childcare help from his parents. It made sense. Or I thought it did. I was sick of the long hours. I don't know if I was thinking clearly. Having a toddler can fuzz your brain.

It wasn't until a few years after we got up here that I started to wonder if Henna was right after all. Maybe I had thrown it away. Friends from my old job were making money I couldn't even comprehend. They took their families on vacations all over the world. They didn't worry how they were going to send their kids to college. But by then, I'd come to love the way the tree shadows tracked the yard all afternoon, and how my children ran back and forth from our house to their grandparents' covered in mud. The duplex I'd grown up in was dreary with cigarette smoke, a five-foot yard. I wasn't allowed to walk half a block to the paved playground. And my grandparents? Sometimes they sent a card from Delaware. My kids' childhood was the opposite.

Maybe it was a mistake. All of it. Except the kids. I don't know. But I guess when I think about Sierra, I think of home. Of knowing the people who make my hand soap. Of people stopping me at the farmer's market asking about my mother-in-law as they handed me a jar of honey. Maybe it was a mistake, but maybe life is a gift we are charged to make a mistake or two with.

Honestly, I hated the vase. Caprice always teased me about it. But you have to keep something if Henna gives it to you. She sent me a bowl when she heard about the fire. Maybe I'll sell it to retire. But probably not. It's beautiful, this one. Bright as the hills in spring.

And anyway, what's life if not an opportunity to miss some chances?

THREE AND A HALF WEEKS AFTER

"How's school going, Caps?" Mom glanced at me in the rear-view mirror. The windshield wipers squeaked. It was raining again. A week after the fire, the skies decided to open and it had rained most days since, like the planet was trying to apologize for all those months without rain, and what had happened because of it. Mom was exhausted from work. It sounded liked it sucked trying to help teachers set up emergency classrooms, trying to help the school find families so they could keep in touch, trying to figure out what it meant to be a school tech coordinator without a school or much tech. I imagined it felt something like being a high school senior suddenly attending classes in a movie theater where no one had supplies or books, and everyone looked haunted and talked about resilience and grief cycles instead of American government or statistics. And you spent most of the time trying to determine if that buzzing sound was inside or outside your head.

This was the first time we'd gone out—only the four of us—since the fire. Other times Adrienne was there, or Alicia, River.

Friends of Mom or Dad. Sometimes even Gram. With only the four of us—Dad up front with Mom, Beckett and me in back—I was edgy.

"Caprice?" Mom stopped short and my head bounced forward into the strip of hard plastic between the front and rear doors.

"Ow!" I said. But hey! The sound in my head was gone.

"Learn to drive, lady," Mom seethed. I wondered what was up with her. She was a mess like all of us, but she usually wasn't angry at strangers. "Cappi, you okay?" she called.

"Minor concussion. No big deal. You going to share some of your special gummy bears with me?"

"Nice try," Mom said, turning left toward the restaurant.

"She wouldn't take them," Beckett chimed in. I resisted the urge to stick out my tongue. My brother watched my jaw twitch. "And neither—for the record—would I."

"How do you know I wouldn't? Maybe I love THC now."

"Caprice!" Mom said.

"What? I'd be following your example."

"I'm an adult. It's legal."

"You know, Caps," Dad said, "this concussion Mom gave you—it was an accidental favor. It'll be healthy to not look at the phone for three days."

"Right, 'cause I didn't have a phone during the fire and for a week after. Wasn't that awesome?"

"Every time I look at my phone," Dad continued, "it's pictures of fire, or a missing pet that's never Cheerio. Sometimes,

I—Look. Maybe I'll throw mine out." He rolled down the window and stuck his phone out.

"Dylan, stop." Mom's voice was hard.

"Yeah, imagine if someone in this family actually decided to face what happened," Beckett said.

"Beckett Alexander, everyone!" I thrust my arms in his direction. "Disaster sage!"

"Caprice Alexander, everyone," Beckett said. "Teenager." He shoved my arms away.

"Oh, like you have any problem with teenagers—" I began.

"What's that supposed to mean?" Beckett elbowed me. Alicia and Beckett were spending *lots* of time under the tree behind the shop. And sure, I encouraged it, but if he was hooking up with a teenager, then he couldn't be a jerk about me being one.

"Sometimes," Dad said, studying his phone, unaware he was behind on the conversation, "you've got to look away."

"When I'm on my phone, I'm looking for Gramps or making a new college plan," I said. "Because even though our town disintegrated," I rambled, "I still need something to do next year. And without the app—" I stopped because no need to say how hard it was going to be to pay. We all knew it.

"It'll work out, Caps," Dad offered. Easy for him to say. Mom and Dad would get insurance money—but that was for a new house. Earlier in the week, I'd overheard Mom say she wasn't sure the school would need her next year—the district numbers were falling and expected to nosedive after the year ended, what with the fire. Dad was taking unpaid leave from work to help deal with Gramps missing, and getting Gram resettled. I understood why no one was talking about college with me. They figured I had it together. I always did. But still. My parents hadn't even said the word *college* since before the fire. If I was still going, it was definitely all on me.

"I'm thinking of applying to Oregon," I said. I hadn't told River this, or anyone. I hadn't even looked at the out-of-state tuition.

"Aw, the perfect child never stops planning," Beckett said.

"Planning to sneak off with her boyfriend to more than the yard," Mom said.

"Really, Mom?" I dropped my head into my hands. It wasn't even a plan yet. More like my dysfunctional mouth spewing things I wasn't ready to share.

"Lay off her, Irene. She deserves something good. Oregon's nice," Dad said. "If only slightly less flammable." We ignored the joke attempt.

"Does River know about this?" Beckett asked.

"I said *thinking,* not *planning.*"

"Hmm," Beckett said. "Interesting."

"Don't tell him." I swiveled to give my brother a hard look. "I know you're friends, but I'm—"

Beckett put his hands in the air. "Look, what you do or don't talk about with him is none of my business."

I turned to the window and crossed my arms. What did he know?

"Maybe we should have gone to the vegan place," Mom said, pulling into the parking lot, where a line snaked out the restaurant's door. With most of Sierra living in Willow Springs without kitchens, the wait for food everywhere took forever.

"Yeah," Dad said, "but then we'd have to eat vegan food."

"Better for the environment," Beckett offered. I tried not to groan as I climbed out of the car. I didn't disagree—after what happened to us, you'd have to be a real ass to not think about the environment. But Beckett's move from "individual actions do nothing" to refusing to buy new clothes felt like the guy-friend equivalent of Alicia and me wearing matching outfits all of third grade. *IF blue shirt THEN pink pants.*

"I'm tired of food I didn't cook myself." Mom stopped, cocked her head. "There's a sentence I never thought I'd say!"

"I miss our countertops." Dad shut the passenger door. "Is that strange?"

"They were really nice," Beckett agreed. "I remember Gramps installing them."

"You do?" Dad said, and he looked sad. "You must have been what? Five?"

Beckett shrugged. "He yelled at me. I was in the way."

"My father and his workspace," Dad said, looping his arm through mine and touching my forehead as if to make sure Mom hadn't broken me. But I felt broken. My memory was porous. Full of holes.

Dad made his way to the hostess's desk. I stayed outside. The rain ran down my scalp in big drops. Layla Montoya was eating at a window table with Cameron Christopher, who owned the lumberyard. I wished the rain would put out my memories. They kept reigniting. I opened my palms to the sky.

Dad called to us—five minutes later? Two? Fifteen?—and the hostess led us to a booth. Maroon, plasticky covers, dim light, one of those LED candles on the middle of the table. I had the urge to smash it. I stepped back to let Beckett into the booth first, so our elbows wouldn't bump. Then I flipped off the plastic candle.

"Do you think I'll ever find candles relaxing again?"

"Or backyard campfires?" Beckett said. "How about no on the Solo stoves."

"I'm not sure I'll ever sit around a campfire again," Mom said.

Then one of those pauses in conversation that made my stomach turn to lava as our parents exchanged a *Should we tell them now?* glance.

"Do you guys have news or something?" I said, interrupting my mother's audible inhale.

"We got—" Mom began, but looked to Dad with pleading eyes.

He nodded and fiddled with his fork. "A call," he finished. He held on to the edge of the table. "They found Gramps's truck a few days ago—"

"Wait, what? A few *days* ago?" Beckett's mouth stayed open.

"And you didn't tell us?" I said. "How? We're almost always five feet from each other."

My dad held up his hand. "Caps was going back to school—and we didn't want to alarm you if there wasn't—if he wasn't—"

"Right, because nothing that's happened lately has been alarming," I said, maybe because I didn't want to hear what was coming next. If they'd found the truck, they'd check it for remains. If they found something, it'd need to be confirmed, and even the new rapid DNA tests took time to verify identity. Mom and Dad were trying to spare us more unknowns. But we didn't want to be spared. Beckett glanced at me, and I knew what he was thinking: *Effing parents.*

"Yeah, that checks." Beckett said, shaking his curls. "Everything's been so calm lately. Better not make waves."

At least we agreed on something. I pressed my spine into the bench seat but still I felt like I was slipping out of myself, back in time. Into fire. I pressed my feet into the ground and inhaled slowly, determined to stay in the booth. To be present. To not remember. To feel my hands. To not think about how in a fire like ours there weren't many bodies left behind. There were bone fragments.

"Look," Mom said, "there's no field guide for how to handle this. We want to protect you even though—" She took a wavering breath. "We're doing the best we can. I'm sorry we didn't tell you right away." Her mascara was clumpy. And the bags under her eyes dark. I reached across the table to grab her hand.

"Yes, well—" Dad said. "Today—they—" But he stopped. The creases around his eyes made sharp V's.

"We heard today," Mom said.

"He was there," Dad continued. "It was confirmed— He— must've been worried about Gram. He went to her—" He swallowed, and when he spoke again, his words came out in little gasps. "They found him—in—the truck—right—in the—parking lot."

"Wait," Beckett said. "Gram's parking lot?" My brother looked at me, eyes saucer-wide.

I pressed my head back into the vinyl covering of the booth, squeezed my eyes closed. *See nothing,* I told myself.

I saw nothing.

"We think—" Mom said. "We don't know, but we think maybe he had a heart attack. So he couldn't drive out."

"Or he burned alive," Beckett said. "That seems more likely."

My stomach turned. I wanted to slug my brother. He was probably right. But our parents were trying to soften the blow. Why not let them? They were going through it too. My dad especially. Gramps and him were tight. If our parents didn't want us to picture what happened, I got it. I didn't want to picture it, but I was. God. I blinked hard. As if that could stop the horror of my imagination.

"Look," Dad said, reaching for Beckett's hand, "this is terrible. We know—but when we found out where he was"—his lips went over his teeth—"we're so grateful the two of you are safe. We can't even imagine if—" He shook his head and a tear slipped out the corner of his eye.

"You're both here," Mom said. "That's what matters. And we're sorry, so sorry to have to tell you this." She handed Dad a tissue from her purse.

He blew his nose, then he looked up and said, "Thank you,

Caprice, for going back for your brother and for saving your gram."

I thought *But not Gramps* and stopped. I replaced it with: *It's real. We lost him. I lost him.* I ran those sentences on a loop. Said them to myself until I could feel their truth settled on me like ash.

I blinked hard and tried to refocus on the table. Beckett ran his thumb along the stripping. Back and forth. The ball in my stomach twisted. My shoulders brushed against my new hoop earrings. I felt like my body had been run through a cheese grater. My hope shredded.

Mom looked out the window. Raindrops trailed down the glass. I couldn't hold it back: That day flickered through me like a film I was forced to watch with my eyes taped open.

"What can I get for you?" The server appeared with a cheerful smile.

"I'm not hungry," I said.

"Me neither." Beckett dropped his plastic-covered menu on top of mine.

"Um." The server looked between us and then to our parents. What were they thinking, telling us this at dinner?

"We need a minute," Mom said, putting her hand on top of the menus.

"Of course," the server said, turning away.

"I know you aren't hungry." Mom's voice was soft. "I'm not either. Please, order something. We can box it up. This wasn't the best way to tell you, I know, but it's crowded at the shop."

I tried to understand what she'd said. But nope. The logic

still failed me. We should have been told everything. Right away. We weren't little kids. We didn't need to be protected. I was together. I held my shit together. I always did.

"I need some toxic air," I said.

"Me too," Beckett agreed.

"Wait," Dad pleaded, but we didn't look back. I'm pretty sure my mom dropped her face into her palms. Dad sucked his lips over his teeth, his fingers tap-tapping the table. Mom said something like "Give them a minute," but by then I was already pushing past the hostess station, through the crowded front entrance, and into the parking lot.

The rain was harder now, hitting the cement and jumping back into the air. Almost immediately the ankles of my fire jeans were soaked. Beckett's head hung. Water ran down the back of his neck. He covered his face with his hands.

"He's gone," I said. Beckett stood in a puddle. His corduroys soaked up water. They were a good donation find, but too long. He dropped his hands and watched the cars on the road: headlights and taillights. White and red. A honk. I wondered if Gramps had found Cheerio. If she'd died with him in the truck. It was likely. I stepped toward my brother, unsure if I should touch him. "Beck?" I said.

"I know it was just magical thinking, but I imagined when we got back to town he'd still be there, laughing like he'd played the best prank ever. And somehow even though we saw the pictures, part of me thought they were wrong too. That the house would still be standing." He kicked a rock across the wet pavement. Probably thinking about when Mom and Dad showed us the drone images of the property on Mom's laptop. Our house gone, Gramps's too. "Denial talks, I guess." Beckett's curls hung in wet ropes across his eyes. He didn't bother to sweep them away. "Well," he said, "the good news is now we get to move into the pain and suffering phase of the grief cycle!"

"Wow, yeah, that does sound great." I nudged the rock into a puddle. "How have we not already been there?"

"It's more waves than stages."

"How do you know?" It was out of my mouth before I could stop it, before I could think. Beckett froze, then reanimated, finally jerking his hair out of his eyes.

"Caprice, seriously?" He didn't look angry. He looked exasperated.

I bit my lip. "Right, your accident."

"Yeah, my accident. Have you ever really thought—" He lifted his hands. "Never mind. Forget it."

I crossed my arms. "Of course I've thought about it. All the time. You could have died. Mason—" I stopped. How did I say it—*was practically dead?*

Beckett turned back to the traffic. "I lost my only friend. The only real one. But there hasn't been a funeral. He's there but not—"

"Like Gram but worse."

"Yeah." He turned to me. "Sort of." I remembered how Mason would amble in the front door without knocking and help himself to the Oreos in the kitchen cupboard. If Beckett was outside, and he often was, Mason would share them with me. It's hard stuff to wrap your brain around. That someone, or something, can be gone but not, altered beyond recognition. Gram. Mason. It was how I'd felt about Beckett too. But then he came back. I thought I'd lost him, but he came back, and I was afraid it could happen again, but when I tried to say any of that, my throat closed up. Now we'd lost our gramps, and our town. At least what it was before. We weren't dead, but so much of our lives were gone. If this pain made me want to evaporate, what was it doing to him? I shook off the memory of the fire. What Beckett had said. What I did and didn't do to get us out. I needed to focus. Feel my feet. Talk to my brother.

"Beck?" I said, and my voice hurt. "Are you going to be okay? Are you going to—I mean, do you want—"

"I want a drink more than I want anything in the world, Caprice, if that's what you're asking. But right now, right now I'm not in there ordering one. Right now, I'm standing in the storm with you. And later, maybe Alicia will come by. And hopefully, I'll keep going, choosing something better, one step at a time, even if I sometimes want to obliterate myself. Because this sucks. It hurts. And it's going to keep on hurting."

I laced my arm through my brother's. "Thanks for the pep talk."

"That's what I got," Beckett said, but he put a wet arm around me. "Come on. I need to piss, and we're getting soaked."

"Which does make us less flammable, so that's a perk."

Beckett bumped his forehead into mine, and when he pulled away one of his wet curls stuck to me. I reached up to wipe it off but we'd already broken apart.

"I know this is awful," Dad said as Beckett and I slid back into the booth after the bathroom. The restaurant looked somehow like it was filling with smoke. But that wasn't real, was it? No one said anything. But I couldn't trust my eyes. I knew they could shut off. Blink out. Lose focus. I felt for my feet on the floor. I fought to stay upright.

"But we do have some good news," Mom added.

"Isn't that nice, Caps? They considered balance!" Beckett elbowed me.

"That's what years of yoga practice will teach you," I said.

"Come on, I know this is hard," Mom said. "But do you want to hear it or not?"

"Makes no difference to me. Nothing you say will make this objectively terrible day better." Mom reached across the table for my hands again. I shoved them into my lap, numb blobs.

"We got a hotel room," Dad said.

Yep. Not better. Now River would be out of my sight for hours a day.

"Imagine, a bathroom we don't share with customers," Mom said. Okay, that was positive. A shower for only four people wasn't bad either.

"Our own microwave and minifridge," Dad said.

"You know I'm not sharing a bed with Beck, right? He kicks."

"We'll bring a cot," Dad said.

"For you," Beckett said, elbowing me again. I knew we were better off than loads of people. Our insurance was covering the hotel. We were lucky. All things considered. But living in a hotel room was not going to be anywhere near as good as my room, my shelf of favorite books, my desk under the window where my LEGO man flashlight sat, and the music box Gram had given me when I was six with a bouquet of flowers spinning inside instead of a ballerina.

It was only stuff. I'd exchange any of it to have Gramps back. Or Cheerio. But I didn't have any of it: my home, my gramps, my cat, my town.

I wanted to crawl into a hole. I wanted my skin to turn to chitin. I either wanted that or to feel my feet, to be whole again.

Beckett drummed his silverware and I thought of the kit my parents had bought when he was fourteen to get him interested in more than choir, but the drums stayed in the family room untouched unless Mason was over. Then they would beat them loudly to try to get me out of the house. It usually worked. I'd find Gram, and we'd work in the garden or go on a walk with Gramps along the canyon.

The server placed a raspberry lemonade in front of me. My parents must have ordered it. How strange that my gramps was dead. I wasn't going to see him again. Not even a changed version of him, injured or out of it. Not even the way I could see Gram. Or Mason. Or even Sierra, when it reopened. But raspberry lemonade. That was always the same.

"So what happens now?" Beckett had stopped drumming.

"Adrienne and I are working on a funeral plan," Dad said. "We're hoping you two will think about how you might contribute."

"Contribute? Uh, no thanks," I said. I'd contributed enough. There was a tin taste in my mouth and the buzzing filled my head.

"I'll sing," Beckett said. My dad put his hand over my brother's. "Maybe I can get Alicia to play," he added.

"Alicia's not playing. You know that."

"She might for Gramps."

"You mean for you." I crossed my arms.

"Okay—" Beckett drummed his silverware again. "Since you guys are all about planning all of a sudden. What's your plan? You rebuilding? Or moving to Cincinnati or what?"

"No one is going anywhere until Cap graduates," Dad said.

"And no one is going to Cincinnati, ever," Mom said.

"What do you have against Cincinnati?" Beckett asked. "Or are you following Caprice to Oregon? Because that seems to be her plan," Beckett said.

"It's not a—" I started, but Mom held up her hand. "Caprice doesn't need to know her plans yet."

"I ran into an old friend at a meeting last week. He's looking for a roommate." Beckett folded and refolded his napkin. "I'm considering it."

Mom shifted in her seat. "Are you sure that's a good idea, honey?"

Wasn't that discouraged? Living with other people in recovery? I'd read that somewhere, right? But I kept quiet.

"You always have a place with us," Dad said. Both of my parents held on to his hands.

"Except," Beckett said, "you don't have a place. We're upgrading from a storefront to a hotel room." He had a point. "And Caprice wants her own bed, so—"

"I'm fine on the cot," I said. I pulled in a long breath and slowly sucked down my sweet drink. I watched the rain, my parents, my brother. I could almost see how the silence hung between us like a thin film, like plastic wrap stretched across a bowl, taut and smothering.

There was so much I wanted—to know what was going to happen next, to have a plan, to have my white-and-orange duvet and Gram's teacup collection, my grandpa at the table, alive and laughing, my gram to look at me and say my name, for Beckett to be okay.

But I knew, like I knew not to smash the fake candle on the table, that the only one I could really hope for was Beckett being okay. So even though I felt like I was shattering, even though I wasn't sure if I could breathe, I sat quiet. If I talked about my terrible mistake, about how Gramps's death was my fault, and maybe Beckett's too, if I started to say any of that, it would puncture this thin film, and that would hurt him more. So, we sat. The weight of our loss stretched tight between us, each of us bearing it a little bit. And up on the hillside, the fire that killed Gramps, that leveled our town and destroyed our home, was finally out.

Alicia:

CAPYBARA!!! are you okay???

Caprice:

I mean compared to what?
A vaquita in a gill net?

oh you poor lonely panda of the sea!!

do you want me to come over????
I'll cut you loose.

I don't know. Beckett
probably wants you to.

I was asking you

So I've not been displaced?

we've all been displaced!!

I'm on standby for all hours.

the parents said no curfew!

We finally found the disaster
to shatter their rules?

yeah!!! it only took a firepocalypse??!!

If only we'd had this insight before—

would arson have negatively impacted college admissions?

pretty sure the charge would be arson and manslaughter—

Sorry did I take the macabre humor too far?

never.

At least some things don't change. Talk soon.

or maybe see you—if Beck wants me to come by

Pretty sure your parents wouldn't let you break curfew to hang out with him

look I can't control what they assume when I say Alexanders

but if I don't see you,

keep away from rabid gnomes in the night.

They'll be after me now they know

it's our last night in the shop.

I love you Caps, I'm so sorry.

OBJECT: House Plants
LOCATION: 51 Plumule Way, Sierra, California
RESIDENT: Dylan Alexander

I had plants in every room. I guess it's one way I'm my mother's son. The back windows along the kitchen and dining room were full of them. I even threatened to stick one in that ugly vase Irene said was worth thousands, but she'd probably have left me if I drilled holes in it. I liked to joke about it though. Sometimes I'd stick a spider plant inside it to freak her out. When I started driving a truck, I taught Caprice my watering and fertilizing schedule, and she took over. I had a mother-of-thousands, ficus, orchids, and more ferns and jades than I could count. But also, spiderwort and snake plant. Purple hearts. Crassula umbella. That's the wine cup succulent and it's a real looker. Lemon and lime trees that we moved outside in summer and inside in winter. A white wizard, four feet tall. It took years until I found the window with the perfect light balance for that one's variegated leaves. The hours I spent trying to list all those plants for insurance. And separately the pots that held them. We had a spreadsheet, and Caprice remembered as many as I did. You can't replace a plant you've been growing for twenty years, though. Not really. But I guess wherever we end up, we'll start again slowly. Little shoots in tiny pots. Seaweed fertilizer. Spray bottles. All things to put on the list. Look, most days I'm just happy that my wife and kids got out. Thankful. But that house—I spent half a lifetime growing that house into a home. When I think about it, I get this pain between my eyes. Sharp. Chicken and hen. Peace lily. Aloe. I wonder if I'll ever be able to name them all.

Back at the shop, Mom and Dad slipped into the corner and began to talk in these tense whispers. Maybe they thought we couldn't read their tone, or maybe they really thought whispers weren't fighting? My stomach soured. I wished I'd been able to say, *Hey, let's sit here and play cards*, but there was no way I could focus.

"What are you doing?" I asked as Beckett trailed me to the shop's back door.

"Chaperoning you," he said, all glint and good humor. My arm hairs rose like porcupine spikes.

"To the wet shop yard?"

"I'm assuming you're meeting your boyfriend, so yeah."

"Seriously?"

"Come on, Caps. I don't want to be in there," Beckett said. He sounded so tired. Fine. He could come. Eventually I'd be alone with River. If I waited my brother out.

Beckett crossed the dirt to the scrub oak and laid his hands on the trunk. I wondered if maybe we should try to actually talk. But when I opened my mouth, I didn't have words. I watched him lean into the tree, my mouth open. My voice gone.

"Hey Alexanders," River said as the door clicked shut. Spock ran over to sniff my knees.

"Hey," I said. Behind me, River slipped his arms around my waist, and I inhaled—mint and pine—to feel more solid.

"I'm so sorry," River said. He dropped a kiss on my head and I felt him nod to Beckett. "I really hoped—somehow—he'd turn up."

"Yeah," I said.

"Us too," Beckett added. The rain had turned to a light mist.

"Our parents are fighting," I offered.

"Which definitely makes everything better."

"But at least this time it's not my fault." Beckett flashed jazz hands like he was back on stage with the Sierra High Singers.

"They're modeling unhealthy coping in face of our confirmed traumatic losses," I said, arching an eyebrow. River let go of me and crouched down to pet Spock.

"Correct," Beckett said, crossing back through the mud to where River and I stood on the patio. "But it's not like Mom and Dad ever had the best coping skills."

"Huh?"

"Oh, come on Caprice. Do you really think the gummies and wine-mom thing is normal?"

"In my experience, that's normal, yep," River said. "Maybe not the wake-up gummies."

I shrugged. I mean, Mom's drinking was never like Beckett's, and River was right—most people's parents have a glass or two and maybe some get stoned. Except Alicia's parents. As far as I knew, the only time her dad got drunk in his life was the day of the fire. Other than that, Jake and Mariana had one craft beer with dinner on Fridays. That was it.

"Well, it's normalized, Caps. But that doesn't make it healthy. Dad literally disappears when things get tough—that's what his job is about. Twenty bucks says he'll be back on the road as soon as he gets the funeral planned."

"He—" I stopped. Dad always said he left Alexander Construction for trucking because of the insurance, but Beckett was kind of right. He could have easily been with us a lot more if he'd stayed working for Gramps. How was I supposed to get through all this loss without Gramps? Gramps, who saw me, even when Beckett was taking everyone's attention. Gramps, who always remembered.

"And of course, nobody wants to talk about me," Beckett said.

"Are we in the same family? Because everyone is always talking about you." Part of me immediately regretted saying it, but part of me didn't. And the part of me that didn't felt like it could actually breathe. And it was so easy—how it had just slid out after all this time, like water down the flume, and now it was out, evaporating into the air. Beckett dropped his head to the tree and River touched my elbow and shook his head, as if to say I was too harsh. But was I? I held so much in. For so long. For always. Was it so bad to let a little out?

Beckett faced us. "Everyone's been good trying to trust me.

But no one, not even you—talked to me about Mason or even the three years of my life after I dropped out of State. No one wants to hear it. When I bring it up, you look like you might fall apart if I say more."

"I—" All the words I thought I'd had dried up. I was sorry. But that didn't help. When Beckett was working as a prep cook and descending deeper into alcohol, I'd been a high school kid trying to plan my escape and prove to my parents that having a teenager did not need to mean a lot of screaming. What did Beckett want me to ask him? More about how a meth lab smells? My head buzzed again. He was right. I didn't want to know. I really didn't. I crossed my arms over my stomach.

"Um, do you two want a minute?" River stepped toward the door. Spock jangled beside him.

"No," my brother and I said at the same time.

I almost laughed. At least we agreed on something. I wanted to move closer to River, but everything in me felt suddenly heavy.

Beckett rubbed his hands together, tilted his head in my direction. "It's part of me, Cap—you know? It doesn't go away because you pretend it's not there."

"I know that."

"Really? Because any time I start to talk about it, you get that worry triangle above your eyes, and it feels like the last thing you want is to be anywhere near me. I know I acted terrible, and it's hard to love me, and I'm sorry about it—"

"It's not hard to love you, Beck."

He shuddered. "Caps, come on. You don't have to lie."

"I'm not lying!" My head felt like it was going to drift off my neck, but I was telling the truth. Beckett was easy to love. It's part of what made him so frustrating.

He shook his head. "Look, I need to know—"

"That I'm lying when I'm not? How will that help?"

"God!" He put his hands in his hair. "How do you not see that you're doing it again! I'm trying to talk to you, and you're interrupting because you don't want to hear me."

Suddenly the pressure on the bridge of my nose felt intense enough to power Willow Springs for four days. I touched my third eye. I guess that was the trigger to run the Say a Bunch of Terrible Shit To Your Brother Program, because I did. "This isn't about you, Beckett. Our gramps died and our town is charcoal. But since you're making it about you, well then—you think our parents see me? No. They see only you. They worry only about you. But Gramps. Gramps saw *me*. He always did. He barely understood what an app was, and he listened to me talk about it anyway. He even got Cecil to invest. He knew what was going on with me. He was the only one. I went to yoga with Mom every Tuesday and got straight A's, and everything was *always* still about you. You want to talk about not being listened to? Every time I tried to be alone with River, you were there—Gramps even tried to distract you, to get us a moment alone. I'll forgive you for that—but during the fire, after we left Gramps at the house, and I saw—"

"Stop it. Caps. Stop. You couldn't see anything. You couldn't. You didn't."

"Gaslight much?"

Beckett kicked the tree. "There's no way that's what you saw—"

"Really?"

"Caps, please. I'll take ownership for a lot—I've made a ton of mistakes—but this—this is not my fault, or yours, it's shit luck." Beckett didn't look mad. He looked hurt. The curls he'd tucked behind his ear fell forward. "If you can't see that, Caps, that's your problem. Not mine."

"Doctor Alexander lays down the law," I said.

His hands went to his temples. "I have to get out of here." He turned to River. "You'll stay with her, right?"

"Oh, because I'm on suicide watch now?"

"No," Beckett said. His voice sounded exactly like our dad's when he was trying to keep Beckett from breaking things. "And you know not to joke about that. Saying it at all means you need support."

"You don't know anything," I said.

"I know it wouldn't hurt you to actually talk about the fire, or—and here's a real challenge for you—consider how life in our family was always a thousand times easier for you."

"I—" My words stopped there. This time I knew not to say what I was thinking. Not to Beckett. But he must have read something on my face. Did it mean we'd become closer? Or could he always read me, some big brother trick that never worked in reverse?

Beckett shook his head. "I need a break, okay. I'll be back."

"Fine, leave. I don't need your trauma-informed brothering right now."

"Good one, Capybara," he said, chucking me on the shoulder as he passed. I stood in the mist, staring at the broken hen house. Already I couldn't stop wishing for a do-over. Another one. And another. A chance to run a different program. I'd kept that wish tucked inside me since the fire, afraid to say it aloud. Afraid that everyone would tell me what I should have done. To get out faster. To save my gramps. The knot in my center began unfurling, unrolling, sluicing into a slow, steady poison. Because *I knew,* even though Beckett said I didn't, there was a more elegant program. Something I could have done differently. The outcome changed. IF, IF, IF, IF, IF, IF, IF.

"Beck, I—" I wished we had that sibling sixth sense that would make him see how much I needed him to stay. "Beckett, please—stay."

I heard the yard door open, and then my brother's voice. "You didn't want me to come out here in the first place. Don't freak out. It's not like I'm going to go missing."

Wasn't it? The door snapped shut behind him. Hadn't Beckett walked off with Mason and left me? Hadn't he disappeared into addiction? And Gramps had gone missing, and now he was gone too. That's what happened to the missing. First they were missing and then they were gone. River came closer now. I felt the warmth of his hand on my back. I leaned into him. I wanted to curl into this boy like a snail into its shell. I wanted to be something so simple, it carried its home on its back. I wanted to count the seconds until my brother came back, then figure out how I could actually talk to him.

River pulled me into a hug. "He'll be back," he said into my hair.

"Probably—but what's he going to do?" I took a step away, pulled out my phone to text Alicia.

River touched my hand. "Come on, let's go inside."

"He's going to talk about me with Alicia."

He squeezed my fingers. "Maybe. I thought you were encouraging that."

I was. But I guess I didn't think about what it meant that Alicia and River were now friends with Beckett in a way my brother and I weren't.

And now Beckett was going to Alicia to talk about how I never listened to him, how everything was easier for me. And she would probably agree. Because yeah, maybe I was the golden child, maybe I worked hard and tried hard not to screw up, but I was also responsible for the most horrible thing that had ever happened to our family, and no one believed it. No one saw that it was my fault. They thought I did something good instead. But l knew. I knew. I was sure. And that knowledge was a fire that had been burning me from the inside since the moment we left our gramps in our driveway.

River let out a ragged exhale. He lightly touched my elbow. "Cappi—can I be honest?"

I nodded, taking another step back, wrapping my arms around myself.

"If Beckett needs his space, I think you should give it to him." He ran his hands across his forehead. "No one's thriving."

"I'm a picture of complete togetherness."

"It's okay to be a mess."

"But you're not." It sounded like an accusation.

"I kinda am, but my gramps didn't die, and I mean, I was the new kid."

My eyes burned, but I wasn't crying. I wasn't sure I could cry. River was saying the fire hadn't destroyed his whole world, his whole history, but I knew what he wasn't saying—that his moms had finally had a home. A place. And now it was gone, and they might not be able to rebuild it. But still he was here. With me. So steady. Even though he'd lost so much too. Somehow I said, "IF your town burns down and your gramps dies THEN it's good to have a River."

He smiled. "Please." He stepped closer and slipped his arms around me. "Please come inside with me? We'll watch a movie, and I can resketch my water-filtration design while we pretend your parents aren't on the other side of a bunch of cannibalistic gnomes."

"I've been wanting to ask—can I smash the gnomes if they come for me?"

"If those little beasts move an inch off the shelf, your fists can become gnome slayers." I smiled my fake yoga smile. River put his arms around me. "He'll come back."

"Okay," I said, shivering in my wet sweatshirt. "But I'm probably not going to be able to focus on the movie. And if

Beck disappears, I'm breaking up with you, which would be annoying because I'm applying to Oregon."

"Wait—what?" His hands fell away from me. A leaden weight dropped from my breastbone to my pelvis.

"Look, I hope it's not too weird, and honestly, I don't know if I'd want to go, or if I'd even get in, or if there's any way I could afford it but—" I was talking so fast, so worried he would say *I don't want you to come,* or that he'd be annoyed that I was complaining about tuition when my parents had insurance. A pain in my belly filled me up, and my ears rang. I didn't even register how he leaned forward and stopped my words with a kiss.

Then I was kissing him back, getting lighter with each touch, and more aware of my hands and feet and lips. Yes, I had lips. And River. I had River to kiss. It was compulsive, this kissing. More than a hunger. A fix. We stayed there for a long time, and the rain picked up again and finally Spock barked, looking at us with big eyes, as if baffled by these silly humans kissing in the rain.

Program for Coping with Fighting Parents in a Tiny Hotel Room After a Wildfire Destroys Your Town and Kills Your Grandpa

IF possible leave *AND* make sure location sharing is on.

IF parents are reluctant to let you leave, ask to visit Gram. This is usually allowed.

ELSE distract parents with pressing questions about college applications.

THEN cross arms until last year's household income is provided OR searched for.

IF fighting parents aren't distracted by college applications questions *THEN* ask for an item that you need but no longer own: Running shoes. A raincoat.

AND tell them you need this item immediately.

THEN go get it.

ELSE insert earbuds, turn on favorite playlist, *AND* drown out the voices while keeping everyone in sight *AND* curl into a fetal position *AND* wait for the fighting to stop.

IF fighting does not stop *THEN* imagine smashing the pottery shop gnomes one by one *OR* focus on the muted fruit basket painting on the hotel wall *AND* imagine the number of these laser-printed bowls that exists. Piles. Mountains. More fruit basket paintings than objects you own. *THEN* stare at the painting until you feel calmer. Notice the shading of the orange. The grapes: green and purple. Life stilled.

FOUR WEEKS AFTER

"Hi Aster!" Alicia said. "How are you?" Gram didn't look up. It was a few days—three? Five? Since we were told Gramps was dead. I was losing track of time, of minutes, of what was happening right in front of me.

"They treating you well, Gram?" Beckett asked, walking in behind Alicia. Gram stayed motionless in her wheelchair, eyes open, head hung.

"It appears to be a bad day," I said to Beckett. River and I had been with Gram for—I looked at the wall clock—could that be right? A half hour? What had I been doing? River sat next to me on Gram's empty bed with his sketchbook, re-creating one of his designs. Beckett said nothing. My brother and I lived in the same room. We had the same friends. And after our fight in the shop yard, we weren't talking much. I'd taken to ironically singing *the more we get together, together, together, the more we get together, the happier we'll be* . . . into the silence, but Beckett didn't join in, didn't even tease my tonelessness. He didn't even bother to throw a pillow at me.

Beckett grabbed the handles of Gram's chair now. "It's depressing in here. I'd have a bad day too." Was he talking to me? Alicia? He wasn't wrong. Gram wasn't allowed to make a flowered wall like she'd had before—and twice the orderlies had thrown out bouquets before they'd even wilted.

"She probably knows if she's in a sad room," Alicia said. "And this is like death by beige."

"Right? Like a sensory deprivation tank," Beckett said. "Let's take her to the common room."

"I don't think it matters," I said, standing to follow, and as I did my mouth filled with this salt and metal taste. I blinked away a dizzy wave.

"If we go to the common room, we can practice," Alicia said.

"For what?" I asked.

"Alicia agreed to play at Gramps's funeral," Beckett said. "When I sing. Remember? I told you?"

"No, you didn't."

"Uh, yeah, I did." When? We barely spoke except *Pass the remote*, and *Your night for the cot*. Or me singing *My friends are your friends and your friends are my friends*.

"No, I'd remember that. The last thing I heard was Ali was never going to touch a piano again."

"Caps"—Alicia's voice was soft—"I'm pretty sure I also told you at school that I can't let Beckett sing unaccompanied. Or with a pianist who didn't know your gramps."

I blinked. Maybe she had said that. "I was supposed to know that meant *you're* playing?"

Alicia gave a big-eyed nod.

River's hand tightened on my shoulder. "School"—his voice was tentative—"can be a hard place to talk. It's loud."

Alicia and Beckett exchanged a look, but I couldn't figure out what it meant. In my head, a whole symphony orchestra tuned their instruments. I pressed my temple. "Thanks, Al."

"Yeah, going back to town—" Right. Alicia and her family went back as soon as they could. Yesterday? Two days ago? River's family had gone too. They'd found a garden gnome still intact, but then on the way home they hit a bump and it shattered. Just cracked into pieces. I guess some things only look like they survived the fire. The losses just kept coming. Over and over. My stomach roiled. I strained to return to the room. To hear Alicia's voice. ". . . seeing my piano—or you know—the strings and ashes, I—I thought about what I'd had planned for this year, how now I couldn't do so much of it. But I could still play. And that meant I should probably play for your gramps . . ." She shook her head and I tried hard to follow her over my own loud thoughts. ". . . possible, like Classical Fest."

"What?" My question was so loud, even Gram looked up.

"Yeah. I'm going to do Classical Fest. I won't win, I'm out of practice, but you'll see, Caps. When you go back. It can change things."

"No." I crossed my arms, tucking my numb hands into my elbows. "Sorry, but not going." I couldn't. Not after Gramps. Not after my part in it. Not if it meant I might find things that had survived only for them to break apart.

"Come on, Caps, you have to," Beckett said.

"She really doesn't," River offered. "And yeah, it's—" He put his hands to his temples to mime his head exploding. After he'd been back to town, we met up and spent an hour making out behind the tree in the shop yard. When? Yesterday? Two days ago? I didn't know. I only knew when we were together like that I could feel. And it was good.

Now, my chest ached. I leaned into River. "What about conservatories?" I asked. My words were rushed but I congratulated myself on my ability to change the subject.

Alicia shook her head. "That feels too—I don't know, selfish."

"Music's not selfish," Beckett said.

"No," she said. "But—after this? I need to help people. Like, with more than fundraising and benefit concerts. Like my parents do"—she pursed her lips—"but maybe without all the blood."

"Oh, a surgeon for the bloodless? Great idea," Beckett said.

"What undergraduate major is a pathway to that?" I asked. Then opened my jaw wide as if popping my ears could stop the noise in my head. The orchestra had been replaced by a loud, familiar buzzing.

"Entomology?" River said. "Because insects don't have blood, and because global warming is causing insect populations to drop, so we need people to study them. They might be the key to using less pesticides and trying to put things back in balance. Without insects we lose all the birds and small insect-eating mammals." I put my arm around his back and squeezed. I wondered if he could feel his feet. Because I still couldn't. Not my hands either.

"Oh, everyone's here," Adrienne said from the doorway, with a giant floral table arrangement of zinnias, dahlias, and miniature sunflowers in her arms. "You all look as miserable as this room. This might help."

"Where is that even going to go?" Beckett asked. The bouquet was twice as big as the tiny table in Gram's room.

Adrienne turned sideways to get the flowers through the door. "No idea, but the word is out about Gramps and the whole floral community wants to send something to Aster here. Look, Mom. Aren't they beautiful?"

Gram looked up and the flowers must have flipped some switch inside her, because she said, "I must have done something really good to get these."

"Or someone else did something really bad." My words sounded like echoes through the tin-can phone Beckett and I used to run from the treehouse to the ground.

"Oh no," Gram said. "They never do me wrong."

But I had, hadn't I? I'd run the wrong program. Listened to the wrong voices. And now my gram was getting flowers because Gramps was dead, and she didn't even know it. My feet disappeared. I closed my eyes. The room flickered. The edges of it blurred, then blackened.

"Mom and Dad are going to town tomorrow. You coming too, Adrienne?" Beckett said.

"Yeah," Adrienne said. "We need to go as a family."

"I'm not," I said in a weird faraway voice. "And Gram won't be. So that's not the family, is it?" I thought, *How could we go as a family when Gramps isn't there?* And then the room was bending, and my knees too.

"Caps?" Adrienne said. I felt inside a cloud, damp and cold. My vision melted away, folded in from the edges. As my knees hit the floor, the only sound I heard was a deep hum. I don't know the rest. How long did I stay like that? An hour? A minute? Three? Seven? Eventually the room opened up again—from a spot at the center, the beige filled in.

"I'm okay," I said from where I sat on the floor. Was I? Adrienne was kneeling beside me, her hand on my shoulder.

"Let's see if we can get the nurse who's been flirting with me to give you a once-over," she said. "Here, scooch your butt— lean against the wall."

"You okay, Caps?" Alicia asked.

"I'm not as breakable as Gram's teacups," I think I said. My head ached.

"Where are my teacups?" Gram asked. "I have the nicest teacups, you know. Glenn buys them for me when he finds the pretty ones with flowers on them? Asters are my favorite, but the violets and dahlias are nice too."

"They're in the cupboard," Beckett said.

"I'll be right back, Caprice," Adrienne said. "Nurse Joe's always happy to see me."

River sat down on the floor next to me. Or maybe he'd been

there already? He rubbed my shoulder. Beckett rolled Gram toward the door. At least Gram didn't know what was going on. She couldn't remember me, didn't know what I'd done. What we'd done. For once, I was happy to be forgotten.

OBJECT: Goats Aren't an Object, and They Didn't Burn, So I Guess I'll Say the Barn?

LOCATION: 4 Bella Vista Canyon Road, North Sierra, California

RESIDENT: Violet Homesteader

My parents didn't want either of their last names—because the patriarchy—so I got stuck with their chosen last name: Homesteader. They thought it was cute. Heather, Forest, and Violet Homesteader. A family name perfect for our goat dairy's coffee-table book. Summed up our lives and made a nice logo for Homesteader Farms too. They didn't think what it'd be like to be a kid in hand-me-down clothes with a metal lunch box full of homemade goat cheese and the name Violet Homesteader in grade school.

At least I had Caprice Alexander as a friend. We were bonded by odd names. And I guess that helped us grow into them. For me, at least, you start helping goats into the world when you're a little kid and you learn some lessons about how to be tough and what matters. Some kids were even impressed by my stories of resuscitating newborn goats. But what helped most was that by eighth grade I had a sewing machine, the internet, and a seriously good sense of fashion. Anyway, the thing is, somehow the house made it, so I still have my sewing machine, and rescue workers found the goats bloated and hungry but alive and kicking. My parents didn't have time to load them up as they fled. They let them out to pasture as the barn caught fire—the truck, trailer, and tractor too. Once the goats were found, we didn't have anywhere to put them. They can't live in a vehicle, and even though the house was still standing, we weren't allowed to live there until it was inspected and we fixed the smoke damage, found out if the soil was safe, all that.

Some people were camped out illegally, and my parents thought about it, but the town didn't have water. Can't have goats without water. They spent a few weeks in the emergency shelter at the fairgrounds and then we sold them off. That hurt the most, knowing they'd made it, but we couldn't have them. Belly Bit and Starla Kit—I was planning to show them at the fair, and had already made a new pair of olive-colored overalls for the occasion. Their mom, Darla G, and aunts, Maggie May and Carly Simon—good milkers. And the boys—Flavius Ferriweather and Mobius Parks. Mom says maybe we'll buy them back if we decide to stay. She showed me a picture of them happy on their new farm. That felt good to see. But I don't know. It's hard to imagine going home even though it's there. To look around and just see empty space where our neighbors once were, to drive through all that destruction every day. Dad says we're worse off than if everything had just burnt. The property value probably tanked, and insurance is hell to deal with. We can't just take a payout. And if we want to make the place safe for animals again? Get *recertified organic? It's going to be a whole thing. And I don't know. I never thought I'd leave Sierra, but now? Maybe. My art teacher told me about a school out in Missouri with a program in fashion design. Seems like a gamble, but staying would be too. I don't know. All I know is, I've sold goats all my life. I know when a sale is final.*

SIX WEEKS AFTER

The pink adobe church sat at the edge of downtown Willow Springs. "It smells like Frank's in here," Alicia said, lacing her arm through mine. Beckett and River followed us in through the heavy wooden doors.

I took a deep breath. I closed my eyes and imaged being in the flower cooler—the fog on the sliding glass door, the buckets of roses: red, orange, yellow, and white. I swayed. Pressed my feet into the ground. I didn't tell Alicia, but it was a good thing she'd convinced me to get some Birkenstocks instead of heels. The Birks were sort of ugly, but I was in less danger of falling.

"I've really got to pee. Performances do that to me," Alicia said, squeezing my shoulder.

"I know." My voice sounded far away. "Please don't joke about putting yourself on a catheter."

"Not today," Alicia said. "But maybe for Classical Fest."

I looked at my hands. Were they even attached? The nurse at Gram's place said all my vitals were normal and that the fainting was probably just anxiety. Just. I hoped I could make it through the service without passing out again.

I tried to focus on where everyone was. Dad pacing the front of the church. Mom and Adrienne greeting guests at the back. I felt River's hand nudge me gently toward the front row—how long had I been standing there? I shuffled forward toward Gram's wheelchair. I focused on River, now casually telling me how hard it was to remember his old designs, and how my mom was recommending he try hypnotherapy to retrieve the ideas. But it was like I could only hear every third sentence. I was about to sit down next to Gram when someone said my name and I turned to see Cecil Ito, in a new suit, jacket buttons undone over a Grateful Dead T-shirt I'm sure he'd ordered in honor of Gramps.

"Caprice, I'm so sorry," Cecil said.

"Yeah, well—" I wanted to climb into the pew next to River and disappear, maybe put my head on his chest and close my eyes and listen to his heartbeat. *Thunk. Thunk.* But I'd been meaning to talk to Cecil and apologize for not finishing the app, to ask how I could get the money back to him, so I stayed standing.

"I know this probably isn't the time or the place, but—"

"I have money for you—how should I—"

"Oh." Cecil straightened. "You don't—I—ugh, wasn't—"

"It's okay," I said, touching his arm. "There's no point in finishing it now. You could help someone else." I thought about River's family without insurance. Or Violet's family—living in her van, first in the Walmart parking lot and then at a shelter. Now rotating through Willow Springs friends' driveways as they waited for people to be allowed to stay back in town.

"Okay," Cecil said. "Of course, we can put it in the Rebuild Sierra Fund. I wanted to talk to you about that. See, I'm working to get people back to town, and we could use someone with your talents."

"I, uh—" My vision blurred. My forehead ached. I didn't even want to go back to town. How could I help?

Cecil fidgeted with his coat. ". . . wrong time, I know. We'll talk about it later. Might not be a bad way to honor your old gramps. To have a job where you could stick around and help Sierra regrow—"

". . . Oh, right, I guess? I'm sorry—"

"That man loved Sierra more than anyone I knew." I nodded and focused on my dad straightening the poster-sized portrait of Gramps on the dais. It felt like the chapel was growing bigger, or maybe I was shrinking. Maybe I was little again, pretending to be Alice in the flower cooler, nibbling a cookie and changing my size.

"You have my number," Cecil said. A chuck on my shoulder. Awkward. He grimaced.

I managed a nod, then turned to Gram. She wore a red dress and held a bouquet of dahlias, all different colors.

"Death by dahlias," I muttered, dropping a kiss on the top of her braids.

"Oh, Adrienne," she said, patting my arm. I wondered if

she remembered that that's what Adrienne called work at the flower shop when she was my age. I looked around for my aunt, still at the back of the church. Right. Gram was forgetting me again. I should be used to it. And thankful for it now.

The backs of my knees sweated. My legs tensed. They shook. The church filled up. "Where's Beckett?" I asked, turning to River, who'd settled in the pew behind me. Or maybe he'd been there all along.

"He'll be right back," River said.

"He should be here," I said, my breath unable to fill my lungs. Beckett. Too far away again. But could I blame him? He knew I'd told Adrienne not to hire him. He knew I was mad at him for what happened in the fire. Why would he ever want to be around me again? I tried to fill my lungs slowly. I tried to feel my feet. I was disappearing. I needed my brother. I needed to know where he was even if he didn't need me.

I stood and strode out the side of the chapel. Passed through the door into the dark hallway. I ran my hand along the cold adobe, searching for a light switch. The restrooms were unlocked and empty. A whistle, and then a sound familiar as rain on the roof—Alicia's laugh. I followed it.

"Oh, come on, you two, is this really the time and place?" I said, channeling Normal Caprice, stepping into what looked like a Sunday school classroom.

Beckett in a child-sized chair with Alicia in his lap.

Alicia stood and straightened her skirt. "Sorry, Caps."

"Gramps would approve," Beckett said, his palms in the air,

curls across his eyes. How could he be so casual? The pain in my belly turned to heat.

"Oh, you're the expert on Gramps now?"

Beckett stood. "Caps, please."

"No, don't. You know we wouldn't be here if you'd listened to me—if you'd—"

"Cappi," Alicia said. "Stop. It wasn't like that." She crossed to me and Beckett was right behind her.

"Alicia, he said it would do me good to face this. So fine. Let's face this."

"Says the girl who refused go back to town with our family?" Beckett said, taking a step back as if he was worried I might slug him. Alicia turned to face him, and just like that I was locked out of the older-siblings fort.

"ALLIIIIICIAAA! Where are you?"

"She's down here, Jenny," I called. My voice didn't feel like my own. Jenny's new patent leather shoes made *sh-sh-sh-sh* sounds as she sped up. When she reached the doorway, I tried to smile.

"What's wrong with your face?" she asked.

"Funeral smile fail," I said. Jenny frowned and launched herself into my arms.

"Thanks," I said, swinging her a little.

"You better hurry," she said as I set her down, "'cause Mom says no one likes to be at a funeral longer than they have to, especially when the whole world is poopy."

"She said *poopy*?" I said.

"No, she said *shitty*, but I'm not allowed to say that—so—"

"Oops," I said.

Jenny giggled, but then she covered her mouth. "Is it okay to laugh at a funeral?"

"Always," I said, flashing my fake yoga smile.

"Our gramps would be honored," Beckett added, his voice artificially calm. Look at us, shredded on the inside, trying to appear like we weren't disintegrating.

"Even the last show has to go on, huh?" Alicia said, grabbing Beckett's hand. I stood there. Jenny chanted, "Alicia and Beckett sitting in a tree, K-I-S-S-I-N-G."

"Jenny, hush," I said. "Kissing is definitely not for funerals."

"And don't you dare tell Mom," Alicia said.

"I won't," Jenny said, dragging her shoes along the slick hallway. I don't know how Alicia was keeping Jenny quiet about Beckett. Must have been part of their sibling deal. Impressively, my own parents hadn't caught on yet. Or maybe it wasn't that impressive, given the stress and grief and quantity of edibles they were consuming.

We walked down the dark hallway like kids dreading the grown-up party. I felt sick. The world appeared underwater as we stepped into the sanctuary. Everything muffled. Hazy. My breath went shallow and uneven, but I made it back to the pew and slid in next to Gram.

River still sat in the row behind our family. He reached up and brushed his hand against my collarbone as I sat down. All my muscles hardened against my bones. I wanted to leave. To get out of the church. To drive. To not cry. To not feel. I wanted to go home. Drive through the familiar. Walk in my red front door. Pour myself a cup of tea. Curl up on my bed with my cat. I closed my eyes. I was practically there. I inhaled.

Gram tapped me with her dahlias. "Why are we here?"

"Because of Glenn," I said.

"I'm married to a Glenn."

"You are."

"He's not here, though. I haven't seen him in a while." She frowned.

"I know."

"Those are beautiful flowers you're wearing." She touched my corsage. "Aster, like me."

"Thank you."

She held up her own wrist. "I've got some too." I tried to smile. "I must be a guest of honor."

"You are." I couldn't bring myself to explain why. Dad had, but she'd forgotten.

"Welcome," Dad said from the pulpit. I don't know how he stood, composed in his linen suit, flowers pinned to his lapel. Could he feel his feet? Could all these people feel their feet? The church walls blackened at the corners, disappeared. I was only half-aware of anything anyone said. Dad. Adrienne. Then Beckett and Alicia got up.

The room entered a slow tilt as Alicia played and Beckett sang, "Well, the moon is broken, and the sky is cracked."

The church melted into sound and my field of vision shrunk.

My brother sang. His tenor ragged. Some of the old guys joined in. I saw Gram through a pinhole. Her mouth moved. She didn't know the words, but she was trying to sing, the bouquet in her hands swaying—and on her face, tears tracked through her wrinkles. And again, like I'd eaten one of the White Rabbit's biscuits, the sanctuary expanded back into focus and it grew and grew and grew as I shrunk down and down and down. I was a puddle of molten lead in the pew. A speck. I was disappearing. I could feel fire around me. Smoke. My hands shook on the steering wheel.

What I did. What I saw. What I didn't do. My stomach turned.

Gramps told me once about the "don't think of the elephant" problem. If someone tells you not to think about an elephant, you can't help but think about the elephant. If you don't *want* to think about the elephant, you will think of nothing *but* the elephant. For the past month I told myself not to think of the fire, but I thought of nothing else. The fire was inside me. All the time. I tried to tamp it down. But that was impossible. The fire was everywhere. The fire took almost everything. I'd tried to not see it. To shut it down. What I did. What I didn't do. Gramps standing in the driveway, in the smoke and embers. I sat through the song now, sat with the knowledge that Gramps's death was my fault. Shrinking in the pew like those Shrinky Dinks people Alicia and I used to draw on and then bake. I hardened as I shrank. It wasn't Beckett in danger of shrinking. It was me. And I was a jerk to him. To Alicia. They *should* be mad at me. Alicia played the final notes then and I needed to get out of there. How could I mourn? I didn't have the right to mourn. I was responsible.

I squeezed my hands into fists. Then I reached into Mom's purse, felt her keys in my hand—they jingled but not enough for her to look up or notice. She dabbed her nose, patted my father's back. I glanced to the pew behind me where River fidgeted, his hands a steeple, then people, a steeple, then people. I slipped my phone out of my pocket and texted: *Be right back.*

Gram wiped her eyes with the sleeves of her dress. It was enough to shatter me: the bright dress, her wet eyes. How some part of her knew, but not all. Did she know something about Sierra too? How it was now? Mostly gone? My throat filled with lead. I couldn't speak, so I dropped a kiss on Gram's head as I slid past her, ducking. I made my way down the aisle, and then I drifted out of the church.

OBJECT: Piano

LOCATION: 42 Plumule Way, Sierra, California

RESIDENT: Alicia Johnson

The piano was an extravagant birthday gift from my parents four years ago when I was sure I'd go pro. And I guess they figured I had a chance at it too. Long before that, piano was what I did, it was who I was. My "draw yourself at 100" picture to celebrate the hundredth day of school in kindergarten showed me, white-haired, in a fancy dress at a piano. At five, I couldn't remember not playing, not being called "good." By the time I was ten, I went to Willow Springs for lessons because no one in town was advanced enough to keep teaching me, and by the time I was twelve I had my first paid gig—at church every Sunday. I replaced Clara Courts, who broke her hip mid-service when her shoe caught the runner. They carried Clara out and I jumped right in. From then on it was my job. Both Sunday services, and sometimes Wednesday nights. By eighth grade I was accompanying the chorus at school.

It's not that the dream disappeared. It's that it was clarified like when you practice a phrase over and over and finally it clicks, automatic in your body. Your hands DO what they're told. That's how it was, I guess.

I can practice again, and I do. But it isn't the same. I bought a keyboard. I like it because I can put on my headphones and play when I can't sleep. And often, I can't sleep because I have these recurring fire nightmares. It's, well—it sucks.

But the truth is, I don't love performing enough to want to really do it. When I started playing again, I learned something else—the music stayed inside me. When everything else disappeared, it was still there. Now when I can't sleep, I play. The knots in my shoulders work their way out through my fingers, dissolve into music. And eventually, I grow tired and sleep. When I found my way back to playing, I realized what music could do for me was so much more than performing.

When I found the Music Therapy program at Illinois State, I knew it was for me. It was a way to play and help people. Don't get me wrong. It's not good fortune. I don't want anyone to find a new dream this way. But I'm glad I found mine.

I'll always miss my piano; I wear a necklace made from its recovered strings every day. I dream I could make it sound again. I'd give my little finger for our house back, the piano tucked inside it. But I made it out, you know? I survived. My family did too. We even rescued our rabbit. I guess that really is what matters.

The heavy wooden church doors thumped closed behind me. I gasped in the warm air, my mom's keys in one hand, my phone in the other. My head was full of sound. The buzzing. And a symphony. And a whole flock of birds chirping at once. I steadied myself on a sidewalk trash can, winced at the hot metal sting. No one followed me. Good. I didn't want to be followed.

My phone vibrated.

River:

> U in danger of rapid unscheduled disassembly?

I pressed my hands into my forehead. I was at my gramps's funeral. If rapid unscheduled human disassembly were possible, I'd probably do it. But at least he didn't ask if I was okay.

I managed to type out—

> No

> Want me 2 come out?

I imagined River's arms around me—how he would lift the leaden weight. How we could kiss and kiss. But no. I didn't want the weight to lift. Not this time. I wanted to feel all of it. I needed to. And I didn't want anyone to follow me. To worry for me. Not even him. If he came out, I would be with him. It would be easy to look away. I knew I'd run a shit program and screwed up. In a hell world, I'd somehow made the hell worse. I typed:

> No. I'll be ok, back in a sec. :)

The okay combined with the smiley face was probably too much. Pressure tightened like a vise across my forehead. And maybe it was that pain that made me click a program together without fully realizing it, and I tossed my phone. I watched it land in the trash on a crumpled McDonald's bag. That would buy me a few minutes at least. By the time they pulled up my location and found my phone, I'd be gone.

I took a long breath in. I pushed it out, and with one look back at the church doors, I ran across the parking lot to my mom's car.

I didn't know where I was going. Not at first. I wanted to drive fast, but once I was on the highway, traffic was heavy, and I couldn't imagine driving and driving to—where? Canada? Mexico? Dad told stories of all-night road trips to Tijuana, or Vancouver when he was young. They made him fall in love with the road—one of the reasons he took up trucking, or so he said. But I didn't even have a passport. And I hated highway driving.

But driving for Frank's? I loved that. Finding secret routes through Sierra's twisting roads, that feeling like I was headed deeper into nowhere—that feeling calmed me. Gramps's voice in my head sang, *We're on the road to nowhere.* I took the exit that snaked back into Sierra from the south. The road I'd driven out on when I'd fled the fire. When I'd last left Sierra.

The two-lane was vacant except for a few trucks that rumbled past, loaded with debris. I turned a corner and in front of me, the yellow grasses of the valley became a line of black that stretched as far as I could see. The burn scar. Everything I'd been trying to avoid.

My mouth went hot and acidic. I pulled over and dropped my head to the steering wheel. I rolled down the window, and in rushed the scent of charred earth. I opened the car door and heaved. Salt and bile. I wiped my mouth, shivered like I was coming down with a flu.

Then something darted out of the culvert and stopped in front of my parked car. A red fox. I met its eyes. I held my breath, counted one, two, three, four, five.

"Come on," I said. "Have at me." The fox's ear twitched but it kept its eyes on me. I stopped counting. I made my breath slow and shallow. Time disappeared. The fox stared until its ears swiveled and it broke my gaze and darted into the culvert. A few seconds later, a truck loaded with bricks sped down the road. The rubble of Sierra leaving Sierra. Someone's life, home, dream, business. Pieces of our town. I turned the car on and like Alice darting after the White Rabbit, I followed the fox into my upside-down world. I needed to be somewhere that was as bad off as I was. I deserved to face this. To feel it. No one would look for me here.

I drove.

And drove, past the fields black and dotted with lifeless scrub-oak—burnt and twisted against a vacant sky. As I got closer to the outskirts of town—husks of cars. A rubble pile where there was once a house—another—then four in a row and in front of them, in the middle of the road, a police car parked sidesways, lights on. I slowed. I'd reached the town cordon.

I rolled down my window, and Gerardo Monteiro, who must have recently graduated from the police academy at Sierra Community because he was a year behind Beckett in school, sauntered to the car. A pack of PPE in one hand, the other open as he asked for my license and proof of residence. Before I even reached down he said—

"You're Beckett Alexander's little sister—but—isn't your gramps's funeral today?" Then he saw the flowers on my wrist. "Man." He shook his head. "So sorry. Most of the guys on the force are there."

"Yeah," I managed, "Gramps knew everyone."

He motioned for me to put my license away and handed me the PPE. "So what are you doing up here?"

"Service is over." It wasn't an explanation, or the truth, but it seemed to work.

"Okay, well—be careful. Chimneys and trees are all unstable. Since you're alone, you might want to stay in your car."

I nodded. He took a step away, but then turned back.

"Your brother, he okay?"

Ugh. That word again. So useless. I must have made a face, because Gerardo laughed uncomfortably. "Who am I kidding, none of us are okay. Tell him I'm around if he wants to hang sometime. We had fun before—" He trailed off. Before what? The fire? Beck's accident? Before Beckett was lost in addiction? Before middle school? When Beckett was still a 4-H member? He tapped the hood of the car and said, "You've got to leave town by dusk, okay?"

"Sure."

I pulled away from Gerardo, waving as I drove. The landscape was like I imagined Dresden after the fire bombings we learned about when reading *Slaughterhouse-Five*. I'd seen pictures on the news. Pictures on my phone. But seeing it firsthand—the destruction life-scale—it was disorienting. The familiar transformed into the unrecognizable. I couldn't stop trying to piece together what had been what.

When I turned the corner near Junkin's Road, what was once a neighborhood now looked like a graveyard of chimneys. A hillside covered in brick. A monument of ashes. This was once the edge of town—what was it now? Rubble piles and cracked pavement.

My stomach turned. I struggled to breathe. Everywhere I looked, I tried to imagine what was there before, layered over burnt cars, foundation lines, crumbling brick. People said *apocalyptic,* or *catastrophic.* But those words felt like something a newscaster would say, something you'd glance up and see on a TV screen when you were at the airport or out to dinner—and some other part of the world was sandbagging or standing around parking lots looking for shelter. They didn't feel right when it was this personal. They didn't feel enough.

I turned onto what I thought was Junkin's Road and I drove for probably a half mile before I realized I wasn't on the right street. I turned around, searching the roadside for the familiar and then I saw it—Crenshaw. Recognizable only because of the big boulder that had once reminded me to turn for Margie Sanderson's weekly flower deliveries. My hands shook, but I turned. I would follow this to Way Back Antiques and then double back to the Ridge Road. I knew this way. The map was inside me. I just needed to follow the roads.

I don't know if it was the sunlight through the clouds, or if turning onto Crenshaw flipped some kind of switch in my head, but as suddenly as I turned I was back there—in the fire. In that day. Surrounded by the memory of it—the one I'd been pushing out even as it pressed against my eyelids.

The sky darkened. I tasted smoke. I felt the heat. Rivulets of sweat dripped down my neck and pooled on my lower back. My hands slipped on the steering wheel. Something ran across the road up ahead. A dog? A cat? A rabbit? The fox? It couldn't be. I'd driven miles. But I slowed, and there it was. The fox stood in the middle of the road. It met my eye again and ran off like it was daring me to enter my memory, to let it scorch me. So I drove on, hands on the wheel, and let the memory come.

FIRE

My hands gripped the wheel. Gramps was a shadow entering the side door of his garage. Orange firebrands sliced the air. The wind screamed.

"You know how to drive a stick?" Beckett said, climbing into the passenger seat. In the back, Alicia had her arms around Jenny.

"Yeah, Gramps taught me." I shifted the Saab into reverse.

Beckett chuckled. "Of course he would."

"What's that supposed to mean?"

"It means he trusted you. I never got a stick lesson 'cause you can bet he didn't want me near his truck. I learned when I bought the Vanagon."

"Sorry."

Beckett waved his hand in the air. "No, it was probably a good call. I definitely would have taken his truck out. You sure you up for this? I *can* drive, you know."

"So can I," I said.

The wind pressed against the car windows. A dog ran down the street.

"Wait, was that one of Layla's goldens?" I craned to see after it.

"If it was, it's gone now." Alicia said.

"Okay—if anyone sees it again—we're stopping."

"Caps, we can't have a dog in the car with a rabbit," Alicia said. I was about to say, *If we get to the rabbit in time, he'll be in a basket*, but the roof of one of the canyon-side houses caught fire and the flame spread in seconds and my words vanished.

"Yeah. Okay. We're in hell," Beckett said. I focused on the road.

Jenny made a sharp sound like she'd slipped with a knife.

"No, we aren't," Alicia said, reaching through the seat to punch Beckett, but he intercepted, grabbing her fist and squeezing. "We're almost to Rowdy." Alicia retracted her arm. "Hang on." And then she started softly singing.

In the rearview mirror I saw Jenny holding her violin case on her lap—hugging it with one arm like a doll and clinging to Alicia with the other. Beckett cocked his head, listened for a phrase, and then picked up where she was in the song, "*Oh dream maker you heartbreaker.*"

Alicia's eyes met mine in the rearview mirror as she continued. "*Wherever you're going, I'm going your way—*"

"*Two drifters,*" I sang, my voice scratchy and out of key, interrupting their sweet harmony.

Alicia's house was not on fire. At least not yet. Before I was in park, she was half out of the car.

She slammed the door against the wind while shouting, "Stay here, Jenny!" and Beckett followed her into the smoke. I let the car run. If Beckett said anything about idling, it wouldn't matter. The world was already on fire. Jenny's breathing was loud.

"Don't go!" she said.

I put my arm over the seat so she could grab my hand. "I won't. Do you want me to sing?"

She stuck out her tongue. "You really can't."

"Thanks," I said.

We sat there in the roar of the wind, holding tight to each other until Alicia pulled open the door and Jenny cried, "ROWDY!!" as her sister dropped the rabbit basket into the back.

"Drive," Beckett said, passing Alicia her piano folder.

I pulled onto the road. Truck lights in my rearview mirror. "That's Gramps, right?" My stomach ached. Palms wet. He had to be right behind us, didn't he? He said he was just grabbing a few things. That's all Beckett and Alicia had done, and we were already ready, so it probably was him. It looked like him.

A gray pine exploded into flames next to us. I concentrated on my hands. The movements of the wheel. I focused my eyes.

Jenny hunched over the rabbit basket, whispering to Rowdy through the slats. "We'll be okay, we'll be okay."

"Yeah, I think—maybe it's him," Alicia said.

"I can't tell," Beckett said.

"It is." I thought about Cheerio and wondered if Gramps had found her. I kept checking the rearview mirror, but as I neared the Ridge Road, the lights behind me disappeared in the thickening smoke, then reappeared as the wind pushed it on. The headlights were the right shape. Right height. The truck was black. Or dark. Or looked dark anyway. It was him. I felt it in my bones. Gramps was behind me.

At the Ridge Road, both lanes were still headed south, only now neither was moving. Normally the fastest way out of town was to turn into the gridlock. I was about to when the streets I learned driving for Adrienne and working on the app showed me another way—a hopefully less crowded way. When the traffic started to inch forward again, I signaled to the driver of the car in front of me that I was crossing and nudged the front end out.

"Cappi, you aren't turning. Why aren't you turning? That's *the* way." Beckett's voice was tight.

"There's another," I said.

My brother looked like he was folding in on himself. "I'm thinking unless we want to die, we should go the way everyone else is going."

I inched onto the road as the gap slowly widened. "There are three *main* routes out of town. That's one. It took us how long to get here from the high school?"

He pointed to the dashboard clock. "I'm guessing a little

over two hours—and I'm pretty sure that means *if* you don't turn and you get us stuck somewhere in there, we'll die."

"There's a cut-through to the highway below lower Main."

"What about Gramps? He won't go that way."

"He'll follow. He's behind me."

"Where?"

"A ways back."

"You don't know that! It's dark! We can see what? Across the road? You think you saw his headlights but five people on our street have the same truck. How will he see where you're going?" Beckett's voice was high and thin. I was passing in front of a Plymouth with a dented front end. Mitchell's car. Inside, Mitchell had one hand on the wheel, the other in his mouth as he chewed his cuticles. Alone. My stomach turned. I thought of River alone and met Mitchell's eyes. "Follow me!" I mouthed. He didn't switch on his blinker. "Why isn't he following?" I asked.

"Because you're making a stupid choice," Beckett said. And there it was. His voice hard as a picture smashing against a wall.

He was wrong. I knew. I knew Gramps was behind me. I was pretty sure I could see his lights reaching the Ridge Road. I was going slow enough that he would see me. He would follow. When I got off the Ridge Road, I could drive fast. Get us out quick. I knew Sierra. I knew the roads. I drove them when I delivered for Frank's. I was building a map app. I would get us out.

"Cappi?" Beckett's voice wavered.

"Maybe she knows what she's doing," Alicia said from the back seat.

"And if she doesn't?" Beckett turned to face her.

"Wonder why the world is on fire and you're wasting time fighting with your sister. Then evoke all the gods," Alicia said.

"Might want to do that either way," I said. "We're going to need them."

"Caps, seriously. Don't do this." Beckett's voice was like a razor.

But we'd reached the other side of the Ridge Road. I pressed the gas. And then we were moving. Fast.

My shoulder blades relaxed down my back. I had a program again. I felt better. Still about to wet-my-pants-and-find-Jesus-and-believe-astrology, but at least I had a plan. I knew what to do next.

"I don't know if that's your gramps behind us," Alicia said, "but they're crossing the road too."

"It's him," I said. Gramps would follow me even if it was against every rule of evacuation. He would follow me; he would feel it in his bones. I sucked in a breath. My throat ached from smoke. My plan was not at all safe. But neither was sitting on the Ridge Road in traffic unlike anything Sierra had ever seen while a blowtorch wind pressed down on us, and firefighters tried to keep the gas station from exploding. This way, I was at least in control.

A half mile off the Ridge Road, there were no other cars. Nothing in my rearview. At least from what I could see through the smoke, which was probably only five feet. It was hot. There was a crackling sound layered over the wind now. My bones ached. A warning. But I tamped it down like glowing embers. I tried to stay steady. I told myself I made my choice. Picked my program. I was going to let it run. The windshield wipers swiped firebrands and ash. Explosions rattled the car. It sounded like the living room when Dad was watching war movies so loud, the house shook. Like we were on a battlefield. Then another noise. *Crack!* And a wooden power pole smashed down in front of us. I braked, stopping the car inches from its sparking wires.

"Um, why is the power not cut?" I said.

"Oh no," Beckett said.

"Our father who art in heaven," Jenny whispered.

"And where's Gramps?" I said.

"Not behind you," Alicia said. I had stopped, so he should have caught up. But there was no one. He was gone.

"Hell no." Beckett slammed his fist into the dash box. *CRACK*. My teeth rattled. The pole on the street sparked. Beckett rubbed his knuckles, spreading little streaks of red across the backs of his hands. "I told you not to come this way, Caps. Now we're going to have to turn around and be stuck in that line of cars like I said." He might as well have knocked the wind out of me.

"Go slow when you back up," Alicia said. "I don't see anyone, but I can't see that well."

"Beck, can you try and call Gramps?"

He grunted.

Alicia reached forward to touch my brother's arm. Their eyes connected. I turned back to the flaming pole. I could taste smoke. Feel the heat.

"No service," Beckett said.

Alicia's fingers tapped Beckett's arm and then she started to hum, and before I could recognize the song I knew it was from the Sierra High Singers catalog. Beckett looked straight ahead, mouth barely moving, but sang:

"You'll remember me when the west wind moves—"

I held my breath. I forced my thoughts back to the map in my head. Tried to focus until—*yes*. There was another path. I yanked the car into reverse. But instead of heading back the way we came, I turned at this big boulder at the side of the road and onto Crenshaw.

Beckett stopped singing. "Caps, please." His voice struck me like an arrow. "Please get us out."

"I am," I said. "Just not the way you would." Most people didn't know about Crenshaw; it's an unpaved, private road. But thanks to Margie Sanderson's flower-sending children in Utah, I knew it well.

"Caprice, seriously, what are you doing?"

"Recalculating route," I said in my best GPS impression as the car bumped through a divot. "And seriously you guys, 'Fields of Gold' is not the right song for the moment."

"It could be worse," Beckett said. "'Fire on the Mountain.' Or 'Ring of Fire.'"

"'Girl on Fire,'" Alicia said, "or 'Light My Fire.'" Then Beckett laughed and Alicia did too. And soon even Jenny was giggling. Beckett sang, *You know that it would be untrue—you know that I would be a liar—*"

"Stop!" Alicia said.

I drove, somehow I drove, though I could barely see, and I was terrified about where Gramps had gone. I didn't know if he knew about Crenshaw, and I worried that Beckett was right, and I had made a terrible mistake.

I pressed the pedal and drove as fast as I could down the straight dirt road. When Crenshaw reconnected to paved roads near Way Back Antiques, I slowed. We were right by Gram's place.

"What are you doing?" Beckett said. "Don't slow down."

"We need to check on Gram."

"I'm sure they evacuated already. I mean, they couldn't miss the whole sun-disappeared-in-a-cloud-of-smoke-and-embers-falling-from-the-sky thing," Beckett said.

"Maybe not." Alicia put a hand on his arm. "But you ever tried moving an old person who's hooked up to machines and strapped to a bed? Especially if you don't have your own ambulance service? It's not quick."

"Thanks, Doc Johnson," Beckett said.

"It wouldn't hurt to check," I said.

"It might actually," Beckett said, "hurt like death."

"Three minutes, Beck. We'll be okay." I tried to sound sure. Even if she didn't know who I was, I couldn't be this close and not check. She was my gram.

Through the gloom I could see headlights. For a moment I thought maybe it was Gramps somehow behind us again, but when they came up on us, it was an SUV.

"Beck, can you try and call Gramps again?" I said, turning into Gram's place as the other car careened around us.

"Still no service," Beckett said. "Texts aren't even sending." He dropped his phone into the cup holder. Then, "Oh no way." Because as we turned into the parking lot, the place wasn't empty. Not at all. Headlights. Taillights. Shadows of people in the smoke. Nurses. Orderlies. Wheelchairs. Gurneys.

"They aren't gone?" Jenny said. I pulled the car as close as I could to the building's squat entrance. Everywhere, people pushing against the wind, protecting their faces from embers.

"Uh, Alexanders," Alicia said, pointing to an orange glow at the edge of the parking lot. Fire spread out in all directions, climbing across the leaves and brush. A swirl of flame. Radiating.

"If we die, remind me I thought this was a bad idea," Beckett said.

"My ghost wouldn't talk to your ghost." I threw the door open.

The wind hit like a blowtorch. Embers stung my arms. I froze and then Beckett was tugging at me.

"Come on!" He had to shout, even an arm's length away.

We pushed into the building, both of us calling "Aster Alexander!" as we ran down the hall to Gram's room. And there she was. Alone in her wheelchair, sleeping, head hung in a way that looked terribly uncomfortable.

"Thank God she's in the chair!" Beckett called. He pushed

her, and as we reached the entrance, there was a nurse shuffling a man toward the door.

She stopped and said, "I was going for her next"—nodding at Gram—"but—" She shook her head. "I should probably make you sign something."

Gram, startled then, sat upright, and shouted, "What is going on here!"

"Fire, Aster, these kids are getting you to safety," the nurse said. Then to Beckett, "She's your family right?"

"Our grandma," I said.

"Go. Be safe. Here—" She thrust a mask into Beckett's hand and gave him a push toward the door.

"I'm not going!" Gram cried.

"Nowhere to stay, Gram," I said.

"Here, let's get this on." Beck put the mask on Gram and then pushed her into the parking lot.

The wind howled and crackled. All I felt was heat. The smoke was a thick orange brown.

Beckett opened the back door of Alicia's car, and I helped him get Gram settled next to her.

"Watch your hands!" Gram said. "I know all about young bucks like you."

"You don't need to worry about me, Aster," Beckett said. "I promise to keep you safe."

Every inhale was hot. Was all smoke. It burned. But still, somehow, I ran back to the driver's door. I buckled myself in. I drove.

As we pulled out of Gram's place and headed toward the south exit of town, Beckett said, "Okay, so maybe I wasn't for this plan, but—well—good call, Caps."

If not for all the smoke and fire, I might have cut my eyes to him, or jostled his shoulder or something, but we weren't out yet. It took everything in me to drive.

"Where are you taking me?" Gram said.

"Do you want to see my rabbit?" Jenny said.

"Your what?" Gram asked.

"Look," Jenny said.

"Is that the one that's been eating my flowers? Glenn's been trying to catch him."

"No!" Jenny laughed. "He's my pet!"

"A pet rabbit—why on earth would you have a pet rabbit?" Gram said.

"He's cute, see?"

Sweat rolled down my forehead. I drove slow out of the parking lot. As I was turning, I saw round headlights. A truck.

My heart squeezed. *Gramps!* "Beck—those headlights! That's Gramps!"

"Caprice!" Beckett said. "There is no way you can tell that! We can barely see anything."

"We need to check," I said. "We need to tell him we have Gram, and he needs to go."

Someone honked.

"That's not Gramps," Beckett said. "If it is—he'll turn around and get out of there."

"But I was right about Gram," I said.

"And that was lucky. Keep driving," Beckett said. "It's not him."

So I drove. I drove and drove. Even though I knew it was him. Even though I felt it in my bones.

IF I had gone with River—

IF we'd stayed with Gramps—
IF I took the Ridge Road—
IF when the power line fell, I'd returned to the Ridge Road—
IF I had listened to Beckett and not stopped for Gram—
IF I didn't listen to Beckett and turned back when I saw the truck
  lights—IF, IF, IF, IF, IF, IF, IF, IF, IF, IF, IF, IF, IF, IF, IF, IF, IF, IF,
  IF, IF, IF, IF, IF, IF, IF, IF, IF, IF, IF, IF, IF, IF, IF, IF, IF, IF, IF, IF,
  IF, IF, IF, IF, IF, IF, IF, IF, IF, IF, IF, IF, IF, IF, IF, IF, IF, IF, IF, IF,
  IF, IF, IF, IF, IF, IF, IF, IF, IF, IF, IF, IF, IF, IF, IF, IF, IF, IF, IF, IF,
  IF, IF, IF, IF, IF, IF, IF, IF, IF, IF, IF, IF, IF, IF, IF, IF, IF, IF, IF, IF,
  IF, IF, IF, IF, IF, IF, IF, IF, IF, IF, IF, IF, IF, IF, IF, IF, IF, IF, IF, IF,
  IF, IF, IF, IF, IF, IF, IF, IF, IF, IF, IF, IF, IF, IF, IF, IF, IF, IF, IF, IF,
  IF, IF, IF, IF, IF, IF, IF, IF, IF, IF, IF, IF, IF, IF, IF, IF, IF, IF, IF, IF,
  IF, IF, IF, IF, IF, IF, IF, IF, IF, IF, IF, IF, IF, IF, IF, IF, IF, IF, IF, IF,
  IF, IF, IF, IF, IF, IF, IF, IF, IF, IF, IF, IF, IF, IF, IF, IF, IF, IF, IF, IF,
  IF, IF, IF, IF, IF, IF, IF, IF, IF, IF, IF, IF, IF, IF, IF, IF, IF, IF, IF, IF,
  FIRE, FIRE, FIRE, FIRE, FIRE, FIRE, FIRE, FIRE, FIRE, FIRE,
  FIRE, FIRE, FIRE, FIRE, FIRE, FIRE,FIRE, FIRE, FIRE, FIRE,
  FIRE, FIRE, FIRE, FIRE, FIRE, FIRE, FIRE, FIRE, FIRE, FIRE,
  FIRE, FIRE, FIRE, FIRE, FIRE, FIRE, FIRE, FIRE, FIRE, FIRE,
  FIRE, FIRE, FIRE, FIRE, FIRE, FIRE, FIRE, FIRE, FIRE, FIRE,
  FIRE, FIRE, FIRE, FIRE, FIRE, FIRE, FIRE, FIRE, FIRE, FIRE,
  FIRE, FIRE, FIRE, FIRE, FIRE, FIRE, FIRE, FIRE, FIRE, FIRE,
  FIRE, FIRE, FIRE, FIRE, FIRE, FIRE, FIRE, FIRE, FIRE, FIRE,
  FIRE, FIRE, FIRE, FIRE, FIRE, FIRE, FIRE, FIRE, FIRE, FIRE

SIX WEEKS AFTER

As my gramps's funeral continued in Willow Springs, I drove slow through the memory of what I had done, and into a landscape of chimney-stack graveyards. I was getting close to Way Back Antiques and didn't want to go near Gram's place. I turned on a road that I thought would cut back toward my house—but I was disoriented again, turned around completely. I ended up in the heart of town. Naming the ruins: the Elko Station, Hole in the Dam Donuts, Sierra Market, Burrito Junction, Summit Veterinary. All of it: Rubble. Rubble. Rubble. At the remains of Feeney Brothers Law Offices, a metal stairway to nowhere. Sierra Savers Grocery, leveled. The sign still hung in the blue fall sky—BEST DAM PRICES IN TOWN.

Somehow untouched, Liquor of the Dam'd, its neon sign flashing OPEN. I shook myself. That couldn't be right. The town had no power. No one was coming up but residents and workers. Still, the light was on. Was it battery powered and never turned off? At the half-charred Dam Hardware, the front windows were boarded up and spray-painted to say REOPENING

ASAP! WE'LL HELP YOU REBUILD SIERRA STRONG AS A DAM!
#DAMSTRONG #SIERRASTRONG.

I thought, *I left my gramps. I led him to his death. I ran the wrong program. Came up with the worst solution.* There was no chance to troubleshoot. In a situation where mistakes weren't okay, I made one.

On one lot a large, spray-painted sign leaned against a charred tree: WE SHOOT LOOTERS!

I crested the hill near the Anglican church—still intact. Luck? The hand of God? The large parking lot that kept anything from burning too close to the building? I stopped the car in the middle of the road. I could see all the way into the canyon. Before, brush and trees hid deer, like the one that had jumped in front of River's truck here after our meeting with Cecil. That felt like ages ago. Now, foundations, burnt cars, a row of blackened pine that would probably be cut. That's what happened after a burn. The trees were too damaged. Or sometimes they weren't damaged, but people said they were because wood was worth money. My spine curled as I thought of all the trees, their dark wide branches. I gripped the steering wheel. *IF your world is incinerated THEN hold on tight.* My arms shook. I couldn't feel my feet, but somehow, I drove.

All I could see, as far as I could see, in every direction, was burnt. The ground black, the trees black. Cars reduced to gray and brown metal husks. Where my friends had lived, where their parents had worked, our school—I had seen the drone footage of Sierra, the news clips of a charbroiled wasteland, but to be in it? Surrounded by a landscape so transformed from the trees, houses, and hideaways of before? My town was gone. Obliterated.

I turned off Ridge Road and the gaping black-and-gray Plumule Canyon. My stomach hardened. Gramps was always excited to lay a foundation. He loved the measuring, mixing, the careful pour, and how later he would pull the studs away, and there it would be. The outline of a home. A space for hope. Now it was all that was left—cracked, burnt, filled with debris, impossible to reuse.

I drove into my neighborhood. I wanted to close my eyes. The canyon was bare and black before me. The foundation piles lining the roadside—all homes I'd been to so many times. At Alicia's lot I pulled the car over. I let it idle on the square of driveway where we used to ride bikes, and looked over the pile to where her piano once stood. My vision was fuzzing, but I inhaled slow and forced myself on. I drove past the husk of a truck parked at the Hernándezes' house, a burnt wagon in the driveway too.

Then I was home. Quicker than seemed possible. Facing the empty space where my house had been. Where my grandparents' house was. The burnt hull of Beckett's van stood in front of me. The foundation of our house beyond that. And my grandparents' house off to my right. My breath came shallow and quick.

I saved the wrong grandparent. I hated the thought. But there it was. I saved Gram. Gram, who couldn't remember so much.

Who couldn't remember me. Gram, who was like this land, full of fractured stories. Chimneys. Only a foundation and, even that, burnt.

But that wasn't entirely true. My stomach turned over.

If we hadn't stopped for Gram, what then?

If we had lost them both. Sweat prickled along my forehead. I thought of Gram's tears. She knew. She felt it in her bones. She must be disappointed in me too. I felt heavy and sick at the thought. Had I saved my grandma only to break her heart?

My gramps had been near. I'd known it. Felt that in my bones too. But I hadn't listened. I'd kept driving. Maybe I could have saved them both. IF, IF, IF, IF, IF, IF, IF—

I opened the car door now, stepped into the wet ashes in my new Birkenstocks. I sunk into the mushy ground. I left the packet of PPE Gerardo handed me on the passenger seat. I wanted to run into the house, into my room. But there was no house. No rooms. No walls. Nothing to hide under. I was dizzy. A sour roil in my stomach. I kept one hand on the car. It wasn't just how everything was gone. It was also the silence. No birds. No people. No cars. A vast empty. Not even the canyon wind moving through the burnt trees.

The edges of my vision clouded—my house. A ring of bricks that didn't look big enough to contain the world it once held. The bent metal of our stove. Blackened pipes. I squished through ashy mud to Gramps's place; I was thinking about where the deck had been. The garden's barely raised lumps, the wooden boxes burnt away.

I stood at the entrance to the garage door Gramps disappeared into that day. A slant of light escaped the cloud cover, and something in the ashes shimmered.

I pulled up my funeral skirt and carefully stepped over a pile of bricks, making my way toward the glinting object, but the sunlight disappeared again and whatever it was—a shard of mirror, dad's old tuba—was gone. I continued through the ashes. Carefully stepping between cinderblocks and bent metal. My heartbeat pulsed all over my skin. Sweat prickled along my backbone. I neared the chimney stack at the center of the house, moving slow, wondering where Gramps went that day. Did he remember the go-bag (I didn't). Did he think to grab important papers—like his social security card, the cash in the clock? Why did he come back to the house at all? Did he find Cheerio? These were all unknown variables.

I thought of everything turned into the mushy ashes under my feet. The Handyman Encyclopedias, Gram's teacups. The china decorated with red asters Gramps had brought home from Way Back Antiques when we were little—how Gram danced around the kitchen with those plates. She said they never had wedding china, but she supposed that any-day china was better anyhow. That night, we'd set a table in the garden and used those fancy plates and Gram's linen tablecloth. It was October, and Gram was serving food she'd grown, so she decided to call it a harvest festival. When Beckett and I finished eating, we'd run into the shadow of the trees while Gram, Gramps, and our parents talked.

I walked through ruins, but I'd really slipped back into the garden at sunset, the flowers blooming, the soft clink of glasses, the skunk scent of Gramps's pipe. The trees as they darkened against the blue sky, and then the rest of the world disappeared into night as Beckett and I watched, spying on the grown-ups, making our way from tree to bush, toward the table glowing with candles. The way Gram's voice rose in pitch when she told a joke, and how the world filled with the roll of Gramps's laughter.

I was thinking of Gramps's laugh, about how burnt and black trees looked like healthy trees if you imagined night was coming on. I was thinking about this double vision of what was here before and what is here now. I was thinking so much, I wasn't in my body. Everything was numb.

So I didn't feel it when I tripped on a loose brick and tumbled straight into the chimney, smacking my forehead on its edge. I landed on my hands and I was back in my body again, face to the ground. One foot was trapped in the rubble, the pain in my forehead searing and sharp.

Something darkened the ashes below me. Oh. I was bleeding. No wonder it hurt. Yeah. Ouch. That was pain. I thought in Alicia's dad's voice: *Girls, if someone is bleeding, apply pressure.* But with what? My hands were coated in toxic dust, and all scraped up. Also I was stuck. I floundered on my belly, a fish in a dry creek trying escape. But no.

I did get a good grip on my skirt and pulled it to my mouth. Then using my teeth, I ripped a hole in the fabric and tore. It took a few good tugs to break through the hem. I braced myself with one elbow as I wrapped the fabric around my hand, then pressed the layers into my forehead, hard.

Did Alicia, or her dad, say something about how head injuries bleed a lot, and that didn't necessarily mean they're serious? Because this was—a lot. Like trickling down my arm a lot. I reached for my phone to call Alicia and to let someone know where I was. But then I remembered, nope. My phone was in Willow Springs, in a trash can in the parking lot of a pink adobe church.

If Caprice doesn't have a cellphone THEN catastrophe.

I was trapped. Really trapped. In the soggy ashes of my gramps's house, in our burnt-up town, stuck under bricks, probably bleeding out, and no one knew where I was. The world smelled like campfire pits and iron. I thought:

IF trapped inside your personal apocalypse with a head injury THEN consider complete surrender to the terror of the world.

It wasn't funny. I knew it wasn't funny, but the thought made me laugh little hysterical giggles. It must have been the head injury. The sun peeked out again, and something near me sparkled. I reached for it. Squiggling forward on my stomach as best I could, careful to keep a hand on my bleeding forehead. A few empty grabs and I pulled a thin disk toward me. A circle, or half of it. Roman numerals. Three, four, five, six, seven, eight, nine. Half the clock face from Gramps's mantel. The one where he stored his money. Was this the last thing he touched? I ran my finger along the round edge of it, the burnt line. How was half of it left?

It was hard to breathe. Who was I now? Without my gramps? My home? My app? My plans? Who was I when nobody even knew where I was?

I laid my head on my arm. Pressed the fabric there with my free hand. I was stuck. And it was my fault. I'd run the wrong program. Again.

I deserved to be alone. Stuck and hurt. I deserved it because I'd seen his headlights, I'd known it was him. But I kept driving. Even though I'd felt him there.

I wondered if I tried to sleep, if maybe I would get taken away too. I'd hurt my head, after all. *If you hurt your head,* Alicia's dad always said, *don't go to sleep! Don't even lie down.* But maybe if I did, maybe if I let myself go to sleep, I would get an escape. A reprieve.

I lay there and tried to relax my body, one leg curled under, the other behind me, torqued at the hip, my foot still trapped, head resting on my arm. Something sharp poked the soft underside of my bicep. I wiggled farther into it. I closed my eyes around the pain. I thought, *IF you fall asleep THEN have no dreams. IF you hemorrhage inside your head THEN you never wake up.* I imagined being welcomed into a cradle of night: starless and empty.

I didn't register my thoughts as suicidal. Or consider that I could end up in a coma like Mason. It was like I was operating on some flawed, deeply rooted grief program. The one that told me it was okay to give up. The one that wanted me to not see any of this, to numb it out, to drift away. Because it was too much. All the ifs. What might have happened and what did.

I wanted emptiness. The vast blank. I wanted an end to a pain so big, I hadn't even let myself look at it or start to feel it. It was a canyon, that pain, and I was drowning in it. I wanted it to stop. I wanted to not feel guilty. I didn't want to end me, not really. I wanted to be free as I was in the backyard with my brother, as our parents and grandparents clinked their glasses, and the cricket chorus filled the canyon. If I couldn't get back the time the fire stole from me, I wanted to turn time back. And if I couldn't turn time back, I wanted time to end. I shifted my head on my arm. I lay still. I tried to let go.

Then I heard something moving. Not human. I thought of the fox from earlier, the one I followed into the burn scar, and I thought of the fox from the worksite of my childhood. The fox. My white rabbit. Then I thought of whatever killed Beckett's cat so long ago. I unfurled quickly, wincing as my arm released whatever sharpness had bit into it. I looked around, expecting a bobcat to lunge at my throat. Or maybe a mountain lion. I thought, *Some hungry beast smelled my blood and is coming for me.* The hair on my arms rose like daggers. Because despite dreaming of a quiet surrender, the idea of being torn to bits by a wild animal did not sound good. I craned my neck. I couldn't see behind the chimney stack. Was a predator there?

I scanned the foundation of my house and Gramps's. The driveway's square of pavement. Something rustled. I craned farther. Pulled again to try and free my foot, but nope.

"You coming for me? Finally going to grab me by the throat?"

Then I heard it. *Meooww.* I tensed, held my breath. Maybe I was delirious. Hallucinating with impossible hope. Maybe my ears were playing tricks on me. I tried to call out, but my voice was gone.

Meooow-meeep. Meep. I knew that sound. But it couldn't be. Could it?

And then—one, two, three, four feet landed in ash; then *meep, meow* and Cheerio talked her way from the foundation, through the ruins, and right to my side. She seemed to be saying, *I've been here the whole time! Where were you?*

"Cheerio?" My voice returned, raspy, as she rubbed against my arms and legs. She stretched her head to my face, purring. She put her paws around my neck as if she could give me a human hug. She rubbed under my chin, then licked me with her sandpaper tongue.

How was it possible? It had been more than a month. I examined her as best I could. She was thinner but no burns that I could see. No cuts. No missing fur. She'd made it.

"Well," I said, burying my nose into her side as she *meep-meep*ed and kneaded my arm. "You made it."

I hurt. But maybe the hurt was better than drifting away, glitching out. The hurt was better than feeling like someone programmed to look normal and act normal when inside I was burning up. Maybe it was okay to decide what happened to my gramps. Or to try to be okay with never knowing. Maybe it was better than looking at my feet and wondering why I could see them, move them, but not feel them. Maybe the hurt of accepting what happened was no worse than glitching out on if, if, if, if, ifs. Maybe it was better.

I pressed my head into my hands. Ouch.

Pain. Alicia's dad always said the body feels it for a reason.

Cheerio circled me, rubbing her head against me. Purring and purring. I don't know how long we were there, my hands in her fur, her rubbing and rubbing.

"Okay, Cheerio," I said eventually. "Time to get us both out of here."

OBJECT: Cuff Links
LOCATION: Pine Crest Trailer Park, Sierra, California
RESIDENT: Gerardo Monteiro

....

"These will be yours someday." That's what my grandpa said to me when I was little. He'd let me hold the gold weights in my palm. And he'd show me the shirts that were so special, they didn't have buttons at the wrists but were fastened with jewelry. Cuff links, he called them. His were gold, set with a smooth black stone the size of my thumb. He wore that shirt to weddings and funerals, and he'd always ask me to help him clip on the links. "Don't you let them bury me in this shirt," he'd say. "Or if they insist, make sure you have these cuff links in your pocket. They belonged to my dad, you know. Nicest thing he ever owned."

I thought they might be the nicest thing I'd ever own too. Grandpa's three-bedroom house was like a museum compared to our single-wide, and I loved the days I got to go there after school to paw through the treasures of his life. The cuff links were my favorite. The weight of them in my hand, cool under my thumb, and how the shirt he buckled them on had "French cuffs." Everything about them was above ordinary. Funny that a little kid latches on to that kind of thing, isn't it? They became mine one day, of course, and I wore them to my grandpa's funeral, and to my prom. I figured if I ever got married, I'd wear them too, but the fire got them first.

I still couldn't move my foot more than a few inches in either direction. I tried and tried, shifting as best I could. Pulling. Tugging. Cheerio rubbed and purred. Purred and rubbed.

My foot hurt. Scraped. Pinched. I wondered if my ankle could be broken. My head pulsed like a blinking cursor. I ripped my skirt again, shaking it into the air to free some of the toxic dust before tying a new piece around my head.

Then I braced myself against the ground and tried to squiggle free. Nothing. I tried again. Felt my foot lift a bit. Enough that I could almost turn onto my side. But still stuck. The sun was lower in the sky now, only lighting one-half of the canyon. The other was a shadow of charred hillside. Ash was the only smell. It coated the back of my throat.

I reached for a loose brick. Got my fingers around it and managed to pull it toward my foot. I pushed brick against brick and tried to pull free. I felt my skin scraping off, and my foot starting to rise. For a second I thought I'd done it. But no.

A breeze swirled the ash, creaked the burnt trees. And then

something else. An engine. A car. Maybe someone did rounds before dusk. Maybe Gerardo was coming to make sure I was okay.

Cheerio continued her love fest. I strained against the brick. The engine came closer. I inhaled slowly. I moved on to forceful exhales, the voice of our yoga teacher in my head. *Hold on to your breath, move with your breath.* The engine revved. Out on the road the details of the car filled in. Sedan. Gray. Old but sleek. The Saab. Alicia! I inhaled. Exhaled. Pushed hard. The rubble shifted. The Birkenstock slipped off. And I was free.

Also, dizzy and without a shoe. I sat up. My ankle looked like a mangled mess. A wave of nausea rippled through me. I spit into the ashes.

But Alicia was coming. She'd figured out where I'd gone. Of course she would. I turned back to the canyon and listened as the car door opened. I tried to stand, but a dizzy wave knocked me sideways. So I sat.

"Ali!" I called, waving my arms. "Over here!"

"Caprice!" It wasn't Alicia. It was Beckett.

"Beck!" My throat constricted. My vision blurred. "Beck! Look!!"

Then I saw him. My brother in his gray funeral suit as he scurried over the foundation and picked his way through the rubble toward me.

"Caprice—what the—"

I took Cheerio in my arms—lifted her to him like a gift.

"Cheerio?" Beckett dropped to a squat next to me. Cheerio's

purr vibrated her whole body. She rubbed against Beckett. "How?"

I shook my head.

Beckett wiped his face on his sleeve. He blinked, his hands deep in our cat's fur, and said, "Caprice, what happened?"

I tugged the skirt strips from my face, letting them fall around my neck like a droopy scarf. "Where's Alicia?"

"Looking for you—"

Cheerio couldn't decide who to climb on. She wove back and forth around our bodies.

"And what are you doing with her car?" I asked.

"Finding you," he said.

I made a sound that was part chuckle, part sob.

"Look, I found part of Gramps's clock," I said, motioning to the clock face. "*If you're lost you can look, and you will find me—*" I tried to sing.

Beckett's eyes softened. "That wasn't—*too* off key."

"*Time after time,*" I crooned, and the song turned to laughter and soon I was choking myself with my snot. One gasp after another.

"Caps?" Beckett put his hand on my arm and kept it steady until I calmed.

"Yeah?"

"It's a miracle. About Cheerio." His voice was low and steady like he was trying to entice an animal out of a hole.

"Hey, at least we got one."

"We got more than one."

"I never took you for the toxic positivity type."

Beckett leaned forward. "You have a head injury."

"No way!" I pointed to my head. It was starting to feel tight.

Beckett jostled my shoulder. "Seriously, Caps, everyone was—" He shook his head. He was still wearing the boutonniere from the funeral, his linen suit pants were probably ruined now. I reached out to touch the spray of blue aster pinned to his lapel.

He grabbed my fingers. "You threw your phone away, Caprice."

"Oh. Did that seem out of character?"

"Ugh, yeah. After the grief you gave Mom about taking yours away." He shook my shoulder gently. "Come on, let's get out of here. Can you walk?"

"I think. But I lost a shoe."

"Alicia finally convinced you to get a pair of Birks." He reached into the rubble and slipped the fallen shoe onto my foot. Then he stood up. "And Gramps isn't even here to see it. Come on. Get on my back."

"You can't carry me—"

"I need to get you back to the car in one piece."

"You sure that's the way to do it? There're obstacles out here. I got stuck." I pointed to the brick and bent metal around us.

"Trust me," he said.

"I'll get blood on your suit."

"Now that would be a real tragedy. You think I'll ever wear this thing again?"

"Maybe. The way you took over my app, you might have a

future in business." I stood and felt like I was on a boat. Was the ground moving? He held out his hand. I took it.

"Funny," Beckett said, turning his back to me. "Hop up." I put my arms around his neck and jumped with my uninjured leg. He caught me. Cheerio mewed along behind us as Beckett navigated the debris. I thought how home was supposed to smell of pine and dry earth. I wondered when, or if, Sierra would smell like that again.

"How'd you end up in Alicia's car?" We were crossing under the oak. Now a charred line encircled its trunk.

"She took her mom's and gave me hers. River stayed at the shop in case you turned up there. Mom and Dad were"—he pushed out a quick breath—"in no shape to drive. No one thought you'd come up here—but I figured," he said as I slid off his back, "if I did find you"—he opened the door to the car and pulled out an unpainted gnome from River's mom's shop— "we could finally lay waste to one of these beasts."

"And if you didn't? You were going to smash it alone?"

He shook his head, his curls covered his eyes, and he reached back into the car and pulled out an unopened bottle of Hell Boy. "Naw, I figured if I didn't find you, I could at least obliterate myself in peace."

"Beck—don't."

He spun the bottle by the neck. "Yeah, maybe not today. Cheerio's alive and you are too, so turns out this isn't the worst day of my life."

"Only the second-worst," I said.

"Naw," Beckett said. "Probably third." Right. Mason. "Wanna smash it?" he said, extending the arm that was holding the gnome. But I grabbed the Hell Boy instead and twisted the cap off.

"Caprice!"

"Relax, I'm not going to drink it." I tugged my makeshift bandage off and leaned over, then poured the alcohol over my gash. What came out of my mouth was a stream of curse words that would have made any sailor proud. I hopped on my good foot. Drawing out the "UUUUU" of my final expletive before it crashed into the hard "CK." Cinnamon whiskey burns.

I capped it with half the bottle left.

"You get rid of the rest," I said.

He stuck his hands into his pockets, clamped his teeth on his lips, cleared his throat, and said, holding the gnome in front of him, "What are we going to do with him?"

"I don't know—he doesn't look so murderous up here. You know, separated from his friends. Maybe we should let him live?"

"Really?" Beckett held the gnome up so he was eye to eye with it. "Huh." He set it down. Cheerio rubbed up against it.

"See, Cheerio likes him. Maybe we should paint him and let him watch over things up here?"

Beckett gazed out over the ashes of our house and our grandparents'. He fixed his gaze on the burnt hull of the Vanagon. "I sort of like him unpainted like this, he blends in with the, you know—" He gestured to the rubble and bent down, rubbing Cheerio's ears. "Caprice, there's something I—should say."

My throat burned. There were lots of things I should say. *Sorry* and *thanks* and—

"Gramps left us the house. Well, the land, and whatever we'll get from insurance, I guess."

"What?" I nearly dropped what was left of the Hell Boy. I stood stunned for a second, then said, "It should go to Gram, right? She's still alive and—those places, they're so expensive."

"Gramps had it all figured out. Long-term care insurance or something. But mostly he didn't think she'd outlive him. Well, that's what Dad said."

"Huh." I leaned against the truck. "We own land. Gramps's land."

"And Dad's trying to figure out what's happening with the insurance, so I think your college fund is more than replaced, especially if we sell—" He gestured around.

I leaned more of my weight against the car. I didn't want my college fund back. I wanted my life back. The bottle clinked on the front bumper.

"You going to break that?"

I held the bottle up to the gray sky. "We're not going to sell."

"Caps." Beckett put his hand on my shoulder. "No offense, but I'm not sure you're in any state to make decisions."

"And you are?" I said, waving the bottle in the air.

Beckett grabbed it, spun it by the neck, and for a second it looked like he was going to unscrew the cap and tip it up to his mouth—"Beckett! Don't!" I said—but instead he hurled it at our house's chimney stack. It shattered. Leaving a wet mark down the side.

"I am," he said.

"Maybe." I crossed my arms. "But if you are, then I am too."

"Yeah, I'm not sure it works like that. 'Cause, see—you're the one with the head injury and I'm the one who is continuing to be sober despite how hard it is. But that"—he nodded to the chimney—"felt great. You sure you don't want to take some rage out on our friend here?" He jostled the hat of the gnome.

"Nope," I said, hobbling over to my brother and the gnome. "This guy's got to watch over our land." I turned him so he was facing Gram and Gramps's chimney stack. I set the half-burnt clock face next to him.

"Let's agree to table talking about this—" He gestured to the land again.

"Fine." I knew I wasn't going to change my mind, but I could be civil.

"So we'll leave Mom's car up here and bring Cheerio back in Alicia's."

"I can drive—" I pointed to Mom's car.

"Uh, the only way I'd let you drive right now is if I dropped dead. And even then, I might waylay you with my spirit until our parents showed up."

"Taking that protector job seriously all of a sudden?"

He smiled.

"Can we make one stop first?" I asked.

"Um, you're bleeding from the head, so no."

"It's only *seeping*."

"Yeah, and that's messed up. You look like you've survived a war."

"Feel like it too. We'll be quick. Your phone." I held out my palm.

"If you're messaging River, no sexting."

I tried to shove him, but it came out more like a press. "Yeah, nothing gets me in the mood like a funeral, a burnt down town, and a head injury."

Beckett gave me the side-eye. "Don't kink-shame, Cappi."

That glint. Ugh. Beckett. "I'm texting our parents! How are we even related?"

"I'm not sure," he said, handing me his phone. "But I think it's got a lot to do with luck."

My vision went blurry then, and it took me a minute to text.

Caprice to Mom and Dad:

Caps here. Beckett rescued me.

Dad:

Thanks, Beckett.

Dad! It's really me.

Your sister wouldn't phrase it that way.

!!!

Mom:

CAPS! I was tearing out my hair

Don't do that

you have really nice hair

We have a surprise but—

Don't freak out—

But I probably need stiches

Might have a concussion?

Maybe a sprained ankle

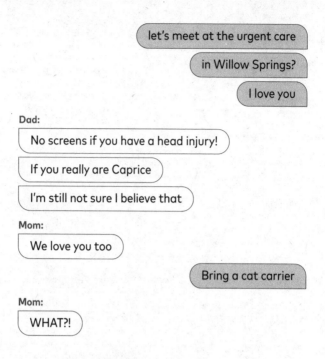

I sent a picture of Cheerio in Beckett's arms.

"Are you sure?" Beckett pocketed his phone and helped me into the passenger seat.

"Would there be a better day?" I said.

He opened his mouth, then shut it.

"Don't say never. You're the one who's—"

"I was going to say"—he handed Cheerio to me—"that maybe when you aren't in need of stitches, and we don't have a cat with us, maybe then. But it does fit with the day of the funeral, so—"

"Let's put the fun in fun-eral!"

"Caps," he scolded, climbing in the driver's seat.

"Okay, Dad."

He scowled.

"Sorry." I touched his arm. "It does seem right, though. To go today."

He nodded.

By the time my brother got to Way Back Antiques, I was shaking. Cheerio yowled and kneaded her claws into my skin.

"Still sure?" Beckett asked, downshifting.

I thought of Gramps's headlights. I thought of how Beckett and I probably saved our gram, but we would never know for sure. Just like I would never know if I saved Beckett, because if Gramps got him, they could have both made it—or both would have died.

We turned into the parking lot. I remembered the fire, but also the grass, the bird houses, the pathway I would hurry down when delivering flowers to Gram.

"I'd like to get out. If it's okay with you."

"I think I have to," Beckett said. He parked close to the four burnt cars in the parking lot. Two sedans, spray-painted with neon zeros, an SUV with the same circle. Then Gramps's truck, a large one across the hood. Because he was there. He'd been there. He died there. At the sight of that number, my vision fogged at the edges. Head hummed.

"Ready?" Beckett asked as he put the car in park.

I nodded. We got out carefully, making sure Cheerio stayed. As soon as the door latched, Beckett was there holding my arm, and together we crossed the pavement to the truck.

We stood in silence. In the strange, birdless, windless, evening sky, Venus blinked bright and a whisp of clouds ran across a half-moon. "Could it really have been a heart attack?" I asked.

"I don't think we'll ever know," Beckett said. "Alicia's dad said maybe."

"I guess our parents weren't the only ones trying to make us feel better."

"Maybe not."

We stopped within arm's reach of the cab. It was black, white, and rusty brown. A queasy ripple spread from my belly into my throat, pressed across my forehead, my lungs, chest, and then hardened. I leaned into my brother; his boutonniere smashed against me.

"Caps"—he swayed—"I'm so sorry. I didn't listen. You knew he was here and I—"

"I didn't know. Not for sure."

"But—"

"No, I'm sorry for all sorts of stuff. But about this, I think—I'm going to decide you were right. Maybe it wasn't his truck—maybe he came later. But even if it was? There's no guarantee we would have saved him. What if he knew he was having a heart attack and drove here to be with her?"

"You think?"

"We'll never know," I said, and I felt something loosen in my chest. I inhaled. I leaned into my brother. "Gramps wouldn't blame me. Or you. We both know that. So, I'm going to try not to blame us either. Here," I said, unpinning his flowers. "It seems right to leave these."

We set our flowers on the metal springs—all that was left of the truck seat. We stood together, Beck's arm across my shoulders, mine around his waist. We are a family that sends energy, and good thoughts, and believes in what you feel in your bones.

And what we felt right then hurt. A nearly impossible hurt. But it was also necessary. To feel. To accept. To be present. To try as hard as we could to not go numb. It wasn't easy. It would never be easy. I wished I could change it. I'd probably never stop wishing that. But I couldn't reprogram or recalculate the past. I could only move forward. One foot in front of the other. Best that I could.

"Someday," Beckett said, breaking the silence and squeezing my shoulder. We turned back to the car. "It'll feel more possible."

"What?"

"Everything."

"Thanks, Doctor Beckett. You going for that psych degree now?"

He chortled. Then after a few steps toward the car he said, "I'm going for my contractor's license."

"Really?" I asked as he opened the car door, reaching in to keep Cheerio from bolting.

"Well, I'm not a real big planner, but it sure seems like Alexander Construction might have a chance at some business. You think Dad might take it over with me?"

"I don't know, maybe. You'd be good at that." I got in and shut the door. Cheerio didn't even try to escape. She settled on my lap. "You'd be a good therapist too."

"Thanks. Not sure about that one, but—well, who knows? Life's long, right? Well—hopefully." Beckett put the car into gear.

"Hopefully," I said. We drove out of town. I thought of our gramps telling me he never thought he'd live long enough to see me grown up, and I thought of my parents saying they weren't going to decide their plans until I decided mine. I thought of what Cecil had said at the funeral. What had he said? Something about how I could have a job here if I wanted. I'd need to ask him to repeat the details. Gramps's voice in my head sang, *Should I stay or should I go?*

TWO MONTHS AFTER

A gnome in a purple hat grinned at me from the passenger seat of River's truck. A Saturday afternoon, partly cloudy. A dampness to the air. River and I were headed back to Sierra to help his moms sift through the ashes. I wasn't sure I was going to be able to keep myself from drifting away. But I could try. And it would be easier with River next to me. I climbed in and took the yard ornament into my hands. It was cold. I ran my thumbs over the red-and-white mushroom.

"Careful!" River said, leaning over to give me a quick kiss. As he pulled away, he added, "He's still a little afraid of you."

I cradled the gnome. "Oh Aldo, first I fear you. Then you me. Is it my new scar?"

River ran his hand across the red line on my forehead. "The scar's tough. Comic book hero cool. But threaten to smash a guy every day for weeks and he's bound to be wary."

"Fair. But with his twelve blank-faced brothers—"

"Hush!" River put a finger to my lips and pointed to a box on the floor. "Tuck him in here or he might decide you're a foe before we get to my house—I mean—our property."

My fingers tingled as I settled Aldo into the newspaper-lined box. I wiggled my toes. Still there—barely. I kissed River's recently shaved cheek. Pine aftershave stung my lips. I pulled back, settling in the passenger seat.

"So, before we meet up with your moms, want to go to Impregnate Point?" I said. River's expression shifted to something between confusion and horror.

"Why?"

"To talk." I tugged the sleeve of his Angry Birds sweatshirt and made my eyes big. The therapist Mom somehow got me into immediately after Gramps's funeral (I suspected one of Alicia's parents had pulled some strings) helped me to come up with this plan to talk to River. Really talk. I owed it to him. We all had been through it, but just about every time he'd tried to have a real conversation with me since the fire, I glitched out. "Talking *has* happened at Impregnate Point before. Plus, I've heard it's better up there."

"Than what?" He paled. "A lobotomy?"

"After all this, a hole in the head doesn't sound so bad."

River gave me the side-eye but started the truck and said, "Okay, but I might only be agreeing because I'm not super excited about sifting."

"I'll indulge your avoidant behavior. Just this once."

We hit the edge of Willow Springs and the sky dimmed. We passed where the National Guard had set up a temporary base in the field off the highway. Giant trucks. Tanks. The air felt thick. I turned up the heat. Fiddled with the truck's fan. Turned on a playlist River had made me on my phone—volume up. The truck only had a radio. But nothing helped. Maybe because most of the songs on the playlist were in a minor key. *Designed to make you melancholy,* Alicia would say. The music played and played into the silence.

The car felt heavy. Of course. This drive, it wasn't easy.

After the checkpoint, we drove up Main. I put my hand on River's leg as we passed the pile of metal that used to be the lumberyard, the high school, where somehow, the wooden beaver remained a sentinel in front of the scorched buildings.

We passed Hole in the Dam Donuts; one orange umbrella stood in front of a pile of half-melted kitchen equipment. At the strip mall where Even Frank Wants Flowers used to be, the store sign lay sideways and smashed. It read: EVE.

I focused on breathing. On telling myself to see what was there. I'd started practicing this at therapy, twice a week, and daily alone—because Doc Sydney is into homework. But it was hard to see what Sierra was now, with my memories etched over the destruction. Staying present was almost impossible. I wanted to drift away. And so I did. The numbness crept in. My stomach tightened as it grew heavy. I worked to pull myself back. To soften.

"So I met with Cecil this morning," I said, and I was present. Back.

"Yeah?" River's hands tightened on the wheel.

"He offered me a job doing some tech work for the Rebuild Sierra Fund—"

"Oh." To our left the trailer park where Mitchell had lived now looked like a field of scorched siding, brick, metal bed frames resting on heap after heap.

I let myself see it. I pulled in a slow breath, calling myself back to the conversation. "The job could be full-time. If I stayed. I could save and go to college later."

"Huh."

I squeezed River's leg. "It wouldn't be easy to work up here. But Cecil says their office will be in Willow Springs for a long time—and he said maybe we could work something out part-time during the school year, even remote."

River's Adam's apple bobbed and he nodded. As we got closer to the point, there were fewer burnt shells of cars along the roadside, or standing in old driveways in front of foundation piles, and there were more trees—pine and oak reaching into the sky, though their trunks were black and their branches burnt-bare.

Finally, River said, "What are you going to do? Take the job or . . . ?"

"I don't know," I said. But I thought *IF one possibility grows another THEN you don't need to decide right away.*

River pulled out onto Impregnate Point, parked, and wrung his hands along the wheel. I rolled down the window and in blew the scent of damp fire pit.

"It's not quite as magical as it was," he said, gazing out at the gray-and-black canyon. "Do you think it's still the second-best place in Sierra?" I gripped his hand as we peered out at the ridgeline—houses once hidden in forest now showed off their skeletal remains. I thought of all the people up here, tucked under the trees, our friends and family, and those we didn't know who lived on these nowhere roads. I thought of that time Cecil took Gramps and me up in his plane, how the trees had hidden the whole town. And then the fire laid everything bare. At the bottom of the canyon, the river still shined blue, still bent its light back to us, still flowed.

"Maybe. We went on this field trip in sixth grade to a burn scar to learn about how the forest comes back after a fire."

"Huh." I saw River swallow.

"Some trees don't even germinate without it."

River's gaze was fixed over the canyon. He looked like he'd drifted all the way down to the water. I was pretty sure he hadn't heard anything I'd said. This must be how he'd felt trying to talk to me these past weeks.

"Riv?"

He cleared his throat and swiveled toward me. "I know you wanted to come up here to talk, but can you listen first?" The green in his eyes was swirling and serious.

"Okay." My knees leaned against him. I felt that dull heat.

He wiped his hands along his jeans. "You never let me explain why during the fire I didn't go with you—to get Beckett."

"You don't need to—"

He held up his hand. "*Please* let me finish." I nodded and he took a breath. "I was completely into you—from that day Beckett bombarded me in the street. Then after we were up here"—he squeezed my hand—"I was tired and not thinking straight. I guess I thought if we went back for Beck, and something happened to us, then what? I wanted us to be safe, but as soon as you left, I kept thinking, *What if something happens to her and I'm not there?* Right away I knew it would be so much worse to lose you that way, because then it'd be my fault."

"No, it—" I started, but River dropped his head, so I stopped. I listened.

"So yeah—the whole drive, I felt like I should've turned around to find you. I tried calling and calling, Alicia then Beckett, Beckett then Alicia—but—"

"I know." Technology failed us.

"When I was waiting at the shop—hoping to hear from you and my moms were telling stories of people running from the flames or getting in their swimming pools hoping the water would help them survive—I—I—just wanted a do-over."

"You were glitching too," I said. God. All this time I'd been *if, if, if*-ing about my own choices, drifting off inside myself, it hadn't occurred to me River could be doing the same. I knew he'd been upset. We all were. But he'd seemed so much more accepting of it all. "Riv, I was so far gone, I didn't know—I'm sorry. I should—" I stopped myself. Doc Sydney said *should* was a dangerous word, like a slide straight into the *if, if, if, if, if*-land of impossible programs. "I thought I could just . . . *decide* not to think about it. That if I didn't talk about it—if *we* didn't talk about it—if we just stayed close and shut it out, then it might all go away, and when we were alone together, then—"

"It was easy to find a distraction."

"Yeah—because you were like this one good thing. When we'd both lost so much and when I felt like I was losing pieces of myself just by walking around—I mean, I swear, spraining my ankle was almost awesome because for the first time in weeks I felt my foot. But with you—I—I could feel something that wasn't pain, it was . . . *release*, and it was so good. I—I wasn't thinking about what we needed to do to make sure that good lasted, that it wasn't, like, just a temporary fix."

River stiffened. Pulled his hand away.

I took in a long slow breath and said, "I used you. For my own comfort, to cope. I'm sorry."

"But I want to help you cope. That's what boyfriends do."

"Yeah—but not talking? That doesn't make the good last."

The cab went silent. No breeze. No engine sounds.

"Caprice?" River's voice cracked across my name. "Are you breaking up with me?"

"What?" I gripped his leg. "No! I—"

"But you just said we weren't—that we didn't make the good last."

"I didn't mean that we're too late! That's what I wanted to say—why I wanted to come here. I mean, I realize now that you might have needed to talk, and all that time, I wasn't ready, and so I hid it because it was so much easier to just kiss and kiss. I craved it. It was easy. But I don't think it was good. It didn't protect us. It just distracted us. I think that was wrong. I was wrong."

"I didn't mind that much," River said, putting his arm over my shoulder and pulling me close. He was joking, but there was something serious in his face too. Some kind of hurt, some kind of relief.

"Yeah, well, we're not short on chemistry. But if we can't talk, if *I* can't, we won't last."

"You want us to last?" His voice pitched higher. "I thought you weren't sure—"

"I want us to last as long as it makes sense. I don't know what that'll mean. You might already be sick of me."

"Uh." He pulled back, looked at me, and shook his head. "Yeah. No."

"Okay." I fought the urge to respond to that with a kiss. "But if I get into Oregon, what I do—it won't have anything to do with you."

He raised his eyebrows.

"I mean—next year—I would love to be in the same place as you, but you can't be *why* I make the choice. I need to make my choice. Even if it means we're not together, it's not going to change that I love you."

He went still. And for a second I wished I could roll back the words. But then River lifted my chin and said, "I wish I could change my plans for you, but—"

"I wouldn't want you to—you have your scholarship, the awesome environmental engineering program."

"Caprice, I wasn't finished."

"Sorry."

"I was going to say it doesn't mean I don't love you." We kissed then, a soft kiss, euphoric and sad at the same time. Then we sat together in the silence, River's arm around me, my head resting on his shoulder as the light moved across the blackened canyon.

"You know the difference between humans and computers?" I asked.

"Humans can kiss."

"Huh. Yeah. Okay. But also, humans understand *maybe*."

"So you're saying we don't need a plan?" He dropped his head onto mine.

I nodded against him. "Not now. Now we just talk."

"And we did. At Impregnate Point even!"

"I told you it could be done." I thought about how the canyon had seen fire before and had come back green and red and growing. "Oh! I forgot to tell you—Cecil refused to take the money back for the app."

"Really?"

"I told him Gramps said never take money for a job unfinished, so he agreed to accept it as a donation in Gramps's name to the Rebuild Sierra Fund."

"That fits. Sorry you had to give the app up."

The sun emerged from behind the cloud splashing the far

side of the canyon in a golden light, and like a seed cracking open, an idea nearly split me in two. "Riv?"

"What? Do we need to get out of here before there are rumors that I'm going to be a dad?"

I laughed. "I don't think anyone is around for miles. But I have an idea." I pulled out my phone, clicked the demo app I'd been working on before the fire (thank you, cloud storage). A map of Sierra showed on my screen. "What if I make a new app—not for tourists, but us. Sierra's people, to record what was here—"

River's tongue appeared between his teeth. "Would you ask for the money back?"

"No! It's not about the money. It's—see I'm thinking people could upload memories—of things they'd lost and where—so people would still tag the location on the map but it wouldn't be about tourism, it would be about memories. And then if people have the app, they can tour what was here as they drive around."

"That," he said, "is a fantastic idea." He turned to kiss me. All softness. I leaned in for more. Mint sweet. His eyes closed. Those two freckles. I kissed his eyelid. His lips. The truck warmed and River's hands smoothed the skin on my back—but then the wind gusted, sudden and sharp. Like the night we'd stayed here. And I shivered. The wind. I forced myself to pull away. I wondered, if the fire hadn't interrupted us, would it have been different? How many nights would we have come up here? Would I have taken some of those condoms from Adrienne? Would we be using them? Or would we still just be kissing any chance we got? Hidden in backyards, and quickly at stoplights? Or maybe everything would have been slower? Anticipating school dance invites and trying to fit in dates between practices, app building, and my brother always being around?

"We should probably go," I said. "Your moms are waiting on us."

Now, after all we'd been through, it'd be hard. To accept things might not work out, that plans might always change. River and I were just a high school couple, and that meant there was only a 2 percent chance we'd stay together. But we'd escaped a fire. We'd made it this far. Maybe it was worth playing those odds. I didn't know. I couldn't know what the future would bring. I only had so much control, but that little bit—I'd use it to choose what I'd do next. To keep trying, keep going.

River put the truck in gear. We drove down the Ridge Road past what was left of the elementary school—a few buildings, a scorched jungle gym—and The Last Dam Stop—a pile of bent metal and ash. He turned on his dirt road and bumped up the hill.

Like most of the town, everything familiar where River had lived was gone. The house and tumbling-down garage, the three pines—they were dark shadows against the sky. Kate and Megan were there already, dressed in their white suits, setting up a long trench for sifting in the house's footprint. River parked.

"Suit up!" Kate called as we climbed out of the truck. "We're hoping to find Megan's wedding band. She kept it in a dish by the bathroom sink when she went to work. So maybe somewhere in the middle here."

We pulled on the white PPE. We looked like twisted beekeepers trying to avoid the sting of this. When we were protected and masked, River shuffled back to the cab and pulled out Aldo.

"So where should he go?" he called.

"Only one place." Megan pointed.

River settled the gnome in the ashes of the old garage, where his predecessor had been. The gnome gazed back at the footprint of the house, taking stock.

"Now," I said. "Let's see what we can find."

It's one of those buildings that was rumored to still be standing because the front wall was. When you drove by, it looked intact, but from the back, it was hollowed out. That really got to me. Maybe even more than seeing what was left of my own house. It was the place where my kids took gymnastics, went to 4-H meetings, where we held community potlucks. I'd been the head fundraiser on the project. It took years to raise that money, but I was on the town council for two decades. Boy, am I glad I'm not anymore. We didn't plan well enough for this kind of thing, I guess. Thought we did with those hours of meetings and escape routes and investments in new warning technology. Some said there wasn't a town in California more prepared than us. Others said we made terrible mistakes. Maybe both are true.

I hope they can build the community center back soon, so the kids have a place to go. Somewhere to have suppers and tumbling classes, or aikido, or whatever it is kids are into these days. E-sports. Dodgeball. Fencing. I can't keep up. Lots of people my age say they don't have the energy to try to bring Sierra back. But I do. For an old guy, I've got lots of energy. Maybe it's because my dad's parents had their property seized during the war. I don't know. That was before I was born, but growing up with that story? You value a home. A community.

It's going to take some time, but it'll be worth it. It always was. Used to be when I drove down Main and saw that center, I'd think, Cecil, you've done good in your little corner of the world. You've given back. And I did. Now my boy's moving out to Idaho. We thought about going with him. But we found the house in Willow Springs, and we'll live there until we're done rebuilding. The grandkids will have a place to come when they grow up. A home in Sierra. Who knows how long it will take, but I'm here for the long haul. Might as well be. I bought our plots in the cemetery long ago.

I hope someday, someone is listening to this with the new community center standing right in front of them. I hope they know how good it can be to work toward something. To build it together. If you can see it now, I hope kids are running in and out of the front door and their parents are carrying covered dishes or costumes like they used to. And if it's not there yet—well, I hope you'll do something about that. I hope that you give a damn about this town.

FIVE MONTHS AFTER

The banner for our Dam Days' float read:

Join Alexander Construction and Even Frank Wants Flowers in Celebrating Our Survival by Contributing to Sierra's Memory MapApp!

A QR code below it led to the app store. Along the side, an image of Gramps and below that: *In Loving Memory of Glenn Alexander: Husband, Father, Gramps, Community Builder, Friend.*

"Help your brother with the other banner, Caps," Dad said. We were gathered in the old parking lot of the community center before the Dam Parade, putting the final touches on our float.

"Yeah, Caps, make yourself useful," Beckett said.

"Never mind. We've got it." Alicia grabbed the end opposite Beckett and pulled so a picture of Gramps appeared, blue eyes gazing out from the side of the truck.

"It's sagging." I tugged the banner up in the middle. My hands tingled. Someone bumped into me—Kim Chase—she squeezed my shoulder and apologized as she headed toward the chorus group assembling at the end of the lot. There was still a dull ache behind my breastbone, but it was nice to see this place so full of people again. After months of temporary living and working spaces, we'd come home—even if we weren't staying, not yet. Even if it didn't look like the home we'd had.

Beckett tossed a roll of duct tape. I caught it. But couldn't feel it. Okay, I told myself. Notice: My brother in his new Carhartts, curls cropped short above his eyes, leaning against the truck. The sky a pale blue with these little whisps of clouds. The breeze that carried the scent of mud, donuts, and charcoal. Three pine trees standing still. I closed my eyes and clasped my hands together. They were back. I was back.

What was left of the community center had been trucked away, and the ground where it once stood was upturned and red like a wound just starting to heal. Rubble remained. The piles the fire had left behind, the shells of cars. It felt like we'd gone through a few lifetimes in the past four months, but the work of rebuilding had barely begun. Dad had said, "It takes a long time to truck away a town. Longer still to build it back." The power grid wasn't back up. There was no water, and no one was even allowed to live on their properties pending safety evaluations, though some were anyway.

"Since Glenn's not here, can you wheel me next to that fine young thing?" Gram pointed at River in his SHS STILL SINGING! T-shirt.

"No, Mom," Adrienne said, handing me one of the flower crowns she'd hung from Gram's wheelchair. "We don't trust you."

"Oh pish—" Gram swatted the air. Her braids were up over her head, and Adrienne had tucked daisies into them.

"It's okay, Gram. No one trusts me either," Beckett said.

"I trust Beckett with my life." I pointed to my scar, a white line under my flower crown. The doctors said it would fade, but they always lie about things like that. Once Beckett stabbed me with a pencil and they said the graphite would dissolve, but I've had a gray freckle ever since.

I leaned into River and said, "I won't be jealous if you let Gram feel your muscles."

"How could you let Gram objectify your man like that!" Beckett said.

"He's not a possession," I said.

"He's a nice decoration," Gram said.

"Um—how is she following this conversation?" I looked between my gram, my parents, and Adrienne.

"This old fruit basket's not full of flies," Gram said.

"She's on a new medication," Adrienne said. "And the lucid moments appear to be more lucid. She even asked for her job back."

"Don't worry, Gram, if Adrienne doesn't reopen, you can have a job at Alexander Construction," Beck said. He settled a flower crown on Alicia's head—yellow rosebuds and miniature sunflowers.

"Mom always said the best part of having a husband in construction was watching him work."

"That is nice." Alicia smiled.

"Gross!" I said.

"Oh, you don't want to know about how hot Beckett is swinging a hammer?"

I made a face like I'd bitten rotten citrus.

"Caps," Beckett said, "I'm even thinking about using some of River's designs when we build."

"Huh. What was it you said about individual actions not mattering?" I asked.

"What if today"—Alicia held up her hands—"a vaquita did not die because some fisherman was convinced to put away the gill net?"

Beckett crossed his arms over his chest and said, "A decent argument, but if River and I become a corporation, then our actions won't be individual."

"And we'll develop sustainable housing all over the world like that Earth Ship guy." River rubbed his palms together.

I looked at each of them. "Who's riding the fancy scooter around the flood zone now?"

"It's a veggie oil truck and a burn zone actually," River said, putting his arm around me. "And it's an excellent plan." I leaned into him.

"Yeah, Caps, you should join us," Beckett said.

"You haven't had enough family togetherness these past few months?" I asked.

"*The more we get together, together, together, the more we get together*," Beckett sang. He was still staying with us in the hotel room. But he did go to Davis every few weeks to see Mason and his mom. On those nights I got the hotel bed.

"Huh," Adrienne said. "If Caprice joins any family business, it'll be mine." She pulled me out from under River's arm.

"You're not even sure you're going to reopen," I said.

"Leave the girl alone!" Mom stepped between us, touching our shoulders. "She's got enough options."

"Caprice here is one step ahead of us all anyway. She's working for the town," Dad said.

"Typical," Beckett said.

"There's always a third way." I twirled briefly, my long skirt spinning wide, and bowed.

"That's your Libra moon speaking," Mom said.

I stopped spinning and cut my eyes to Alicia, who grinned.

"Hey!" Cecil appeared from around the side of the Rebuild Sierra Fund float. "Line at the Hole in the Dam truck was long. I figured I'd buy up a few boxes and pass them around. Take some!"

We descended on the open box, murmuring our thanks.

"So, Cecil, why didn't they go with *my* slogan for the buttons this year?" Beckett asked. Dam Days Buttons were a town tradition.

"Uh, no one thought *Hot Dam* was a good choice," Alicia said.

"I did," Adrienne said.

"And you weren't alone," Cecil added. "But *I Give a Dam* just felt like the right fit. So thanks, Caps, for that."

My cheeks warmed, but I didn't look down. I smiled. Since starting with the fund, besides coming up with the slogan for the buttons—which, yes, Beckett tried to get in on—I'd set up a simple website with an easy click-through donation page. It wasn't hard, but it was apparently magical to my new coworkers.

"And Caprice, the app looks great. Excellent work."

"She's a builder like her gramps," Dad said.

"Speaking of building, Cecil, I hear you all found a house."

Cecil shook his head. "It's temporary. Hard to say we live in Willow Springs now. We got lucky finding something." I felt cold and my feet were gone again. I shook out my hands.

"*Lucky* is one word for it," River whispered in my ear. This was the same since the fire: Everyone wanted to go home. But none of us could, not yet. Maybe never. Even Cecil, with his luck—okay, money—could only buy a house in Willow Springs and line up an architect and contractor for when building permits started to be issued again in Sierra. We were all waiting. Waiting to figure out what would happen next. Waiting to make decisions. Dad and Beckett wanted to get back to work. To build here like Gramps had. River's moms were hoping for some FEMA money and considering whether they should sell their property, or hold on to it, praying that and a possible settlement from the power company might get them enough for a down payment to rebuild. That familiar tingle started in my fingers and toes.

It wasn't standing in Sierra that made my feet keep disappearing. Doc Sydney said I could expect this pain to claw at me for a long time, to invite me to drift away. And sometimes I might. What mattered is that I'd work to bring myself back. To see how my aunt was leaning down to offer a bear claw to Gram, how Gram smiled, taking it in her hand, how Beckett and Alicia stood shoulder to shoulder, and how the light was bright and warm on my cheeks.

Some people wanted to let the town's incorporation go. Close the post office. Some said we had no right to rebuild now that this had happened. That it was unethical. Lots of people said they wouldn't ask that question if we were a town with money, or tourists. That much was probably true. River told me one-third of all homes in the U.S. are built in what's called the Wildland Urban Interface—trees, foxes, twisting roads, and fire danger. Was the answer to move everyone out? Stop building? Or figure out how to live here better? As usual, people were divided. And the rest of the world had opinions too. The united Sierra we were during and immediately after the fire hadn't lasted long. Old splits resurfaced about the codes to enact, the roads to change. I wanted a more resilient Sierra and I wanted to hold on to what connected us, because I knew, as I struggled to keep my feet firm on the ground, that part of me would be in Sierra forever. On the canyon, over the flumes, in the river, running with the foxes and bobcats. I was part of the town that built me.

***

Dad drove the truck through the parade. The rest of us walked alongside. We passed out flyers with the QR code to the app.

I'd love it if the map filled up with stories. I didn't know how many people would add to it, or how many more would look through it. Maybe someday kids would use it in school when they learned about the fire. Maybe it wouldn't matter what happened to it. If it just languished with all the other unused apps of the world, it'd still be worth it, even if no one got anything out of it but me. Making it helped me through. That was worth something.

More fires would come. The world was still warming. We knew this. It was frustrating. No single action would fix it. Change would be slow. But I'd do what I could.

As I walked down Main past the remains of businesses and the trees tagged for removal, I could feel my feet on the ground, and in my bones I felt something too.

"This might sound woo-woo," I said to Beckett, "but I swear I can feel Gramps here walking the parade route with us."

He bumped his shoulder into mine and whispered, "I can too."

As we walked Main Street, you could see mountains in the distance that you never could before. It was different here. The sky bigger. And I swear I heard my gramps say, *Isn't it amazing, Caps! A man like me can have a view like this?*

Adrienne tapped my shoulder and gestured for me to take Gram's chair. I took the handles and Gram reached up and squeezed my hand. The thing is, when Gram forgot me, I'd thought she was gone. I didn't see that so much of her was still there. But now I know just because something isn't recognizable, it doesn't mean it's gone. At least not completely.

Beckett clapped his hand on my shoulder. Alicia laced her arm through my brother's, and River, after the first few songs, lagged so far behind the choir that he was with us too. Alexander Construction and Even Frank Wants Flowers united for once in the Dam Days parade.

Someone called out "Dam good float!" And I looked up at the people lining the sidewalks in front of the remains of Main Street, and I saw what was there: my town, my family, my friends. And in my bones I saw what had been there, and also what may be. And I felt for the first time since the fire that I had done my best. I had done everything I could under the circumstances. I felt my hands as they pushed my gram in her chair, and my feet walking down the road, the one that will lead me away from Sierra. And the one that will bring me back home.

Unprogramming My Future

Maybe I'll go to Oregon.

Maybe I'll stay and work full-time for the future of Sierra.

Maybe I'll leave and work remotely.

Maybe River and I will stay together no matter what happens.

Maybe not.

Maybe Beckett and I will be as close as Dad and Adrienne.

Maybe Adrienne will reopen Frank's.

Maybe we will rebuild on Gramps's land.

Maybe not.

*Maybe Alicia and Beckett will stay together, and she'll end up my
sister and we'll all have barbeques in a New Sierra.*

*Maybe they'll have a terrible falling-out and it will be hard for the
three of us to ever be in the same room again.*

Maybe I'll be a programmer.

Maybe AI will get so good, there will no longer be programmers.

Maybe not.

*Maybe it's okay if I don't know who or what I'll be as long as I
know that I can get through hard things.*

Maybe I'll be okay. Probably. Most likely. It seems like maybe, I will.

OBJECT: Teacup Collection
LOCATION: 53 Plumule Way, Sierra, California
RESIDENT: Aster Alexander

I don't know where they put my teacups. They must be around here somewhere. I have a whole collection and they all have different flowers. Some have blue and pink roses. One has yellow sunflowers. Glenn would pick them up at yard sales and such and bring them to me with garden flowers tucked inside. My girl, she loved tea parties and we'd set a table in the yard, and Glenn, he'd pretend to be the Mad Hatter. Dylan, he'd play the Dormouse or sometimes the March Hare. The tea, I grew it myself—mint, lemon balm, rosemary, bergamot, chamomile. I dried it on racks in the garage and brewed it in a pot the old-fashioned way. We'd sit in the garden under a big umbrella and Glenn, he'd say things like You might as well say, I see what I eat is the same as I eat what I see. And we'd all try to twist our sentences around like that. Neighbors would stop over and let me treat their dogs, and you might as well say their dogs were my treat. See, I'm not so gone as they think I am. Not so mad really. I'd send those neighbors off with a flower or two. We haven't done that in a while. We should. Maybe you could join us? Do you think you could come by for tea?

A NOTE FROM THE AUTHOR

On November 8, 2018, my hometown of Paradise, California, was obliterated in a matter of hours by the Camp Fire, the most destructive and deadly wildfire in the history of the state. Eighty-five people died. Ninety percent of the structures were destroyed. And 50,000 people were displaced. At that time, I was living across the continent in Maine—with little ability to help those impacted. I tried to do what I could to support my hometown. Nothing felt like enough. What everyone needed most—a home, their community back intact—was simply impossible to give.

So, like many who loved Paradise, I did what I could. I supported from afar—sending money to local organizations, sponsoring Christmas for a family who lost everything, and listening to the stories of my loved ones who were displaced. When my friends asked if I could write a poem for their child's teacher as a thank-you gift for reopening school in her home, for providing stability for children who needed it deeply, I got to work. The response to that poem allowed me to believe my writing might be used to support my hometown in some way, however small.

It wasn't easy to find the story that eventually became

this book. I wanted to honor my town. I also wanted to raise awareness about the realities of climate change. And it was vital to write an authentic, gripping coming-of-age tale. I *didn't* want the story to be stuck in a single historical moment documenting the past. And I *didn't* want to be narratively tied to the facts of the Camp Fire specifically. So here's what I did:

I started by changing the name of the town to Sierra. Anyone familiar with Paradise and the story of the Camp Fire will be able to see that the two are closely related. But this work is fiction, and I have made choices that separate Sierra's story from Paradise's in order to craft the narrative to my best ability. In my mind, Paradise and Sierra are like twin towns, one whose disaster I witnessed from afar, and one whose disaster I lived through, navigating alongside my characters.

But this book is not just a story of fire. It's a story of family, community, and first love. Because one thing I have learned is that disaster isn't the whole story. It's an important part of it. But the people, their lives, their loves and struggles, and how they get through them—*that's* the story. And it's a story all of us need. We all face our own disasters. We all must find a way through. And we all must learn to be okay with uncertainty, or learn to accept, as Caprice does, the possibility of *maybe*.

In the years it took me to write this book, the instances of catastrophic wildfires have increased worldwide. This impacts every one of us. The fictional story of Sierra reflects not just Paradise (though certainly most closely), but also Stinnett, Texas; Lahaina, Hawaii; Greenville, California; Berry Creek,

California; Detroit, Oregon; Vida, Oregon; Phoenix, Oregon; Talent, Oregon; Superior, Colorado; Louisville, Colorado; Santa Rosa, California. And the list is incomplete because not only are there many more, but also because I'm writing this in the spring of 2024, unaware of the fires that will come between now and the moment you're reading these words. One-third of the U.S. population lives in the Wildland Urban Interface, communities particularly prone to this type of fire. Every year, the fire seasons are growing longer, and more communities are being impacted.

Even for those not in danger directly, the smoke from fires causes real health problems. In the novel, some of this is depicted via River's character. Studies estimate wildfire smoke contributes to between 16,000 and 30,000 deaths per year, a number that's expected to grow should human-caused climate change not slow. We all have lungs, after all.

I don't tell you this because I don't have hope. I do. I wrote this novel because I *do* have hope. People can come together and make change. They can support one another and build a better world. This book was one small thing I could do with my skillset to try to bring attention to these issues. I've learned through my research, through the stories of my friends and family, that when we share our human stories, true healing can happen.

For more information on Paradise and how you can help fire-impacted communities, or if you or someone you love is struggling with substance use disorder, please see the following pages.

RESOURCES

If you or someone you know is struggling with suicidal thoughts, call the Suicide and Crisis Lifeline at 988 for support.

If you or someone you love is facing substance use disorder, here are some resources:
- Al-Anon and Alateen
  Al-anon.org
- Alcoholics Anonymous (AA)
  aa.org
- Narcotic Anonymous (NA)
  Na.org
- National Alliance on Mental Illness (NAMI)
  Nami.org

For those of you wanting to know more about Paradise and the Camp Fire, I recommend these books:
   Paradise: One Town's Struggle To Survive An American Wildfire
       by Lizzie Johnson
   Fire in Paradise: An American Tragedy
       by Alastair Gee and Dani Anguiano

And these documentary films:

All Its Name Implies, director Ev Durán

Rebuilding Paradise, director Ron Howard

Tips for supporting other fire-impacted communities:

Gift cards are better than donations of "stuff." They allow people to get what they need.

Donate to local foundations connected to the community. On the next page, I've listed some organizations supporting the ongoing rebuild and community development efforts in Paradise that I've contributed to. Join me if you're able, find similar organizations in another community, or find your own unique way to make an impact:

- Rebuild Paradise Foundation

   Rebuildparadise.org

- North Valley Community Foundation Butte Strong Fund

   Nvcf.org

- The Gold Nugget Museum (historical preservation)

   gnmuseum.art

- Scholarships for teens living in the Camp Fire

   footprint: The Paradise Scholarship Federation

   Paradisescholarship.org

ACKNOWLEDGMENTS

I wrote this book out of my love for my hometown and across years that included: COVID, finishing a second master's degree, a cross-country move for a new job, and often wobbly attempts at remaining a decent spouse, parent, and professor. That it exists in your hands is a testament to the love and support of many people.

My thanks to:

My editor, Jessica Dandino Garrison, who pushed me to make this story the best I possibly could and never gave up on me. My agent, Elizabeth Bewley, who stood by me every step of the way and connected me with the brilliant Sterling Lord intern Kelsey Mitchell whose notes were perfectly timed, astute, and encouraging.

The entire team at Dial Books and Penguin Young Readers. Especially Squish Pruitt, whose insight and engagement bettered this book at several stops along the way; Nancy Mercado; and copyediting genius, Regina Castillo, and proofreader extraordinaire Kenny Young. Kristie Radwilowicz, whose cover design embodies so much of this book for me, and David

Curtis, cover artist—thank you for making this book more beautiful than I ever dreamed. Maya Tatsukawa for the stunning page design of the interiors.

My writing group—AKA—the best thing to come out of 2020: Alex Richards, Jennifer Moffett, Eva Gibson, and Shannon Takaoka. Thank you for reading so many versions of this and for the endless support.

Shannon Schuren, your thoughts made this project better. Thank you endlessly.

My new STL-area writing community, for support in this new place and hours of writing dates: Ciera McElroy, Catherine Bakewell, Michelle Mason, and especially Meredith Tate, whose notes on a later draft were critical to my getting over the finish line.

Helena Fox, your kindness and support was unmatched. You embody what author community should and can be. Thank you.

My students at the University of Maine, Farmington, particularly those in my Writing Seminar: English 100: It's a Disaster—thank you for engaging in the story and theories of disaster alongside me. Special thanks to my student assistants Zoe Stonetree and Hannah Paige, whose research on teenagers experiencing PTSD and PTSG after natural disaster was essential, foundational research for Caprice's story. And thanks to my former student turned friend Alexandria Mac for critical early developmental feedback.

Lindenwood University's MFA in Writing Program: A day

job that aligns so well with the dream is truly a dream. Thanks for giving me a home.

Moriah Reusch, my first teen reader, thank you for reading this early in the process, and again when it was getting close to what it is now. I'm endlessly grateful for your keen insights, honesty, and engagement.

Christine Schwab for lending your keen eye for piano and medical insights. Anything that's wrong is my fault, and I'm grateful for your time with this.

Lynn Rockwell for insight on rehab programs.

Richard's Florists in Farmington, Maine, for letting me shadow you for the day. Fuller's Flowers of Paradise, who I delivered flowers for on holidays as a teenager—I'm glad to know you're still keeping the ridge in bloom.

To Steph Dunn, who helped talk me through some of Caprice's technical knowledge. And to the University of Maine's M.Ed. program in Instructional Technology, the coursework for which informed Caprice's interest in computers, and gave me foundational knowledge in the field.

The Novel 19s for support and for donating new books in the wake of the Camp Fire to Ridgeview High School, and Gina Lefebvre for ensuring they got to the school for us. Stories are hope.

Main Street Books, Saint Charles, and Devaney, Doak and Garrett Booksellers in Farmington, Maine. Thanks for all you do for local authors.

Beth Mooney, Paradise girl, chosen sister, your attention to many drafts of this novel, responding to countless texts, sharing resources, brainstorming, and being honest about your own journey, but most of all reminding me over and over again that I could write this. You've fed my soul since the day we met on the Ponderosa soccer field. Thank you for always being my oak, modeling resilience, and sharing your wisdom.

Julie Prestopino Van Roekel, thank you for your willingness to read this, your supportive notes and sharing some of your story with me. You've made this book better. I'm honored to have you in my Paradise circle.

Lindsay Cunningham for the photo of the gnome that inspired me, and for helping me describe the flumes. To Chris Hoffman for your expert read on the author's note. I'm hiking flumes with you all in my dreams.

Claire and Dave Neal for asking me to write a poem, and for sharing the story of your cat that served as inspiration for Cheerio's narrative.

Thank you to so many other Paradise friends who have inspired me with your stories and resilience these past years, as well as those of us who've found our place elsewhere but came together in the ways we could to support our home. If I named you all, these notes would never end, but I do love every one of you. You give me hope.

I'm grateful for the foundational public education I received in the Paradise Unified School District. Much gratitude to all my teachers. I know I wasn't always easy.

My parents, Doug and Kristi Youngdahl, for raising me in

Paradise. Sonja Ljungdahl for reading multiple drafts of this and giving another Paradise perspective.

My husband, Nathaniel Teal Minton, who read drafts, talked through countless narrative problems, kept me from giving up over and over, all while feeding our girls, and holding down the fort while I traveled to do research and write. You make this possible. Thanks for a half-lifetime of love. Let's keep it up.

My daughters. I love you both beyond measure. Thank you for all the ways you helped me get this done. To Adelaide Minton, who became a teen when I was writing this book and so was put to work as a reader. Your feedback was incisive and excellent. It's almost as if we raised you for this. To Elodie Minton, my biggest cheerleader for signs of support, flowers, artwork, and your unwavering faith in me. It made all the difference.

All those working to rebuild a thriving community and help kids build a future in the Camp Fire footprint, and in communities with similar stories all over the world. Let's continue to love and support one another.

Paradise Forever.

SHANA YOUNGDAHL is a poet, professor, and the author of the acclaimed novel *As Many Nows as I Can Get*, a *Seventeen* Best Book of the Year, a New York Public Library Top Ten Best Book of the Year, and a *Kirkus* Best Book of the Year. "Deeply authentic [and] marvelously complex, [this is a] smart, poignant story [that] readers shouldn't miss. . . . Grief, addiction, first loves, and traveling an unplanned road are among the many themes explored," *Kirkus* raved of Shana's debut. *A Catalog of Burnt Objects* is Shana's second novel. She hails from Paradise, California, and now lives with her husband, two daughters, and a cat and a dog in Missouri. Visit her at ShanaYoungdahl.com.